UNBELOVED

UNDENIABLE #4

MADELINE SHEEHAN

Dedicated to Undeniable love.

PROLOGUE

It was misery that washed her color away, leading her off her path and astray. So she wandered through her life, unknowing and unsure, until realizing her path had always been right there in front of her from the start. Hidden in the shadows of despair, she found her path, her color, within her beating and beautifully bright red heart.

I WASN'T ALWAYS BROKEN; WE ARE ALL BORN PURE. IT IS our journey that burdens us and leads us astray. Our mistakes that beat us down and cover us in guilt and shame, burying us a little more with each successive hardship. It is up to us to dig ourselves out, to come to terms with our faults, to embrace not only our imperfections but those of the ones we love, and to once again find the path we strayed from.

I had been a simple girl. I grew up in a small town in Montana surrounded by down-to-earth, simple people with small, simple dreams. I loved my mom, my dad, and my big sister with all my heart. I loved books with happy endings and romantic movies, and couldn't wait to fall in love.

Unlike my ambitious older sister, I was a born romantic. I'd been in love with the idea of love for as long as I could remember, full of flighty, fluffy notions of what happiness truly was. And to me, happiness could only be found within the arms of a man . . . a man who loved me.

I wanted butterflies, holding hands, stolen kisses in the backseat of a car, late-night phone calls, all of it. The anxiety, the desperation, that beautiful, agonizing ache called love. And so I romanticized everything.

I had no aspirations, no big dreams. There was nothing I was working toward, no great goals or accomplishments. Instead of college, I dreamed of marriage; instead of a career, I yearned for children.

Visions of traditional white weddings and babies danced in my head. I wanted three babies—one boy, two girls—a nice house with a white picket fence, a cat, and a dog. By the time I was fourteen, I had it all planned out. The cut of my bridesmaids' dresses, my wedding reception's seating chart, the color of my living room curtains, the decor of my children's bedrooms . . . no detail escaped my attention. I wanted to live the fairy tale, to become someone's everything and anything, to be his princess.

I wanted my happily-ever-after.

There was only one problem.

Instead of finding my prince, I found a whole mess of trouble. At the age of fifteen, I'd found myself pregnant; by eighteen I was married to a man I didn't love; and by the age of twenty, I was running around on my husband with a married man.

Then, at the age of twenty-four, I gave my heart away to yet another man, a mistake that would once again drastically change the course of my life.

My weaknesses, my choices, and my decisions—the ones I made and the ones I didn't—all took me down a rocky road filled with regret, heartbreak, and pain. And eventually, they nearly killed me.

Would I change things if I could? Would I turn back time and do things differently?

Never.

This isn't just my story, the story of a broken woman who lost her way. It's also the story of my children, the men I loved, and the friends who were more family to me than my own.

This is the story of us all, all our fates intertwined. And for that reason alone, pain and death be damned, I wouldn't change a thing.

CHAPTER 1

IT WAS A BEAUTIFUL DAY. MONTANA WAS IN FULL BLOOM, with nothing but green as far as the eye could see. The sun was shining, children were playing, and laughter was plentiful. All in all, it was just another typical summer barbecue at the Hell's Horsemen motorcycle compound that, as usual, everyone was thoroughly enjoying.

That is, everyone except for me.

For me, the sun was too bright, the children were a painful reminder that my own daughter wasn't present, and the laughter was just too darn loud. I felt suffocated by it all, wishing I were anywhere else, wishing I *was* anyone else . . . anyone but me.

"Dorothy?"

"Hmmm?"

I glanced up at the small group of friends encircling me:

Kami, Mick and his wife, Adriana, and Eva, who was peering at me curiously. Those eyes of hers, too big and shockingly gray, seemed to see straight through me; no matter how desperately I tried to hide my feelings, she was always able to discern them. Although I supposed it came with her job.

Married to Deuce West, the president of the Hell's Horsemen, one of Eva's unspoken duties was keeping us women in line, ensuring any emotional problems we might have didn't interfere with the men and their business.

All the same, she was the closest thing I had to a best friend, even if I wasn't hers.

Kami, her childhood friend and the wife of another club member, held that precious title. I wasn't jealous; I was just happy to be included in the inner circle. It hadn't always been that way. Before Deuce had brought Eva home, life was very different inside the club for those of us who weren't lucky enough to be married to one of the boys.

Women like me—sometimes called side pieces, muffler bunnies, seat warmers—were essentially club whores. Even though I had a somewhat elevated position within the club as a den mother of sorts, and was paid to cook and clean, I still had been considered a second-class citizen, expendable and easily replaced.

Eva had changed all that. She'd changed a lot about the way things worked, and during it all had become more like a sister to me than my own had ever been.

"I'm fine," I lied, trying to smile. "The little one is kicking, is all."

Being eight months along in my pregnancy, it was easy to blame my moods on the baby, but Eva was far from gullible. With her eyes full of pity, she nodded and turned away.

I did the same, my gaze seeking out the reason I was here, standing amongst a club full of criminals and their families.

Already looking in my direction, Jase's smiling eyes met mine. When his gaze dropped to my swollen stomach, his smile turned to a rather devilish grin.

Even after nearly seventeen years together, it was still painfully apparent how Jason "Jase" Brady, a married man with children, had been able to convince the dutiful wife and mother I'd once been to become his "club whore." So much so that all I had to do was close my eyes and I could once again hear the bells jingling on the door, feel the wooden floor bend and creak below my feet, hear my own voice call out as it had on that day so many years before . . .

"Mornin', Joey," I had called out as I'd entered the neighborhood convenience store.

From behind the counter, Joe Weaver, a former classmate of mine, had glanced up from his *Playboy* magazine and flashed me a mouthful of crooked yellow teeth. "Mornin', midget," he'd said cheerfully. "You bring me any muffins today?"

"Sorry," I said over my shoulder as I headed for the medicine aisle. "Teg's got the flu. Poor thing has been throwing up all night."

Grabbing what I needed, I headed toward the counter and began pulling my money from my pocket.

"Pete home with her?" Joey asked.

I shook my head. "He's over the road again, this time for a month."

"Who's he haulin' for now?"

"Not sure," I said, shrugging.

My marriage wasn't a typical one. We were more like roommates than anything else, roommates who couldn't be bothered with each other.

His job hauling freight cross-country gave us the luxury of living apart from each other while still appeasing our parents' wishes: to raise our daughter together.

But Pete usually didn't tell me what he was doing or where he was going unless it directly concerned me, and I didn't care enough to ask.

"He's with a smaller company now," I added. "Hauling paper, I think."

While ringing up my purchases, Joey nodded distractedly. "So, your folks got Teg?"

I snorted softly. The idea of my parents ever willingly helping me was laughable. On a good day they considered me an embarrassment, but on most days, a failure they wanted nothing to do with.

"She's with Mary."

At the mention of my older sister's name, Joey grimaced, and my lips twisted as I fought the urge to laugh. Mary was no one's favorite person. Like most people in Miles City, she was religious and a right-wing conservative, but she took it to another level entirely, talking down to people who didn't share her viewpoints, incessantly preaching to anyone who would listen, and even those who wouldn't. Needless to say, she wasn't Miss Popularity, but she was the only real estate agent in town and so, whether they liked it or not, people were forced to interact with her.

"Poor kid," Joey muttered, handing me my change. "Sick and forced to hang with Mary, Mary, quite contrary."

"You gave me the wrong change," I said, handing him back my receipt. "You still owe me three dollars, look—"

The shop's doorbell jingled loudly, and I glanced over my shoulder half expecting to see Marty, the town drunk, stumble inside to beg for his morning freebies.

Instead, a young man dressed in military fatigues stepped inside the small shop. Carrying a large green duffel bag, he paused upon entering and pulled his kepi off his head as he did a visual sweep of the store. When his gaze reached me, my breath caught in my throat.

He was gorgeous. His eyes were a deep, brilliant shade of blue, his dirty-blond hair was cropped close to his head, and his features were hard and chiseled, tanned to a perfect golden hue. His figure tapered nicely from broad shoulders to trim hips. The man was absolutely gorgeous, and I was stunned.

Furthermore, I didn't recognize him, and this was Miles City, Montana, a small town where everyone knew everyone. As far as I knew, we didn't have any new arrivals.

"Bathroom?" He raised his eyebrows.

In answer, Joey pointed toward the back of the shop, and we both watched as he shouldered his duffel bag and started through the store.

"Stop droolin', D." Joey's voice was pinched, as though he was trying not to laugh. "You're lookin' like a bug-eyed leprechaun. And it ain't a good look for ya."

My cheeks burning, I shook my head. "I was just wondering who he was, is all."

"He's one of Deuce's. Transplant from the Wyoming Horsemen chapter, or so I heard. Name's Jason Brady, and accordin' to some of Deuce's boys who work at the auto shop in town, he's in the Marine reserves."

Deuce's boys.

Deuce, the president of our town's local motorcycle club, was one of the most frightening yet intriguing men I'd ever met. And I used the term "met" very loosely; I'd had very little contact with the leader of the Hell's Horsemen, only minor encounters here and there around town. Deuce was a very private person, but as far as I knew, he was a decent enough man.

Unlike his father, Reaper, the former club president, Deuce took care of Miles City. He'd taken control of several failing businesses around town and brought them back from near bankruptcy, he constantly donated money to the public schools and library, and a few years back, when my parents' neighbor had lost his wife to cancer and was about to lose his farm due to her exorbitant medical bills, it was Deuce who had picked up the tab.

Even so, there were rumors that Deuce was involved with business that danced around the law, but Deuce and his boys were good to us, so other than the rumors and the idle chitchat between the gossipmongers, usually no one gave it a second thought.

"Sell smokes here?"

Jason Brady emerged from the bathroom no longer looking like an American hero. Dressed in leather boots, leather pants, a tight black T-shirt, and his leather Hell's Horsemen cut, he now looked like one of Deuce's boys. Except he was hands down the most clean-cut biker I'd ever seen. And he appeared to smell good too.

But that was pure assumption on my part. Or maybe wishful thinking. Because for some reason, I really wanted to get close enough to give him a sniff.

"Name's Brady," he said, smiling over my head in Joey's direction. "Jase Brady."

"Joe Weaver." Pointing at me, Joey said, "And this here's little Dorothy Kelley Matthews, resident ginger midget."

Jase's friendly gaze dropped down to where I stood and he looked me over, an embarrassingly slow and thorough perusal of all five foot nothing of me, from my head to my toes and back up again.

I felt my face heat. Not only were my holey jeans and plain tee covered in the remnants from a full morning of cleaning, but my hair was piled on top of my head in a messy bun, and I was sweating from the midday heat.

"Nice meetin' you, baby," he said, his lips curving. The tip of his tongue appeared and he very deliberately ran it across his full bottom lip.

Then it wasn't just my face overheating but my entire body. Feeling suddenly drugged and my thoughts muddled, I pressed my hand over my stomach and swallowed hard.

"You . . . too," I whispered.

"You got a nickname, little Dorothy Kelley Matthews?" he asked. "'Cause that's a fuckin' mouthful right there."

My breath shuddered from my lungs in small spurts of air. What was wrong with me? Why couldn't I speak? Or move?

Jase's lips split into a grin. "Not that I mind a mouthful of pretty girl . . ."

Oh dear God. How did one respond to *that*?

From behind me, Joey let out a loud and amused-sounding cough, startling me back to reality. Back to Jase and his knowing grin, fully aware of the effect he had on me.

"Excuse me," I muttered. Snatching my purchases off the counter, I hurried quickly toward the door and pushed blindly through it.

What was wrong with me? I'd been flirting! And with a total stranger!

And worse, I was married. It might not be a love match between Pete and me, and he might be on the road more than he was home, but we had a daughter together and he took care of us financially. I should respect that, and yet here I was acting like a teenager with a crush, entertaining thoughts that I had no business thinking. I shook my head in dismay and let out a large pent-up breath that did nothing to calm my rapidly beating heart.

Reaching my truck, I tossed my purchases inside the open window, and was about to open the door when I felt a touch on my left shoulder. Startled, I spun around and came face-to-face with . . . Jason Brady.

"You forgot your change," he said.

When I tore my gaze from his grin and looked down to his outstretched hand, I found three wrinkled dollar bills. But my focus wasn't on my change, it was on the man standing in front of me. He was so close to me, too close, and watching me too intently for me to feel at all comfortable.

And yes, dammit. He did smell good. An understated, yet softly spicy bouquet wafted off his skin, and along with it, the faint odor of sweat and the crisp scent of leather.

Swallowing hard and with a slightly trembling hand, I reached for my money and when I did, his free hand came down on top, his hands caging mine, his touch freezing me in place.

"You should stop by the club and see me sometime," he

said, his eyes lazy, his smile filled with less-than-honorable intent. A smile that had my stomach flip-flopping.

I cleared my throat and managed to choke out, "I . . . I'm married."

Jase's smile never wavered. "Baby, I ain't tryin' to marry you."

Releasing me, he held up his left hand and wiggled his ring finger back and forth. His wedding band, a thin band of platinum, glinted menacingly in the sunlight. "Got the battle scars to prove it too."

I stared up at him as foreign thoughts infiltrated my brain, thoughts of him and me naked, sweaty, our bodies colliding. I saw heated kisses and furious groping and—

Instantly disgusted, more so with myself than at his audacity, I had spun back around and quickly jerked open the driver's side door. Yanking it closed behind me, I'd thrust the key into the engine, slammed the truck into reverse, and hit the gas. As I had burned rubber out of the parking lot, I could see him in my rearview mirror, still standing where I'd left him.

Laughing.

What an absolute scumbag.

What an absolutely, perfectly sculpted, beautifully smelling . . . scumbag.

Since I was young and unhappy in my marriage, it had only taken Jase a few months of pursuing me before I'd succumbed, and an even shorter period of time before I'd fallen head over heels in love with him. A love I'd chosen above all else—my marriage had ended and my family was lost to me, viewing me as an adulterer; the utmost disgrace.

And my dignity, I'd sacrificed that as well.

And for what? To be a club whore?

I might be off-limits to the other boys, belonging only to Jase, but the painful truth was that he'd never be mine. All these years later he was still married, still armed with a litany of excuses as to why he couldn't yet leave his wife, and still promising that he someday would.

It was a promise I'd recently given up on.

I could either accept my fate and status in Jase's life—always a club whore, never an old lady, forever waiting for what little crumbs he would toss my way—or I could leave him.

But how could I leave him? After all I'd given up, all I'd sacrificed for him, the sheer lengths I'd gone to, to ensure that someday I would be his one and only, how could I simply walk away?

The truth was that I couldn't.

Leaving him meant losing the security he provided me. I'd lose the apartment he paid for in town, and my only source of income: my position at the clubhouse.

So as I made nice at a barbeque I had no interest in attending, I matched his happy expression, hoping from this distance that it would appear genuine, and that unlike Eva, he wouldn't see through my facade.

I shouldn't have been worried. As usual, Jase was oblivious to my wants and needs, only ever focused on his own. So much so that he was unaware of my biggest secret yet.

The secret I carried inside my belly.

Unbeknownst to Jase or to anyone other than myself, the life growing inside me was not a product of my relationship with Jase. It was the result of an affair with another member of the Hell's Horsemen. It had begun as a drunken slipup, a night of much-needed comfort spent in the arms of another, but over time had become something else entirely. Even years later, it was still something I'd never quite known how to process, could never truly comprehend, but at the same time . . . I'd eventually begun to depend on it. Need it, even.

The other man provided me with an outlet nothing else in my life allowed me. When I was with him, I was never consumed with feelings of inadequacy, fearing that every move I made was being compared to another woman. With him, I felt almost free.

Turning away from Jase, I squeezed my eyes shut, easily envisioning *him*, a beer in one hand, a cigarette in the other, as stoic and as silent as ever.

The dark to Jase's light, James "Hawk" Young's skin held a duskier undertone; his features were more striking, almost otherworldly. Even without the additional height of his Mohawk, he was taller than Jase, larger with bulky muscles and an overall stature that could very easily be construed as intimidating.

At first, I too had been intimidated by Hawk. After our first night together he'd come to me again, wanting more. When I'd refused him, he'd threatened to tell Jase what we'd done. Terrified of losing the only man I'd ever loved, I'd agreed.

And in the end, I'd been the furthest thing from intimidated.

In the end . . . I'd been in love with two men.

It was yet another mistake I'd made.

But even as I thought those very words, I could hear

Hawk, his voice uncommonly deep, his expression forever firm as he stared down at me and said, "There ain't no such thing as mistakes, Dorothy. There's only shit that happens and shit that don't."

I swallowed back a threatening sob, furiously blinking back my quickly gathering tears. No matter what Hawk thought, I knew in my heart what we had done was wrong. Hawk had betrayed the bonds of the brotherhood, and I had betrayed Jase by allowing another man into my bed. Even worse, I had allowed Jase to believe that the baby inside me was his.

But what choice did I have? If I admitted my sins, I would lose everything. As it was, I'd already lost Hawk.

I could still see him, the joyous expression on his face when I'd told him I was pregnant. And then the pain that had shattered his joy when I'd told him the baby wasn't his.

Hawk had known the admission for what it truly was, a bald-faced lie stoked by fear in the addled mind of a confused woman. But even knowing this, he hadn't put up a fight. Instead, he'd left.

I didn't blame him for leaving, for choosing life as a nomad over continuing to live a life full of lies and secrets. I just hadn't realized how drastically my life would change with his absence. I hadn't realized how much I had come to depend on him, and in turn, how much I would miss him.

Good God, what was wrong with me? Almost thirty-seven years old with a grown child and pregnant with another, yet in many ways I was still a child myself. I was without purpose, always unsure of myself and my feelings, giving love away as easily as breathing, all while flitting and flailing aimlessly through my life . . . if you could even call this delusional sham I'd created around myself a life.

The light touch of a hand on my stomach brought me reeling back from depressing musings, to the young woman who'd stepped up beside me. Blonde, beautiful, and dimpled as all Deuce's children were, Danielle "Danny" West smiled kindly at me.

Blowing out a breath to ensure my voice wouldn't quiver, I then covered her hand with my own and gave her fingers a light squeeze. "Only a few more weeks," I said. "I can't wait for this baby to come. I'm too old to be pregnant."

Danny's smile turned sympathetic, but anything she might have said in response was stopped short by the man who walked up behind her. ZZ, her boyfriend, slid his arm around her middle and pulled her tightly up against him.

"Hey, baby," he murmured.

Danny turned in his arms, returning his embrace, and placed a kiss upon his chest.

It was refreshing to see her happy again. Not too long ago, she'd been depressed, constantly brooding, and engaging in destructive behavior that had belied her usually outgoing and upbeat personality.

It was ZZ who'd pulled her out of her funk and brought her back to the land of the living. At first Deuce hadn't been thrilled with the match, but not even Deuce could deny the significant change in his daughter, nor could he refute how good of a man ZZ was. Smart, sweet, and loyal, ZZ was the perfect match for his president's daughter.

But even as thrilled as I was for Danny, I couldn't help but be reminded of my own daughter, Tegen.

Not much younger than Danny, Tegen was away at college in San Francisco. Her phone calls were minimal and her visits home practically nonexistent. Although she'd never cared much for Miles City, always wishing for something bigger, something better, I couldn't help but think it had been her disappointment in me and my life choices that precipitated her hasty departure and reluctance to visit.

"Oh my God!" Kami shrieked. "Oh my fucking God, he's proposing!"

Startled from my reflections, I glanced up, seeking the cause of Kami's outburst. I'd been so lost inside my own thoughts I hadn't even realized the yard had gone quiet, or that the couple who'd been standing right beside me only minutes before were now in the center of the yard, all attention on them.

Down on one knee, ZZ was holding up a small black box in offering to Danny. She stood before him, staring down at him, her pretty features twisted with shock.

My throat convulsed, suddenly dry and scratchy, and I swallowed repeatedly, trying to wet it, trying to keep my composure.

That would never be me. *That would never be me.*

"I'm going to cry," Adriana whispered, and covered her mouth with her hand. Rolling his eyes, yet smiling, Mick wrapped his arm around her shoulders and drew her close to him.

Even Kami, a born cynic, forever bickering with her own husband, looked misty eyed.

"Baby girl!"

My gaze traveled to where Deuce and Eva had come together. Standing side by side, both of them were smiling happily in Danny's direction.

"You say the fuckin' word," Deuce yelled, "and I will

throw that asshole into next fuckin' week! Fact is, whether you say yes or no, I'm still gonna beat the fuckin' shit outta him!"

Eva shoved playfully at Deuce's abdomen and in response he captured her neck, pulling her against his body and into a loving embrace.

Good God, I was surrounded by it. So much love and affection. So many happy couples, both mature relationships and ones that were just beginning. Love was everywhere, literally all around me except for where I wanted it, needed it, most of all.

I couldn't stop myself from crying, not this time. I was too pregnant, the welling emotion too great. So often while at the clubhouse, during birthday parties or barbeques, when I'd been forced to watch Jase interact with his wife and children—and dying inside a little each time—from across the room or the yard, I would find Hawk. Our eyes would meet, and then I was no longer falling apart but instead was centered by Hawk's desire for me, warmed by it, strengthened by it. Again and again, with just one look, he would save me from myself.

I needed that now, his strength, him.

As my tears began to fall, I hurriedly turned away from my friends, searching out the most expedient way back to the solitude and emotional safety of the clubhouse.

That was when I saw her.

Standing at the far edge of the lawn, just outside the circle of gathered people, was Jase's wife, Chrissy.

My tears dried instantly as my breath hitched and my stomach sank. She wasn't here to attend the party.

It wasn't the tears streaming down her pretty face that

gave it away, or her disheveled hair and wrinkled clothing. It wasn't even the wild look in her eyes. It was the simple act of her gaze meeting mine, really and truly seeing me for the very first time. She'd never looked at me before, only in passing glances, and always dismissing me.

She knew. She knew everything.

All these years of being thrust together, living in the same town, attending the same parties, both in love with the same man, yet strangers still.

Not anymore.

Her gaze dropped to my swollen belly. In a mindless instinctive reaction, I raised my hands to cover it. To somehow protect the life inside me from what I knew was about to transpire, to shield its innocence from the ugly secrets that were about to be ripped from the darkness and sent, screaming and bleeding, into the light.

Tentatively, I took a step backward and was about to take another when movement at her side caught my attention.

A flash of light.

A glint of metal.

Shrieking, I turned to run, but above my cry heard a booming crack. As if I'd been punched, my head snapped backward, knocking me off my feet.

Then I was falling and people were screaming. There was so much screaming, it was all I could hear, and yet it sounded far away, off in the distance.

"Dorothy!"

Voices echoed all around me.

Hands grabbed at me.

A face hovered directly over mine.

I knew that face, I knew her, she was my . . . she was . . .

Tears streamed down her cheeks and her mouth was moving, but I couldn't hear what she was saying. I couldn't hear anything. Why couldn't I hear anything?

I tried to ask her why I couldn't hear, but my mouth wouldn't work.

Another face, a man with pretty blue eyes, appeared beside the woman, wildly shaking his head back and forth. I knew him. I couldn't remember who he was or how I knew him, only that I knew him.

Like the woman, he too was crying and his lips were moving, but still there was no sound. I tried to lift my arm, to reach out to him, to . . .

My vision began to blur, distorting and warping the faces around me. I blinked furiously, trying to see, trying to understand.

Something awful was happening, I knew that much, something horrible. And these people, whoever they were, I wanted to help them.

But I couldn't move, I couldn't hear, and black spots floated over me, quickly growing larger, taking over my vision.

I was tired. So, so tired.

I just had to . . . close my eyes . . . for just a second . . .

Darkness enveloped me.

And then, there was nothing.

Not even darkness.

CHAPTER 2

Seven years later

I MISSED THE SNOW. IN MONTANA, IT ALWAYS SNOWED ON Christmas.

In San Francisco, it rained instead. And rained. And rained.

Curled up on my living room couch, a cup of coffee in one hand, my cell phone in the other, I watched the rainwater as it sluiced down the glass in thick rivulets, distorting and blending all the colors of the outside world into one gray mass.

A sort of symbolism in relation to my life, a little too colorful of a life, I mused, twisting my lips sardonically. A life that had started out naive, full of pinks and blues, but as I grew older became full of brilliant reds and yellows, and then later filled with stormy, sorrow-filled grays.

Since my recovery I'd done what I could to wash most of that color away, leaving behind my chaotic life in Miles City, Montana, and starting over in San Francisco, California.

A necessary step in letting go, forgoing the brilliance for softer colors, neutral, relaxing shades. Because when you'd lived through nearly dying, you learned to appreciate the quiet, calmer colors of life.

Letting my cell phone fall into my lap, I lifted my hand, pushing back my thick mane of wavy red hair to finger the long, thin scar that ran the length of my skull.

The lone bullet meant to kill me and the child I'd carried inside me had failed. My son, Christopher, and I had thankfully survived. Christopher had been unscathed, but the trauma had left me with a blank canvas. For a long time, I had been without the knowledge of my life, who my children were, even my own name.

Thanks to my great doctors, therapy, and a strong dose of luck, I'd eventually regained the knowledge I'd lost. And when I had, I wished I hadn't.

They say that what doesn't kill you makes you stronger, and while that might be true for some, for me it had the opposite effect. At first I couldn't face what I had done, the pain I had caused so many, let alone face the people my actions had directly impacted.

For shooting me, Chrissy had been convicted of first-degree attempted murder and had been sentenced to prison. And Jase had nearly taken his own life while in the throes of grief. Their three daughters had subsequently been left without their mother, with an incapable father, forced to transition into adulthood on their own.

And Hawk, after finding out I'd been shot, flew into a very public fit of rage that had shed light on Christopher's true paternity. His disloyalty to his brother now exposed, Hawk retreated even further into himself, and his visits home to Montana became more infrequent.

Unable to deal with the overwhelming sorrow and the crippling guilt I felt, unable to figure out how to move forward, I simply hid myself away, going so far as to feign ignorance even after my memories had returned to me.

It had taken another near tragedy, this time involving Tegen, for me to finally see past my own nose, to realize that I'd spent my entire life in hiding. Hiding from my past, from my present, and any sort of future I might hope to someday have.

Refusing to let history repeat itself, and done with hiding, I moved my son and myself to San Francisco, not only to see my daughter through her rough patch, but to start fresh.

My wish was for the three of us to become the strong and solid family we always should have been, to live in such a way that didn't cause anyone any pain, and for the opportunity to make new memories for us all, this time ones that would be worth remembering.

It took some time, but eventually I got my wish.

Since then, Tegen had moved back to Miles City, was happily married to Deuce's son, Cage, and Christopher was living the peaceful and carefree life of a seven-year-old. Despite whatever resentments still lay between Hawk and me, he was a regular in Christopher's life, which was all that mattered.

Our son had that effect on us, no matter how strained

our relationship with each other. Christopher was our Switzerland, a span of untouched land covered in wildflowers that stretched between two crumbling cities.

Both my children were safe, they were happy, and they were surrounded by those who loved them. There really wasn't much more a mother could ask for.

But like a glass that had shattered, while you could glue it back together, it would never again be what it once was.

I was a shattered glass, glued back together. And my children, while their wounds had healed, had been cut by my jagged edges.

Sighing, I turned my attention away from the window, back to the cell phone in my lap.

It was Christmas morning. Christopher would be waking soon and yet Hawk wasn't here. The last text I'd received from him had been days ago, informing me that he'd be here by Christmas Eve. There'd been nothing since, and every call I'd made had gone unanswered.

However strained our relationship with each other was, Hawk had never ignored my calls, and he'd certainly never missed an opportunity to spend time with his son.

Something was wrong.

Setting my coffee down on the windowsill, I quickly typed out a text on my phone.

I'm worried. Please call me.

Pressing Send, I held the phone in my hand and waited. And waited.

Ten minutes went by and still no answer.

I glanced at the clock on the wall, which was silly since my phone told me exactly what time it was, but old habits die hard and I'd been checking clocks long before I'd had a cell phone to tell me the time.

Six thirty a.m. Which meant it was seven thirty in Montana. Deuce and Eva had two young children, and considering it was Christmas morning, might be up already.

I typed out another text, this one to Eva's cell phone.

Have you heard from Hawk? He's not here. He hasn't responded to my calls and I'm worried.

Then I waited, clutching my cell phone, staring at the lit screen so intently that when it brightened even further, flashing Unknown Caller, followed by the ridiculously loud and obnoxious ringing I hadn't yet figured out how to change, I nearly jumped out of my skin.

"Hello?"

"Dorothy." Deuce's deep, rumbling voice filled my ear. "You fuckin' know better than to text shit like that to an unsecured line."

"Merry Christmas to you too," I said dryly, unconcerned with Deuce's texting protocols. "Now, where's Hawk? Why hasn't he responded to any of my calls?"

"What do you mean he hasn't responded to your calls?"

For such a smart man, Deuce could really be dense at times.

"What I mean is *just that*. He hasn't responded to any of my calls or texts. Not since the day before yesterday."

Silence followed my words, only serving to worsen the sinking sensation in my stomach.

"Deuce?"

"I'm here. I'm thinkin' . . ." Another long pause followed, then, "I gotta go. I'll have Eva call you if I have news."

"Wait!" I cried, but I was too late. He'd already hung up.

"Dammit!" I shouted, squeezing the phone in my hand

22

with frustration.

Why had I even bothered calling? The Hell's Horsemen and their seedy business dealings were never something I'd been privy to. And getting any sort of information out of Deuce was the equivalent of demanding answers from a brick wall. Utterly impossible.

"Mom?"

My gaze jerked across the room. Leaning heavily against the hall entranceway, Christopher regarded me with sleepy eyes and a crooked smile.

Tossing aside my phone, I jumped up off the couch. "Merry Christmas, baby," I said softly. Smiling, I gestured toward the tree and the brightly wrapped presents piled underneath it.

His little face, still slack with sleep, instantly brightened. His green eyes widened, and then he was hurtling across the hardwood flooring. Just as I thought he would run right past me, he skidded to a stop, whirled around, and threw himself at me.

I caught him, but just barely. Only seven years old, but he had the strength and build of a baby bear. Much like Tegen, the color of his eyes and hair were his only resemblance to me. He was every inch his father's son.

"Merry Christmas, Mommy," he said, squeezing my waist. In answer, my heart skipped a beat. He hadn't called me Mommy in years.

I might not have remembered being pregnant when he'd first been presented to me as an infant, but it hadn't stopped me from loving him instantly.

Regardless of all my confusion, the pain from my head injury, the resulting surgery, and my emergency C-section, the moment I'd laid eyes on him, I'd felt instantly connected to him, knowing he was mine.

While everything else around me had felt foreign and new, while my family and friends tried desperately to force my memories, Christopher was the exception. He was as new to the world as I was, expecting nothing from me but love.

Grateful for that, and for him, I'd returned the emotion in spades.

"Merry Christmas," I whispered, running my hands through the unruly mass of long red hair he'd vehemently insisted on growing.

Tilting his head back, he returned my smile. "Where's Dad?"

Keeping my smile firmly in place, I softly brushed a few locks away from his eyes. "He's on his way," I lied. "He said not to wait for him."

"But he's coming, right?"

Not knowing how to answer him, I changed the subject instead. "Your sister sent you that big box over there." Releasing him, I gave him a gentle push toward the tree and pointed to the ridiculously large present Tegen and Cage had mailed out weeks ago.

With an excited shout, the absence of his father temporarily forgotten, Christopher bounded forward. Grabbing the large red bow from the top of Tegen's gift, he tossed it over his head and began quickly stripping off the brightly colored wrapping paper. Knowing them both, I was fearing the worst. A drum set, a dirt bike, something that would undoubtedly make Christopher ecstatic and me miserable.

"Mom! Look!"

It was even worse than I'd feared. Like a beacon on a foggy night, the words "Tactical Paintball Gun Mega Set" glared ominously at me. And I glared right back, silently promising retribution against my daughter and her husband. One day they would have a child and I would be the doting grandmother, buying my grandchild gifts that will surely leave its parents as equally horrified as I felt right now.

Setting the paintball gun set aside, Christopher began tearing into his presents with happy abandon. Grabbing my coffee, I took my seat on the couch to watch him, smiling when he smiled, nodding excitedly each time he showed me a newly opened gift.

But my heart wasn't in it. Every other minute I was checking my phone, hoping to find a message from Hawk, or Deuce, and coming up empty.

I had grown so accustomed to our quiet life, to our dependable routines, that this glitch, this unexpected change was more than unsettling.

In fact it was much worse than even that, the anxiety and worry coursing through me . . . it was all too familiar.

"This is for you, Mom." Christopher appeared in front of me, a small wrapped box held in his outstretched hand. "From me," he said proudly.

The bitter coffee sloshing around in my stomach congealed into a hard ball of dread. A present from Christopher meant a present from Hawk, more than likely something they'd bought together during Hawk's last visit.

Setting my mug down, I took the little box from Christopher into my trembling hand. As I turned it over, noting the messy wrapping job, my lips began to curve in a genuine smile.

"Thank you," I said softly as I did my best to release the wrapping paper without tearing it. It was the little things, like my son's shoddy wrapping job, that I wanted to savor and remember. Things I'd never done with Tegen.

I'd been too caught up in myself, desperate to be loved, unable to see past all the things I didn't have, so that what I did have—Tegen and all her love—had gone unnoticed.

Now I kept every drawing, every note, every little trinket or memento, all of them tucked safely away inside the chest beneath my bed.

In a lot of ways, Christopher represented my redemption as a mother, but even more so as a person. Without him, without the circumstances that his conception had brought about, I might never have realized the extent of my mistakes, and thus would have never had the chance to make things right.

The wrapping paper safely removed, I was left staring down at a small velvet box. Surprised, I glanced up into Christopher's smiling face.

"Jewelry?" I asked, confused. My accessorizing amounted to a small pair of gold hoop earrings that had once belonged to my grandmother. I had always been simple in that sense, not someone who'd ever cared much for flashy clothing or adornments.

Christopher shrugged. "Dad said you'd like it."

Tentatively, I lifted the silky-smooth lid and, upon seeing the contents, felt my eyes prick with tears.

Of course Hawk had known I would like it. Hawk had always known me better than anyone. He'd seen me at my best, at my absolute worst, and all the moments in between.

Whereas no other man, not my ex-husband, not even

Jase, had ever taken the time to truly pay attention to the little things, Hawk had always been watching. Whether we were secreted away together in the shadows, lying beside each other in bed, or when we were apart, from across the room, he always had his eyes focused directly on me.

Using only the tip of my index finger, I gently brushed over the delicate silver chain until reaching the tiny silver heart that hung from it. "Mom" had been engraved in softly swirling letters in the center of the charm. It was beautiful, yet simple. It was perfect.

"You like it?" Christopher asked.

Clearing my throat, I set the box in my lap and reached forward, drawing my son into my arms. "I love it," I whispered hoarsely.

As was typical at his age, our hug was short-lived, and after only seconds he was pulling away from me, his attention once again on his gifts.

Tucking my legs beneath me, I leaned comfortably against the large throw pillow beside me, content for the time being just to watch him enjoy his Christmas.

He might not appreciate it now, but someday he would look back and remember that his mom had always been there for him, was always armed with a hug and a smile. He would remember those times and in turn, he would smile.

Tegen hadn't had that as a child, and after repeatedly disappointing my parents, neither had I. But Christopher always would. I would make sure of it.

Glancing over at the cell phone lying beside me, I felt my chest uncomfortably tighten as my anxiety returned. I just hoped he would be able to remember the same from his father.

Good God, why wouldn't someone tell me what was going on?

It was early afternoon when my phone finally rang, the screen signaling that Tegen was calling.

"Mom," she said softly, too softly. My daughter did not speak softly, not unless something was wrong.

Gripping my phone tightly, I swallowed back a wave of fear. "What's wrong?" I whispered. "Where's Hawk?"

"Mom," she repeated. "This isn't a secure line. You need to come home."

CHAPTER 3

Two days earlier

WITH THE HIGHWAY STRETCHED OUT IN FRONT OF him and nothing but more highway behind him, James "Hawk" Young could finally breathe again.

Whatever craphole town he'd been holed up in for nearly a month now had early on begun to wear on him. So when Deuce had called and told him to get his ass to Vegas, he was more than happy to oblige and leave behind the obscenely clingy bartender he'd been trying to shake since day fucking one. Young and hot didn't necessarily make the ideal companion, and after a few rounds of sex, he'd been more than done with her.

But he was finally free of her, finally back on the road, the only place he'd ever felt he could just . . . breathe.

No, that was a lie. There been one other place, or rather one person, who'd given him that same feeling. Who'd taken away the stifling emptiness with just a simple fucking smile.

It wasn't the case anymore but way back when, when he still had the woman he loved within his reach, that damn smile . . . it was fucking magic.

Usually when he was on the road this late at night, mostly empty aside from him and the occasional car, he would think about that smile, those eyes, that tiny little nose all covered in freckles. And for just a moment, the emptiness would begin to ease.

He'd think about his favorite memory, the one and only morning he'd ever been able to wake up beside her . . .

"Good morning," Dorothy had said, stretching her body.

Hawk had already been awake. He was always up with the sun, and had spent the last two hours just staring down at her naked body, watching her sleep.

It had been the first time they'd ever spent the night together. Between taking care of her daughter and her ridiculous relationship with Jase, spending time together wasn't an easy feat for Dorothy. But for once it was just the two of them; the clubhouse was empty. For the first time what he felt for her, how fucking deep those feelings went, felt real.

"Did you hear me?" She laughed and he loved it. Just hearing her laugh. He fucking loved it. "I said good morning."

Instead of answering her, he pushed her over and onto her back, looking his fill at her tight little body covered in all that soft, creamy skin. Dorothy immediately tried to cover herself, but he pinned her arms down and quickly rolled on top of her.

Then he had tickled her.

And as she'd squirmed beneath him, howling with laughter, he'd whispered, "Good morning."

Closing in on his destination, Hawk hit his blinker and turned his bike onto the exit headed for downtown Las Vegas. The memory evaporated and just as quickly, the emptiness returned.

Another fifteen minutes later, he pulled up behind an old abandoned shipping warehouse. Hawk shut off his engine and glanced around anxiously at his old stomping grounds. It wasn't that he disliked coming to Las Vegas; quite the opposite, actually. Whenever Deuce needed one of the boys to make a run to Sin City, he always volunteered. He might look very different from the kid he'd once been, and sound different, but Vegas would always feel like home.

Because technically Vegas *was* home, and he wasn't truly who he'd spent the past two and a half decades pretending to be.

Yeah, he was a biker. Just another patch on a totem pole full of patched, leather-wearing bikers living as criminals, not for the money or even for enjoyment but because that was all they knew. It was how they survived, how they paid the bills and cared for their families. It wasn't about greed or excess, it was about living a certain way, being a certain kind of man who didn't have to bow down to laws and the government who enforced them. It was a brotherhood, a camaraderie. It was about really, truly living your life the way you wanted to live it.

It was about . . .

Freedom.

But Hawk didn't have that same freedom. It wasn't the same for him. And it never would be.

Like a lot of his brothers, Hawk was just another piece of shit Deuce had fished from the gutter. But unlike Cox or Dirty, Hawk hadn't had a hard life spent living on the streets. At least, not at first. But neither did his upbringing resemble Ripper's, who'd lived a good, solid life, the American dream, until he'd lost his parents at the age of seventeen.

No, Hawk had been born a spoiled and privileged son of a bitch, his mother a cocaine-addicted burlesque dancer who'd fatally overdosed when he was only three years old, and his father an infamous member of the Bratva, a Russian mob boss, the one and only Avgust Polachev of the Polachev cartel.

For eighteen years he'd been a gluttonous whore, reveling in a life of overindulgence, seduction, and sin. Spoiled was putting it mildly. He'd had more money than he could have spent in ten lifetimes, as well as cars, drugs, booze, and women, all at his self-destructive disposal. He'd had it all.

Until he'd lost it all.

The summer he turned eighteen, his father was gunned down inside the man's own home during an FBI raid. His father had gotten greedy and that greed had made him careless, and that carelessness had landed his father with an undercover federal agent on his crew. Actually, several undercover agents.

After the FBI, fitted in bulletproof vests and armed to the teeth, had broken down their door and stormed their home, they'd informed Hawk's father of the stack of evidence they had against him. They told him he'd never again see the light of day, and that a lethal injection would be his last memory of life.

Hawk would never forget what happened next. His father, his only family, had turned to him and mouthed one single, solitary word.

Begi.

Run.

Turning back to the agents, his father had reached for his gun, as had every other man in the room. A flurry of bullets had cracked through the air, and Hawk hadn't waited around to see what was going to happen next. After pulling his own piece, he'd run from the house as fast as he could.

He ran, and because he was a wanted man, not one of his father's former associates would take him in. He was deadweight. His picture was all over the news and there was a price on his head. So he kept running, living in the shadows for two years until Deuce found him hiding out and digging for his dinner inside a casino dumpster.

Hawk had recognized Deuce, and Deuce him, having met each other several times in the past. The Hell's Horsemen motorcycle club president hadn't been a friend of his father's, but a loyal buyer. Because Deuce knew what had transpired in the wake of his father's greed, he'd taken pity on Hawk and took him in.

Deuce's connections provided Hawk with a fake birth certificate and driver's license, giving him a new identity. He'd become James Alexander Young, a New York native who for all intents and purposes was a big, fat nobody. Deuce burned off his fingerprints, gave him a Harley and a haircut, nicknamed him "Hawk," then took him home to Miles City, Montana, where he'd begun the second chapter of his life.

His Russian accent had been the first thing to go. Luckily it was slight compared to the heavy Slavic intonations of his father and friends, developed only because he'd grown up around it. But even so, his transition from mob prince to homeless grifter had been easy in comparison to his transition from homeless grifter to biker.

Learning to ride a motorcycle hadn't been the hard part; the most difficult transformation had been learning to live and breathe leather and chrome, to talk the talk and walk the walk. The Hell's Horsemen, while still a highly profitable criminal organization, were the underbelly of the world Hawk had come from. Whereas his father had once been at the top of the food chain and considered men like Deuce and his boys necessary trash, Hawk was now at the mercy of them. Funny how life worked out sometimes.

As a Hell's Horsemen prospect he'd kept his head down, stayed quiet, kept to himself, and did what he was told. That diligence and intense survival instinct ensured he acclimated quickly, gained loyal friends among his brothers, and was unanimously voted in a full-fledged Horseman.

No one but Deuce knew who he really was, something that Deuce had told him was for his own protection from other MCs looking to make a quick buck or weaken another club. Therefore no one, not even Deuce's top boys, were allowed in on the secret. Which was just fine with Hawk, since even the most loyal of brothers could turn on you.

It was the reason he was in Las Vegas.

Just this morning Deuce had gotten a tip on ZZ's

whereabouts, a former brother of the Hell's Horsemen who, if Deuce got his way, wasn't long for this world.

Over the last year ZZ had been spotted repeatedly across the country, part of the underground fighting circuit. He'd been made a few times in Vegas; only by the time the information had been passed down the line, the fights were over and ZZ had been long gone.

Not this time.

Blowing out a long breath, Hawk toed his kickstand down and dismounted his bike. He didn't want to be the brother to find Z, he didn't want to be the man to have to take the guy out. As fucked up as it was that ZZ had shot Deuce's son, Cage, Cage had freely admitted that ZZ hadn't drawn first, and had even spoken in his defense.

But Deuce wouldn't be swayed. The guy had shot his son point-blank in the chest. Twice. Then he'd taken off, turning his back on what he'd done, and on the club altogether. Now he wasn't just wanted by the law, but by Deuce. The president of the Horsemen was out for blood, and when Deuce had his mind set on something, you didn't question him. You did as you were told or you ended up in the same sticky situation ZZ was in. Sticky with your own fucking blood.

Blood that Hawk was going to have to spill. Merry fucking Christmas to him. His only saving grace was that after this he was headed to San Francisco for the holidays, to see his boy . . . and Dorothy.

As if on cue, he felt his cell phone vibrate against his chest. Reaching inside his cut, he pulled out his phone and found a text message from Dorothy.

Christopher is wondering when you're getting in.

Although he should have been used to this by now, Dorothy's refusal to acknowledge that they'd once shared something more than just their child, he found himself frowning.

All her texts, all their phone conversations, even their face-to-face time, were only ever about Christopher. Even after all this time had passed, she was still going well out of her way to ensure he didn't get the wrong idea.

What he wouldn't give to wrap his hand around her fucking throat and give her a nice, hearty shake. Despite what she thought, he wasn't a fucking moron clinging to some childish hope that someday she'd realize she still had feelings for him. Maybe way back when, when she'd been coming to him desperate for something Jase could never give her. Freedom. The freedom to let go in a way she never could with Jase, because with him she hadn't been trying to win a prize. She hadn't had the same feelings of inadequacy, the constant looming threat that if she weren't as good as Chrissy, as beautiful, as giving and loving, that Jase would leave her.

All that pent-up misery, all that desperation, all that hidden anger and harbored resentment, he'd gotten the brunt of all of it. Once Dorothy had realized he was her safe place, she'd never held back on the crying and the yelling, and she'd taken it all out on him . . . him and his cock.

But that was then and this was now, and things weren't the same. Not even close.

He'd gotten her message loud and fucking clear about who she really wanted on the day she'd told him the baby inside her was Jase's, even though they'd both known she was a damn liar.

Yeah, he'd fucked that all up. Taking what hadn't been his to take, forcing her hand, essentially blackmailing her into his bed, none of it had been the right way to woo a woman you wanted. But even now, older and wiser, he still couldn't bring himself to regret not even one fucking second of it. Not when it had resulted in the birth of his son. Hearing that little boy call him Daddy, seeing those big eyes looking up to him for . . . everything. No fucking way would he ever regret a single moment that had led to Christopher. Not a chance in hell.

Still, he'd always kept his feelings, his yearnings, and his disappointments to himself. Well, other than announcing to all and sundry that Christopher was most certainly his. After finding out Dorothy had been shot, not knowing whether she was going to live or die, there was no way in hell he was going to let a lying, cheating piece of shit like Jase Brady raise *his* kid.

A good thing, too, seeing as Jase couldn't seem to do much of anything since then other than lift a bottle to his mouth.

I'll be there tomorrow.

As he typed out his message, he felt his dour mood begin to lighten. Shit might be in permanent stasis between him and the woman he loved, but that didn't mean he wasn't thankful for the time he got to spend with them in some semblance of a family. When you lived on the road, you learned to appreciate the little things.

"Brother."

Hawk recognized Hammer's voice before the man himself walked out from the shadows. Hammer was president of the Las Vegas chapter of the Hell's Horsemen motorcycle club. With a shaved head, sparrow beard, and built like a tank, Hammer was a fearsome-looking beast of a man. He'd gotten his nickname after beating a man into a bloody, unrecognizable pulp with nothing but his own two fists.

If Hawk hadn't been secure in his own reflexes, in knowing his trigger finger was as steady as a rock and he hit dead center every damn time, he might have feared the man.

"You look like hell," Hammer said, approaching him. "Long ride?"

Sliding his phone back into his cut, Hawk shook his head. "Long fuckin' life, brother. Long fuckin' life."

Hammer snorted. "I hear that. My old lady's been givin' me hell. Knocked up a patch whore, bitch is demandin' money . . . I'm about ready to start eatin' concrete outta here."

"Been runnin' 66 for a grip now," Hawk said, his gaze dropping to his saddlebags. Inside lay his Miles City rocker, the patch he'd given up when he'd gone nomad. "Shit's startin' to wear on me."

Hammer's expression turned grim. "I got you, brother. I like to bitch, but ain't nowhere I'd rather be than here with my boys. You do this job, you goin' home?"

Hawk shrugged. He didn't have a home, not really. As much love as he had for Deuce and the club, after everything that had happened, he wasn't able to sit in one place for too long. He'd start dwelling on the countless things he couldn't change, wishing for things he couldn't have. The road was a better place for him. Running jobs across the country, keeping him busy, too busy to sit down and think about how jacked up his life really was. But Hawk had never talked about his problems, or worse, his feelings, with any-one. And he wasn't about to start now, especially with an asshole like Hammer.

"So this shit's for real then?" he asked, jerking his chin toward the broken-down warehouse. "Z's really inside?"

"Shit's real," Hammer answered. "Seen 'im with my own two eyes. He's lined up now, got two boys ahead of 'im. Coulda put 'bout fifty holes in 'im by now."

Hammer's expression hardened. "Wanted to. Man's got-ta pay the price for what he's done."

Hawk wished he had, wished the deed was already done, and done by anyone but him. But ZZ had been one of Deuce's top boys. Because of that, it had to be one of his own that put him to ground. It was the rules of the road and a code they'd all sworn to live by.

Pulling his smokes out of his leather jacket, Hawk lit one up and surveyed the warehouse. "How many exits?" he asked.

"The whole fuckin' place is full of fuckin' holes and ready to crumble."

"Fuck," Hawk muttered.

"Yeah. I got three of my boys with me, each of 'em hangin' by an exit. But this fucker's a slippery bastard. How many times he been spotted and got away clean?"

"Too many," Hawk said grimly. An intense wave of ex-haustion washed over him, settling deep into his muscles. He took another drag off his cigarette, hoping the nicotine would shake him awake some. After all day on the road, he was more than tired. He was damn near comatose.

Blowing out a breath of smoke, Hawk flicked his cig-arette away. "Let's do this," he said, and together he and

Hammer headed toward the front of the building. As they grew closer, the din of noise that could be heard from outside grew louder, more discernable as excited shouting.

Stepping past the broken and bent steel door, he found the large room empty, other than a few pieces of rusted-out machinery and scattered garbage that could just barely be seen. As he'd suspected, the noise was coming from beneath their feet, from the basement of the building, making him all the more wary of what was to come.

Silently, the two men continued slowly toward the stairway, the noise growing louder and louder with every step they took, until they'd reached the bottom, where it became damn near deafening.

After exchanging a look with Hammer, judging by the man's expression he was more than ready to put ZZ six feet under, Hawk gripped the edge of the already partially open door and pulled it open. The dimly lit, smoke-filled storage room was filled with wall-to-wall bodies, both men and women, pressed up against one another, all shouting at the top of their lungs.

This wasn't the first bare-knuckle cage fight Hawk had been to. The underground fighting circuit was infamous in Vegas, and in his youth he'd taken part in his fair share of illegal betting in abandoned warehouses very similar to this one.

But as Hawk shoved his way through the spectators, his hearing began to adjust, the screams of the crowd beginning to sound less like excitement and a lot more like bloodthirsty war cries.

"Kill! Kill! Kill!" They chanted the lone word over and over again, in and out of unison.

Realization slammed into him like a runaway freight train. This wasn't any ordinary cage fight; this was a fucking death match. All around him, bodies were straining against one another, their arms raised in the air, holding up their money as they continued to trample one another, attempting to get a better glimpse of the gory entertainment.

His apprehension mounting, Hawk glanced over his shoulder, looking over top of the crowd and seeking out Hammer. Due to the sheer volume of people packed inside the room, the man had fallen a ways behind him. Only because of Hammer's size could Hawk find him, violently shoving people out of his way as he made his way toward him.

Hammer having reached him, the two of them stood side by side and charged forward. The size of their combined statures created a human battering ram that allowed them to slam easily through the remaining people, clearing a path to the front of the crowd.

A ceiling-to-floor steel cage had been erected in the center of the room, the floor within stained brown with the blood of past fights, and currently slick with the fresh blood of the battle presently raging inside it.

"There he is!" Hammer shouted, jerking his chin in ZZ's direction.

At least it looked like ZZ—if ZZ and the Terminator had a fuck fest that had produced a love child named "Warmonger" who had been kept on a steady diet solely consisting of raw eggs and steroids.

The man was all deadly muscle, furrowed brows, and fists flying with a single-minded focus. To kill.

One, two, left, right, left. Hawk watched as ZZ

hammered his bloody, swollen fists into his opponent's stomach, chest, and face in that precise order, sending blood and teeth flying with every bone-crunching punch.

Like a machine, ZZ never once paused to catch his breath, never once missed a beat. On and on it went, him beating the other man senseless while deftly avoiding all punches aimed at him.

Watching him, Hawk felt the hairs on the back of his neck stand to attention. Hawk wasn't looking at ZZ; this was not ZZ, this wasn't even a man. Hawk was looking at a slab of meat covered in skin, a walking, talking, still-breathing carcass.

But he didn't have time to dwell on it. ZZ had just cornered his opponent against the cage wall and in a quick maneuver, grabbed a fistful of the other man's hair, forcing his head down and his body to fold over. Then bringing up his own knee, ZZ slammed it into the man's face, snapping his head backward and breaking his neck.

As the man slumped to the ground, his lifeless eyes wide open, the crowd erupted in an explosion of exhilarated cries and shouts. Only Hawk and Hammer remained still, frozen in the midst of the chaos.

What in the holy fuck had he just witnessed?

Seeing his former brother like this, a man who'd once been so damn easygoing, always had a grin on his face and a joke to tell, turned into a ghost of his former self, a stone-faced killer . . .

Well, it didn't exactly leave him feeling all warm and fuzzy inside. Quite the fucking opposite, actually. And he might have just continued to stand there, staring, leaving him vulnerable to ZZ noticing him if Hammer hadn't grabbed him, yanking him backward into the crowd. The cheering people swarmed around him, hiding him from sight just as ZZ straightened and turned to face his fans.

He spared them only a quick glance before abruptly turning away. Outside the cage, ZZ took a wad of cash from some greasy-looking asshole, grabbed a jacket from a near-by chair, and then he was on the move, shoving off the poor souls who dared to approach him before disappearing behind a door Hawk hadn't previously noticed.

"Follow him!" Hammer shouted. "I'll head back upstairs and cover the front!"

Cursing, forcing himself into action, Hawk started maneuvering his way through the throng of people, heading for the exit ZZ had taken. As soon as he passed through the open door, he slipped his hand inside his cut and pulled his gun free from its holster.

He was only a few feet inside the dark hallway when the door behind him suddenly closed with a loud bang. He spun around, his trigger finger ready, only to find Hammer and two of his men standing there.

Confused, he lowered his gun. "Why aren't you . . ."

He trailed off as something hard and cool, undoubtedly the barrel of a gun, was pressed against the back of his neck.

"You thought you had the drop on me, huh?" ZZ's tone and the laugh that followed were so cold and devoid of emotion, chills went skittering down Hawk's spine. But even worse was Hammer's refusal to meet Hawk's eyes.

Well . . . shit. You really couldn't fucking trust anyone, could you? There was no loyalty among criminals. The only man he'd ever met who'd been the exception to that rule had been Deuce.

The barrel of ZZ's gun dug deeper into his neck. "Drop your fuckin' piece."

Thumbing the safety, Hawk opened his hand, allowing the weapon to fall. It clattered onto the floor with a sad, slapping thud that echoed throughout the empty hall.

Grabbing hold of his arm, ZZ roughly turned him, shoving him face-first into the wall. Without having to be told, Hawk assumed the position. After placing his palms flat against the wall, he then spread his legs apart.

ZZ's pat down was quick, yet thorough, and within moments both of Hawk's blades and his phone had joined his gun on the floor.

Hawk blew out a silent, frustrated breath. It was just a phone, but it contained the only photos he had of his son. Living life on the road didn't allow him the luxury of keeping anything that wasn't absolutely necessary. Not that any of that was going to matter if he didn't make it out of this warehouse with his brains intact.

"Whatever you're gonna do," Hawk said quietly, "you best do it now. If not, I got places to be."

"Yeah?" ZZ snorted. "More fool's errands for your prez?"

"He was your prez once too."

"He's out for my blood, meanin' he ain't jack shit to me."

"You shot Cage," Hawk said, "meaning you shot us all. Your brothers. You can't be dumb enough to think that shit was gonna fly with Prez."

"He pulled on me!" ZZ yelled.

"Enough!"

Hawk turned toward the voice just as Hammer and his men parted, allowing four more men to enter the hallway.

Dressed in expensive suits, their hair perfectly styled, these men weren't more of Hammer's crew.

The lead man, a good twenty years older than Hawk, judging by his white hair and wrinkled skin, stopped directly beside Hawk and smiled. It wasn't a friendly smile but a vicious one. It was a smile that niggled at his memories.

"Luca," the old man said, his voice heavily accented. "Is good to see you again . . . alive."

Hawk blinked. That name, his name, his real goddamn name and that thick Russian accent. Which meant . . . this man was mafia. Cut from the same damn cloth Hawk was.

Behind him, ZZ burst out laughing. "To think all those fuckin' years I was livin' amongst mafia royalty."

Hawk said nothing. He didn't move, didn't breathe, too busy trying to compute what was happening. Or better yet, why it was happening.

"You no remember me, do you?" the old man asked.

Hawk stared at his face, his features, trying desperately to place him, but for the life of him, he couldn't. Not until he looked directly into the man's eyes, such a dark shade of brown that the pupil was virtually indiscernible from the iris. Not only were they a mirror image of his father's eyes, but of his own as well.

"Yenny," he said flatly.

As the man's smile grew, so did Hawk's anger.

Yevgeniy Polachev was Hawk's uncle and had been his father's second-in-command. Hawk had been under the impression that Yenny had died along with everyone else in his father's company.

But Yenny hadn't died, he'd lived, and from the look of

his expensive clothing and the armed men behind him, had prospered.

"You," Hawk spat. "You turned on my father, didn't you? You took everything he'd made for yourself!"

In answer, Yenny simply shrugged. "Your father was greedy, Luca. He would have fallen eventually."

Hawk said nothing, the silence stretching uncomfortably between them. In the background, the shouts of the spectators could still be heard, along with the low hum of a plane flying overhead. But predominant was the sound of Hawk's own heart, fast paced and erratic, his blood thundering violently through his veins as he fought the urge not to reach out and strangle the man he'd once called Uncle. Something that would undoubtedly end badly for him, seeing as he was the only unarmed man in a room full of guns.

"Luca!" ZZ continued laughing. "I still can't believe this shit."

Ignoring ZZ, Hawk focused on Hammer. "You set me up? You set this up?"

Whereas every Hell's Horsemen chapter had their own president, their own business dealings, and their own way of doing things, Miles City was the mother chapter and Deuce was ultimately in charge. Hammer's involvement in this wasn't just disloyal, it was traitorous. Once Deuce found out, the Nevada chapter would be gutted and rebuilt from the ground up, if it even was rebuilt at all.

A body slammed unexpectedly into Hawk from behind, forcing him flat against the wall. He felt a gun pressed into his cheek, causing the soft skin on the inside of his mouth to grind painfully against his teeth.

"I set this up," ZZ hissed, his breath hot across Hawk's

face. "Deuce has been buyin' less and less Russian metal since teamin' up with Preacher and those Chinese fucks."

Hawk cut his eyes toward Yenny. "Deuce hasn't been buyin' less. Fact, this isn't about Deuce at all, is it? You want Preacher. You want the East Coast."

"You always were a smart boy, Luca. Such a shame what happened to you . . ."

Yenny's gaze ran up and down the length of Hawk as he eyed his leathers and his cut with nothing short of disgust. Once upon a time, Hawk would have done the same, way back when his name was still Luca. But he wasn't Luca anymore. He was James motherfucking Hawk Young, he was Deuce's boy, and he was unfailingly loyal.

"I'll never help you," he gritted out.

Hawk found himself suddenly spun around and face-to-face with a smiling ZZ. No, ZZ wasn't smiling, he was mocking him with a crude and ugly grin.

"Brother," ZZ said with a sneer. "You already have. Now we wait to see if your prez gives a fuck about you."

"Enough," Yenny demanded. "The car is waiting. Shoot him already."

The declaration caught Hawk by surprise, but he had little time to dwell on it as a shot rang out, and his left leg bent suddenly and then gave out entirely. Searing pain shot up and down the limb as he stumbled backward and slammed into the wall behind him. Falling forward, his body crumpled to the floor in an awkward heap.

Blinking through watery eyes, he tried to assess his injury, could almost make out his shin. The bullet had gone into the left side of his leg, torn straight through, blowing out the other side, taking with it bone, muscle, and a shit ton of blood. Seeing the gaping wound, the broken bone fragments sharply jutting through the gory mess of shredded muscle and blood, all caused his stomach to roil.

Shaking, starting to shiver from the cold quickly taking hold of his insides, Hawk glanced up at ZZ and, despite his pain, attempted a smile. No fucking way was he going to let these assholes use him against Deuce. He would die first.

"Never did see Danny lookin' at you the way she looks at Ripper," he whispered hoarsely. "Must burn you up inside knowin' she loves lookin' at somethin' Crazy Frankie carved up, more than she ever did you."

ZZ's nostrils flared wide as the hand holding his gun began to twitch.

"And Tegen," Hawk continued through chattering teeth. "Shit, brother . . . you packin' light . . . 'cause you're losin' women left and—"

Hawk jerked as a gun discharged and sent ZZ sprawling backward. But before Hawk could see how badly ZZ was hit, Yenny stepped in front of him, blocking his line of sight.

"Luca, Luca, Luca." Yenny sighed and tsk-tsked. "You made me shoot my best fighter."

"Yeah," Hawk rasped. Defeated, he let his head drop back against the wall. "So not fuckin' . . . sorry . . . about . . . that."

CHAPTER 4

Christmas Eve Day

"Just sign the papers, Jason."

Inside a secure and guarded room within the confines of the Montana Women's Prison, Jase was seated beside his eldest daughter, Maribelle, staring across the dull metal table into the big blue eyes of his wife. Eyes that had once looked upon him with utter love and devotion, but now were filled with the bitter sting of resentment.

Chrysanthemum "Chrissy" Montgomery had once been a vision to behold. Never, in the history of ever, had there been a man who hadn't looked her way. That wasn't the case anymore. She was in her forties now, yet looking exceptionally older, hardened to the point where she'd become a woman he barely recognized.

He'd done this to her, ruined her, ruined their family and ruined . . .

A pair of pretty green eyes and a freckled face invaded his thoughts, that face framed in thick red waves. He closed his eyes, shutting out the view of his wife, remembering instead Dorothy, the woman who'd once made him feel so damn alive.

Those green eyes had once looked at him with love too.

Opening his eyes, Jase slumped down in his chair, wishing he were drunk. In fact, the only reason he wasn't drunk was because he'd known he'd never be allowed inside the prison reeking of booze. But as soon as he got the hell out of here and back to the club . . .

He could already picture it, pouring himself a nice tall glass of "drowning his sorrows" because he didn't have anything worth a damn left.

"This is really what you want?" he asked quietly.

Her request for a divorce hadn't come as a surprise as much as Chrissy's request to see him in person had. Every attempt he'd made in the past to visit with her, she'd refused. Then out of nowhere, Maribelle had called him early last week—another surprise since not one of his three daughters had wanted anything to do with him since gaining their independence—and informed him of her mother's wishes.

"Your wife is up for parole in a few years, Mr. Brady. Her ties to you and your club will do her nothing but harm."

Jase cut his eyes toward the pudgy-faced lawyer seated beside Chrissy. "Would you shut the fuck up? This ain't your business."

He wasn't opposed to a divorce, but at the same time, even though he was loathe to admit it out loud, the thought of severing all ties to his wife and quite possibly his children because of it, terrified him. Aside from the club, this was all he had left; it wasn't much, and it might be tattered, shredded to shit, but it was all he had.

But if he were honest with himself, he would have to admit that it had been his own fears and insecurities that had gotten him and everyone around him into this mess in the first place. And that if he continued ignoring the needs and wishes of those around him, prolonging the inevitable, tragedy was bound to strike again.

"Just sign the papers, Jason," Chrissy repeated tonelessly. "You don't want me. You never did."

He stared at her, his stomach churning as his inescapable guilt welled up twice as strong inside him. That wasn't true. He had wanted her. Once upon a time, when they were both still teenagers with endless possibilities ahead of them, he'd wanted her very much.

He'd loved watching that tight body bouncing up and down in her high school cheerleading uniform, and that beautiful, flawless face grinning as she cheered him on from the sidelines. But that didn't mean he'd wanted to become a father at seventeen and a husband at eighteen, forced to spend the rest of his life listening to her prattle on about stupid, insipid bullshit he couldn't give two shits about. She'd taken to married life, to motherhood, like she'd been born for it, and he'd . . .

He'd enlisted in the Marine reserves to escape the hell that had become his life. He'd taken to drinking heavily too. And it was during one of the many nights he'd spent intoxicated at a local bar that he'd run into the local Horsemen president.

Not too long after, he'd found himself a patched-in member of one of the most notorious motorcycle clubs in the country, and a lance corporal in the reserves.

Jase had known he was an anomaly—Marine by day, biker by night—but the truth of the matter was he'd never been able to find a happy medium. Constantly dissatisfied and always itching to be on the move, always looking for something new, he needed the duality in his life. The Marine reserves kept him grounded, forced him to stay in one place, forced him to be the man he knew he had to be for his family, but the club gave him the excitement he always felt he was lacking. Despite his dual life, he found himself still searching for something more.

He'd found that something more in the most unlikely of places.

His Horsemen chapter had fucked up big-time. Two boys had been thrown inside, and word was they'd been about to go turncoat and start singing to the district attorney. Everyone in his chapter had to scatter, especially him. Being a Marine, he couldn't afford to have trouble with the law. He'd been lucky too. Being picked up by Deuce wasn't something that happened every day. At first he hadn't been happy about the move until . . .

Little Dorothy Kelley Matthews.

He should have left Dorothy alone; he hadn't even meant to fall for her, but it was hard not to fall for Dorothy. They had all fallen for her in their own way, every last boy in that club, even the constant flow of whores had loved her. She was a natural caretaker, a mother to everyone. You couldn't help but gravitate toward her, waiting for your turn to be enveloped by that beautiful glow that always surrounded her.

And, as was his usual MO, he'd put his own wants and needs before that of everyone else, and in turn had destroyed them all.

To his left, Maribelle leaned forward, her hard eyes catching his gaze. "Haven't you done enough damage?" she asked, her tone acidic. "The least you could do is sign the papers and give her a fraction of a chance to get out of this place."

Unlike his twin girls, Meghan and Marisa, Maribelle was the spitting image of Chrissy in her youth. Along with her blue eyes and long auburn hair, as well as her natural tanned and flawless skin, she possessed the same tall, slim, yet muscular body as her mother, and the two of them could have been mistaken for sisters if not for the apparent age difference. But that was where the similarities between mother and daughter ended. Whereas Chrissy had always been fun loving, most times bordering on silly, Maribelle was all piss and vinegar. Something else that was his fault.

Glancing from his daughter to his wife, feeling the heat from their hard, unwavering stares, Jase knew he didn't have a choice. So, for the first time since he'd met her, he put Chrissy before himself. It was the least he could do after everything . . . he'd hadn't done.

"Where do I sign?" he asked, his voice cracking mid-sentence.

The lawyer pushed a manila folder across the table. "I've made it easy," the man said. "Anywhere you see a red tab, sign your full name, your initials, and date it."

Muttering about the uselessness of needing both his full name and his initials, Jase opened the folder and quickly skimmed over the first page. It was all pretty cut and dried. She didn't want a damn thing from him, not the house, not one damn penny. As for their children, all three of them were over the age of eighteen.

Fucking Christ, he needed a goddamn drink.

The pen felt cool within his clammy grip, and his first attempt at signing his name resulted in a barely legible scribble. But by the time he'd reached the final page of the document, his grip was firm, his hand steady and dry. Closing the folder, he slid it back across the table where the lawyer picked it up and promptly placed it inside his waiting briefcase.

"Thank you, Mr. Brady. I'll be in contact if any further participation on your end is required."

Jase nodded; what else could he do? What could he say? It was official; Chrissy was done with him. All those years they'd wasted together, him staying only for the children, her loving him, blind to all his faults, only to have it all blow up in her face in the worst possible way . . . and it all crumbled to nothing.

What a fucking waste. All of it.

"Can you give us a second?" Chrissy asked, looking to her lawyer and then to Maribelle.

Surprise flickered through Jase's gut. He hadn't expected her to want to speak with him privately, but he supposed it made sense since she'd requested to see him in person.

The lawyer had no argument; he packed up his remaining things and was gone. It was their daughter who hadn't so much as moved in her seat. She continued to sit, stone faced, glaring at her mother.

"Belle," Chrissy said, using Maribelle's childhood

nickname. "Please."

Her lips pressed tightly together, her eyes flared wide, Maribelle shook her head emphatically. "No," she said tightly. "I cannot think of anything you could possibly have to say to the man who ruined your life."

The man who ruined your life . . .

Not Dad. He hadn't been Dad in a long time now. He was just some man who'd ruined her mother's life. Fucking hell, he could practically taste the liquor he so desperately needed.

"Belle," Chrissy repeated, this time firmer. The two women stared at each other while Jase waited to see whose will would win out.

When Maribelle slammed her hands down on the table, the noise loud enough to draw the attention of the guard, Jase knew Chrissy had won the battle. As the short, stocky, masculine-looking woman standing outside the door turned toward them and frowned, Jase gave her a weak smile, only succeeding in deepening her frown.

Fucking women. They all hated him. Even ones with facial hair.

Dramatically, Maribelle pushed herself out of her chair. "Whatever," she snapped, "what-fucking-ever. Just don't take all day. The weather service is predicting another epic Montana snowstorm, and the last thing I need is to get stuck in Miles Shit City."

Jase watched his daughter storm out of the small room before turning back to Chrissy. As her tired eyes met his, the guilt, the sadness, the regret he felt was overwhelming, stifling in its intensity. He wanted to look away from her, wanted to run from this room, from what he'd done to her.

But like a car hitting a patch of ice, he could do nothing but watch as the guardrail came rushing up to slap him in the fucking face.

Chrissy took a deep breath before slowly releasing it. "Dorothy," she started, jolting Jase. "I want to know how she's doing. And the child? The girls could never tell me much, only bits and pieces—"

"Chris," he said, interrupting her. "Why are you bringing this up?"

Irritation creased her features. "Because, Jason, I shot a woman, a pregnant woman. I could have killed her and that innocent baby, and I've lived with that fact every day, every year, since it happened. There's nothing I regret more than what I did to her."

He supposed that made sense; even so, he didn't want to discuss Dorothy with Chrissy. But this wasn't about him, and he owed Chrissy at least that much.

Shrugging, he said, "As far as I know, she's doin' good."

"You don't see her?" Chrissy asked. "At all?"

Feeling incredibly awkward discussing his longtime girlfriend with his wife, or ex-wife, even after all this time, Jase shook his head. "Not really. She comes into town sometimes, only to see Tegen or Eva. She never stays very long."

"Not you," Chrissy said. It wasn't a question, but an observation.

"Not me," Jase repeated. Even before her memories had returned to her, Dorothy had repeatedly refused any attempt he'd made to speak with her. And then, after Cage had gotten shot, when she'd threatened to kill him if he came near her again, he'd given up altogether.

"You lost everything," Chrissy said.

He stared at her. She didn't seem to be mocking him; she didn't seem angry or bitter. In fact, much to his surprise, she appeared to have expected his answer.

"I lost everything," he confirmed, then added quietly, "and because of me, so did you."

This time, it was Chrissy who shook her head. "I still have my girls."

Jase didn't know how to respond to that other than to nod in agreement. It was the cold, hard truth. When it had all gone to shit, the girls had taken sides with their mother, barely acknowledging his existence even before they'd all left home. As much as it had stung, he hadn't blamed them. He, more than anybody, hated what he'd done.

"For the longest time, I blamed you for everything," she continued. "I hated you for lying to me, for betraying our marriage. Most of all, I hated you for destroying our family.

"But I've had a lot of time to think about . . . everything. And I've come to the realization that it wasn't just your fault. The other women, Dorothy, I let that go on. I knew you weren't happy, I'd always known, yet I chose to ignore it instead of dealing with it. It was only after I'd found out she was pregnant . . ." She trailed off, her eyes glistening with tears as she turned away from him.

"Chris," he said softly. "You don't have to—"

"No," she insisted, sitting up straighter and wiping at her eyes. "I do. I need you to know how sorry I am. I asked Maribelle here for a reason, to give you some time together. I'd hoped . . ."

She swallowed hard before speaking again. "It's almost Christmas, Jason, and I'd hoped that it being the holidays and seeing each other would help somehow."

"The girls don't need me," he said, nearly choking over his words as he fought back a rising wave of intense emotion. Fucking hell, he was so sensitive lately. Hopefully it wasn't an aging thing, because if it was, if he made it to sixty, he'd be a weepy fucking mess. Worse than a goddamn woman.

Chrissy reached across the table and surprising him, covered his left hand with hers. For a moment, he could only stare down at their hands, joined yet both without their wedding bands, and another wave of regret crashed through him.

"They do," she whispered, squeezing her fingers over his. "And it's your job to show them that."

Jase turned to look outside the room, to where his daughter was standing. With her arms folded across her chest, her face a mask of impenetrable stone, she could have easily passed for one of the guards. One of the not-so-manly-looking guards.

"I'll try," he said, turning back to Chrissy.

She gave him a sad smile. "That's all any of us can do now."

"You don't need to walk me to my car," Maribelle muttered, picking up her pace. "I'm not a little girl."

Jase quickened his own stride through the prison parking lot. He didn't want to fight with her, yet knew no matter what he said, it would turn into an argument. It always did. Scrubbing a calloused hand across his grizzled jaw, he tried to think of something to say to her that wouldn't set her off.

"Pretty big storm headed this way," he called out, "and

you got a long drive ahead of you. You got snow tires on that piece of shit you're drivin'?"

Maribelle stopped walking so abruptly, he nearly barreled right over her. Backing up a couple of feet, he braced himself for what he knew was coming.

"Stop it!" she hissed. "Just stop pretending you give a shit about me!"

Feeling both exasperated and exhausted, he lifted his hands in a gesture of peace.

"Belle," he pleaded. "I'm just tryin' to talk to you, is all. It's Christmas Eve, baby. Throw your old man a bone, for shit's sake."

Maribelle's face twisted into an ugly sneer. "You're right!" she shouted. "It's Christmas Eve! And like usual, I get to spend it without my mother!

"Whose fault is that?" she continued. "Whose fucking fault is that?"

Jase opened his mouth, not knowing what the hell he was going to say, but knowing that something, anything had to be said to defuse her anger before they had prison security descending upon them. But Maribelle beat him to it.

"Yours!" she screamed, her hands clenching into small fists. "You ruined our family, you ruined everything, and now you're a sad old drunk who thinks just because it's Christmastime you have some right to talk to me about snow tires? As if you even give a shit! All you've ever given a shit about is that fucking club and that whore of yours!"

"Keep your damn voice down!" he whispered harshly, "before you get slapped with cuffs and I'm bailin' your ass outta jail."

Even as angry as she looked, he could still see the

sadness, the disappointment she was trying to hide from him. It reminded of him of her as a child, learning to ride her bike without the training wheels. Over and over again she'd fallen, skinning her shins and knees, but she had been a determined little girl. Even when he'd been ready to throw in the towel, not wanting to bring her home to her mother covered in blood, she'd grit her teeth, dry her eyes, and get back up on that damn bike. The memories only served to worsen his mood. He didn't have nearly enough of them because he'd never been around.

"Belle," he said, sighing heavily. "I took all that blame a long fuckin' time ago and I never denied it, not fuckin' once. But there ain't nothin' I can do about the past. All I got is right now, and I'm tryin'. I'll never stop tryin'. You're my daughter, my baby girl, and that shit means somethin' to me. Always has."

Maribelle continued to glare at him, seemingly unwavering in her resentment, except for the slight tremble of her bottom lip.

Seeing an opening, he took a step forward and placed his hands on her shoulders. "I know I've no right to ask you for a damn thing, not after everything I took from you and your sisters, but I'm askin' anyways."

Maribelle looked up and directly into his eyes. "And what exactly are you asking for?"

He stared down at her, into the mirror image of his wife twenty years ago, realizing for the first time that if he didn't try to right this wrong, really try this time, his daughter's eyes would continue to grow colder, losing their light the same way her mother's had.

"I'm askin' for Christmas," he said. "I want you home

for Christmas."

In fact, he wanted all of his daughters home for Christmas, but the truth was that the twins took their cues from Maribelle. She had, along with Chrissy's parents, taken over as their caretaker. Jase was persona non grata. But if he could get Maribelle home, the twins would undoubtedly follow suit.

Several long moments passed by in uncomfortable silence, during which it began to snow. Jase glanced up at the darkening sky, worrying about Maribelle's long drive home, and while he was distracted, Maribelle slipped out from under his hands.

"I can't," she said as she quickly backed away. "I'm sorry . . ." She shook her head. "No, I'm not sorry, but I just . . . can't."

Then she turned and hurried off.

Jase remained where he was, watching as she fumbled with her car keys, waiting until she was safely inside the vehicle and halfway out of the parking lot before finally lowering his gaze.

"Back to the club," he muttered. Because there was no way in hell he was going home to that empty house on Christmas Eve. There was no Christmas tree, no decorations, no presents to be wrapped, no turkey baking in the oven, no giggling coming from the kids' rooms upstairs. There was nothing but four walls, dusty furniture, and a dirty floor.

Ever since his two youngest had left home, he'd been at the club more than ever, unable to stomach the ever-present emptiness that had not only taken root inside his house, but inside him as well.

If only he'd realized sooner that it wasn't the house, four walls and a roof, that made a home. It was who had lived inside those four walls, his wife and daughters, the true support beams of the structure. Without them the roof had caved in, the walls had collapsed, and the foundation had crumbled away.

And as he headed for his truck, he found himself wishing for the millionth time since Dorothy had been shot, that Cox hadn't wrestled the gun from his hand.

CHAPTER 5

MY GRANDFATHER USED TO SAY THAT WHEN IT RAINED, it poured. Or in my case, when it rained, it rained like Christmas in San Francisco until eventually it flooded and pulled you under, leaving you flapping your arms and kicking your legs, gasping for a breath you already knew wouldn't come.

After Tegen's phone call, I'd spent the following thirty-six hours flapping and gasping under a waterfall of problems. It seemed as if the universe, Mother Nature herself, was determined to keep me away from Miles City.

First I'd needed to find a place for Christopher to stay. Not knowing what awaited me at the clubhouse, there was nothing on earth that could convince me to bring my son into what could potentially become a dangerous situation, or worse, a devastating one.

This proved to be a problem as I had very few friends in San Francisco. Due to some minor residual side effects from my brain injury and my lack of education, I hadn't been able to find a job that would provide me with a more substantial income than my disability checks already did, which meant there were no coworkers I'd grown close with. I'd made nice with the other mothers at Christopher's school, and I'd gone on a few dates over the years, but there was never anyone serious, and most definitely no one I trusted with my most precious possession.

It was Tegen who'd suggested Hayley, one of her closest friends, and I mentally kicked myself for not thinking of her sooner. Hayley and her husband were kind souls, full of happy energy, who had a young child of their own.

Hayley had readily agreed; it was Christopher I'd had to convince. More time was spent explaining to him why his mother had to leave him, and on Christmas Day no less. I ended up lying to him, something I had promised myself to never do, and told him his grandfather was sick.

Being that I'd had no contact with my family since I'd divorced Tegen's father, something Christopher was aware of, I could tell he was skeptical, as well as feeling put out that I was leaving him behind. But what choice did I have? I couldn't very well tell him his father was in danger or worse. In the end he took it in stride, further proving how very much like Hawk he truly was, and only serving to make me feel even worse for lying to him.

Once Christopher was settled at Hayley's, I ran into a whole other slew of problems. Due to a winter storm that was bearing down on the entire Midwest and spilling into the surrounding states, flights to Montana were either being canceled or delayed indefinitely.

I waited at the airport for hours, my anxiety worsening each time another flight was canceled, until I eventually gave up on the airlines altogether and ended up renting a car.

The next twenty-four hours were spent on the road, only four of which I'd allowed myself a quick nap in a rest area off the interstate.

By the time I reached the state of Montana, I was well into the center of the storm, unable to see more than a few feet in front of me, and unable to drive more than thirty miles per hour. It was slow going for a while; my only reprieve was that the roads were virtually empty, and I was determined to make it to my destination.

Now I was parked just beyond the clubhouse's razor-wire-topped gates. Releasing my death grip on the steering wheel, I released a large breath of pent-up air and looked up at the building before me.

The whitewashed warehouse was massive, the Hell's Horsemen logo painted on the front, huge and intimidating. Nothing about the appearance was warm or inviting, something I'm sure Deuce did purposely.

I'd been here a thousand times before, even after my move to California, but something felt different this time.

I felt as though I were standing on a precipice composed of quickly unraveling thread, and once I passed through those gates, my quiet life, my now peaceful existence and everything I had rebuilt from the ground up, all of it was going to disintegrate and send me free-falling back into the never-ending abyss of the unknown.

That thought, the fear it caused within me, was nearly

enough to make me turn the car around and go back to California.

But this wasn't about me. This was about Hawk and the little boy I'd left behind.

Taking a deep breath, I swallowed my fears and pulled the vehicle forward. Rolling down my window, I reached out into the blistering cold and pressed the call button on the intercom.

The intercom buzzed to life and a gravelly voice crackled through the speaker. "Was wondering how long you were gonna sit out there."

I instantly recognized the voice as Worm's, a longtime brother of the club, and despite my nervousness felt a smile slip past my thinly pressed lips.

"Just mentally preparing myself for those roaming hands of yours," I quipped.

"Welcome home, little D," he said, chuckling.

After an entire day spent driving and worrying, his answering laughter, raspy due to many years of chain-smoking, was a welcome sound.

The latch clicked and as the gate began to slowly swing open, I could barely make out through the heavy veil of falling snow the front door of the clubhouse opening. Like a beacon in the midst of the surrounding gloom, a warm glow of light poured forth, spilling out into the darkness.

As I drove forward, a figure appeared in the doorway, imposing in size, taking up nearly the entire entrance. Despite the absence of the sun and the falling snow impeding my vision, I would know those shoulders anywhere. Those were shoulders that usually bore the weight of the world upon them, yet somehow never fell.

After parking and with my luggage in tow, I began the trek through the snow-laden parking lot, battling both the biting cold and whipping wind until I reached the front door, a mass of quivering skin and chattering teeth.

Deuce took my suitcase from me. As if it weighed next to nothing, he easily hefted it up and over his shoulder and quickly ushered me inside. Once the door was closed behind us, he pulled me into an awkward one-armed hug. I stood there, momentarily frozen in shock by the uncommonly kind gesture. Deuce didn't hug people, at least not if he could help it; hugs were reserved for his wife and children.

"Welcome home, Dorothy," he said gruffly, giving me a hearty pat on the back that if it hadn't been for his large body in the way, would have sent me flying across the room.

Through the snowflakes still clinging to my eyelashes, I looked up his leather-clad body, taking it all in—the tattooed dragons on his bare forearms, the president patch on his cut, the scent of cigarettes and liquor that always seemed to cling to him, before stopping at his icy blue eyes.

His smile wasn't friendly; it never had been. Deuce had always snarled more than he'd smiled. But his eyes were soft and kind. Inviting, even. He'd aged a little more since I'd last seen him; he had to be around sixty now and it was starting to show. His long blond hair and beard had heavily grayed, the lines on his forehead and bracketing his eyes had grown longer, were etched in a little deeper.

Pulling off my knit ski hat, I shook out my damp hair and smiled. "I see my daughter has given you a few more gray hairs."

His smile grew, causing several dimples to appear, and

just like that, the changes in his appearance seemed to vanish. He stood before me the same fearfully handsome young man I remembered from my youth. Elusive and frightening, yet intriguing, he'd taken over his father's motorcycle club and in turn changed the lives of so many.

"Your daughter and that mouth of hers is gonna give me another fuckin' heart attack," he muttered, shaking his head. "Her and my own fuckin' daughters, my sons, my granddaughter, and . . . Jesus Christ, Cox, that motherfucker . . ." He trailed off, grimacing.

"Mm-hmm," I murmured, glancing around the quiet club. Aside from Worm, who was standing behind the bar pouring himself a liquid snack, there was no one else in sight. As I brought my gaze back to Deuce, I found him watching me, all traces of humor gone, and my smile fell away.

"This shit with Hawk, it ain't good, D," he said. "And usually I wouldn't be tellin' any of my boys' old ladies this kinda shit until I had more information, but I'm makin' an exception here. One, 'cause it's Hawk and there's some shit you need to fuckin' know, and two, 'cause it's you and you're family now.

"Let's go to my office," he continued, turning away, "and I'll tell you what I know."

For a moment I only stood there, watching as he walked off, still holding up my suitcase with those pillars of strength he called shoulders.

Family. He'd called me family. True, our children had married each other, would probably someday have children of their own, but still I'd never thought of myself as part of Deuce's family.

Not only that, but he'd referred to me as an old lady.

Hawk's old lady. It made sense, being that I was the mother of his child, and resided in the only other place aside from this clubhouse that he'd put down any sort of roots.

But still . . . I'd never realized . . .

A warm tear slipped out from the corner of my eye and slid down my cold cheek.

Home.

CHAPTER 6

J
ASE WAS GLAD HE WAS DRUNK. IF HE WASN'T DRUNK and had to listen to Deuce explain that Hawk wasn't actually Hawk, but instead Luca Fuckachev or some such shit, the son of the head of one of the most dangerous drug and weapons cartels in the history of cartels, he might have actually been pissed off that Deuce had kept this a secret for so goddamn long, like everyone else appeared to be.

Instead, he found the entire thing pretty fucking amusing. Especially the part about Hawk having been shot. But according to the Russians holding him hostage, he was still alive and would continue to stay alive, as long as Deuce and Preacher both agreed to their terms.

Terms that Jase wasn't entirely aware of since he wasn't paying much attention to Deuce. Something about guns and the East Coast, something about Preacher and his club, the Silver Demons, something about Hawk being killed if Deuce didn't get Preacher on board, and something else about going to war with the cartel, blah, blah, fucking blah.

It wasn't that he wanted Hawk to die, not really. Once upon a time, when the shit had first hit the fan and he'd found out the baby he'd thought was his was actually Hawk's, and that Hawk and Dorothy had been having an ongoing affair right under his goddamn nose, yeah, he might have wished death upon the guy once or twice.

But that was then and this was now. Now he was freshly divorced, without his kids, having spent another Christmas drunker than shit at the clubhouse, watching Bucket and his girlfriend fuck like rabbits on the couch beside him. Good times.

So, no, he really didn't give a fuck if Hawk lived or died. In his opinion, if it came down to the club or Hawk, Hawk could go straight to hell. Personal feelings aside, the asshole wasn't even one of them; instead, he'd been using the clubhouse to hide from the law.

"Preacher's on his way here," Mick announced. "He's on board with the plan and bringing his VP and three of his boys with 'im as a show of good faith to the Russians."

Deuce nodded his thanks in Mick's direction, and in turn, Mick averted his eyes.

"What?" Deuce demanded. "What the fuck is your fuckin' problem?"

Mick shrugged. "I'm your VP, have been since day fuckin' one, and even though we've butted heads a few times, I've always stood by your side. Fuck, Prez, I did time in lockup for you and you couldn't trust me with this?"

Mick shook his head. "I don't know what to think now."

"I never asked you to take that rap for me!" Deuce shouted. "You need to reel your fuckin' bullshit in, right the fuck now!"

Mick jumped up out of his seat and slammed his clenched fists down upon the tabletop. "But I fuckin' did! Because your old man had just kicked the bucket and this fuckin' club needed some stability for fuckin' once, not another prez who was locked up!"

"That was almost forty fuckin' years ago," Deuce said, purposely punctuating each word. Gripping the edge of the meeting table, he leaned forward, bringing him nearly nose to nose with Mick. "Why are you bringin' this shit up now? You want me to suck your dick or somethin'?"

Normally, a comment like that would have sent the rest of the boys into a fit of laughter, followed by more lewd comments or gestures, but not today. Tension was high, and even the most lighthearted of the brothers were sitting stone faced in their seats.

"He never fuckin' told me," Ripper suddenly muttered. "What the fuck . . ."

Out of everyone crammed inside Deuce's office, Ripper looked the most put out, even more so than Mick. Probably because he'd been the closest to Hawk, more than anyone else associated with the club.

Except for Dorothy, Jase thought bitterly. Obviously she'd been a hell of a lot closer to Hawk than Ripper had.

Deuce tore his angry stare away from Mick and pinned it on Ripper. "He was under my fuckin' orders not to tell a damn one of you! Do you do shit I tell you not to fuckin' do . . ."

Deuce trailed off and closed his eyes. "Never mind," he said, sighing. "Of course you fuckin' do."

Seated beside Ripper, Cox elbowed him in the ribs. "He's talkin' 'bout you fuckin' his daughter," he whispered loudly. "We weren't supposed to do that, dude, and you didn't listen."

Ripper shoved Cox and in turn Cox shoved Ripper, and as the two of them proceeded to shove and slap at each other like the two little girls they often acted like, the rest of the room burst into a fit of laughter. The thick tension that had been holding the entire room hostage for well over an hour seemed to evaporate. Even Deuce and Mick, who—other than Jase—were the only two club members not laughing, looked more at ease than they had only moments ago.

And just like that Jase was no longer amused, but instead, straight-up pissed the fuck off. Slamming his palms down on the table, he shoved his chair back and shot to his feet. Of course, since he was shitfaced, he had to continue holding on to the table for a few more seconds to ensure he wouldn't go toppling backward along with his chair.

Heads shot up all around the room as his brothers peered curiously at him with raised eyebrows. He paid them no attention as he stumbled his way to the office door, more than ready to be done with this bullshit meeting.

"Jase!" Deuce bellowed and he paused, his hand on the doorknob. "I didn't say you could leave. This is a meeting and a vote. I made that pretty fuckin' clear."

Jase glanced over his shoulder at his president and narrowed his eyes. "I don't give a fuck what you do with

Hawk," he spat venomously. "Or Luca, or whoever the fuck he is. My vote goes to the club."

Yanking one of the office's double doors open, Jase forced his body into action, managing to stay upright just long enough to breach the doorway and slam the door closed behind him with enough force that the connecting walls shook in response.

With every intention of heading straight for the bar and the copious amount of booze beckoning him from its shelves, he spun away from the still-rattling door and started forward.

"Jase?"

Recognizing the voice, he froze in lumbering midstride and nearly fell over because of it. He'd known Dorothy was here, or at least he'd known she was in town, but had already figured he wouldn't be seeing her, since she usually went to great lengths to ensure she was never in the same place at the same time he was. Never in a million years would he have guessed she would have come to the club.

Slowly, he turned to face her, squinting across the considerable distance between them, and found her standing just outside the hallway that led to the kitchen. He looked her up and down, just drinking her in for the first time in what felt like far too long.

Gone was the fresh-faced girl next door he'd fallen for. She no longer carried with her that aura of innocence and naïveté she'd held throughout her twenties and thirties. No, Dorothy finally looked like the grown woman she was. Her features had matured, sharpened, were no longer cute, but instead a refined sort of beautiful.

"Dorothy," he said quietly, focusing on her face and

those big and beautiful green eyes of hers. Her eyes hadn't changed, and for some reason he took comfort in that. "I didn't realize—"

"The vote," she said tersely, interrupting him. "Did you vote yet?"

Jase's mouth snapped shut as he noticed for the first time the slight tremble of her lips, her rigid posture, the way she was gripping her hands, wringing them together.

She was afraid.

For motherfucking Hawk.

Of course she was. After all, she had come all the way from California just to find out what was going on with him. But what Jase had initially thought was only concern for the sake of her son's father, looked to be something else entirely.

Jesus fucking Christ, did she still have feelings for the man? Did the two of them have something going on that no one else knew about . . . again?

Feeling suddenly awkward, he reached up to rub his hand across the back of his neck, using the maneuver to avert his eyes, hoping she didn't realize the sudden overwhelming disappointment that had gripped hold of his heart.

"I . . . uh . . ." He stumbled over his words, trying to form an answer that didn't include telling her he'd just announced how much he didn't care whether Hawk lived or died, seeing as she so obviously did care.

"No vote yet," he said, clearing his throat. "I'm just taking a piss break."

Nodding, Dorothy's lips pressed tightly together and her eyes perceptibly widened. He knew that look, had seen it hundreds of times before. It was the face she made when she was desperately trying not to cry. Seeing that, something rattled painfully inside Jase's chest, and his insides clenched uncomfortably. He hated that face, he fucking loathed it . . . mostly because he'd always been the cause of it.

"Don't worry," he said quickly. "We'll bring him home."

"Okay," she whispered, nodding more to herself than to him. "I'll just be . . . I'll just be in the kitchen."

He watched her disappear around the corner, listened as the swinging doors to the kitchen creaked back and forth as she passed through them, and shortly after that came the banging of pots and pans.

Something warm burst forth within his gut, easing the uncomfortable tightening that had taken root. She was back, not only in Miles City but inside the clubhouse, and back inside the kitchen no less.

It was so fucking familiar and, goddamn him, so incredibly comforting. After so many years of feeling nothing but the cold shoulder from both her and his family, feeling this semblance of his past, a place where he'd been happy and content, was more than welcome.

And he didn't want to lose it.

Turning around, he burst back into Deuce's office. Ignoring the stares of everyone in the room, he marched forward, shoved Anger out of the chair Jase had been occupying before he'd left the room, and reclaimed his seat.

When it came time for him to cast his vote, he looked directly into Deuce's narrowed eyes, raised two fingers in the air, and answered, "Yea. Bring him home."

What bringing Hawk home would accomplish,

other than putting Deuce and Preacher at the mercy of the Russian cartel, Jase didn't know. All he knew was that it would keep Dorothy around, if only for a little while longer . . . as well as keep her from crying.

At the very least, he owed her that much.

CHAPTER 7

The more things change, the more they stay the same.
— Jean-Baptiste Alphonse Karr

"WEIRD, ISN'T IT?"

Tearing my gaze away from my daughter and the group of young woman who were surrounding her, I glanced to where Eva was seated beside me on a long leather couch. Seated beside Eva was Kami, and to my left was Kajika, a Native American woman from a nearby Indian reservation who Cox and Kami had employed as their nanny, but now held my former position around the clubhouse, cooking and cleaning up after the boys. Something I had only just found out after being scolded for disrupting her highly organized cupboard system. Who knew plates had to be stacked according to size and shape?

"What's weird?" I asked.

Pushing her headphones off her ears, Eva smirked. "Them," she said, gesturing to Tegen and the other women. "And us. We used to be them, young and hot, the center of attention inside the club, and now we're not. We've become the actual old ladies.

"Strangely enough," she continued, shrugging, "I don't mind. I feel like it's the natural progression of things, and we're all exactly where we're supposed to be."

Knowing exactly what she was up to, attempting to distract me while we all waited for Preacher to arrive from New York City, I decided to play along instead of dwelling on the agony of wondering what was going to happen next, or worse, if Hawk would survive it.

Or . . . who Hawk truly was, something that I couldn't exactly bring myself to think on quite yet. I'd sat inside Deuce's office and quietly listened, absorbing the wild story he'd told me about the son of a mob boss he'd found living on the streets. In return for saving his life and giving him the protection he'd needed, Deuce had only asked for one thing in return . . . his loyalty.

Now, Hawk had been kidnapped by an uncle everyone had thought dead or living on the lam, and who was threatening to either kill Hawk or turn him over to the federal government if Deuce and Preacher didn't concede to their terms.

It was a little too much to take in all at once, more so because Hawk wasn't here to confirm any of it, or let me berate him for lying to me all these years.

Although it finally made sense to me why Hawk never insisted on Christopher taking his last name. Young wasn't his actual name.

And for some reason, knowing that was why, because he'd been in hiding and hadn't been able to give his son his real last name, hurt my heart in a way that left me physically aching.

"I don't mind either," I said. It was true that I'd never been one for the spotlight, even in my youth. While most of the other women who'd hung around the clubhouse had always tried to outdo one another when it came to sex appeal, I'd never even attempted it. Being wanted by many wasn't something I'd ever aspired to, despite the way my life had gone.

"Speak for yourselves," Kami retorted. Leaning back against the couch, she folded her bony arms across her chest, purposely pulling down the neckline of her lacy black camisole. "I'm still hot. Forties are the new twenties, ladies."

My eyebrows shot up and I couldn't stop the laugh that escaped me. "Are you serious?" I exclaimed. "Forties are the new twenties?"

My forties were most definitely not my twenties. Most mornings I stood in front of the mirror staring down my reflection, wondering disparagingly where my twenties and thirties had gone to. That wasn't to say I felt myself ugly or lacking. Other than the slight signs of aging around my eyes, I'd been blessed with very fair freckled skin that had kept up its elasticity nicely through two children and four decades, even though not everything on my body was as perky as it once had been. Not that it mattered. Since I was no longer having sex, hadn't engaged in anything more than meaningless kisses after a few awkward dates with men I hadn't felt more than a speck of interest for, since . . . since

Jase and I were last together.

Looking to the bar, where I'd last seen Jase, I found him watching me. Setting down his glass, he smiled kindly at me. The smile didn't sit well with me and, suddenly awash with discomfort, I quickly looked away.

"Ignore her," Eva said, laughing. "She's full of shit. Since realizing she's now the mother of a teenager, every year she's doing something new and ridiculously expensive to try and stop the aging process. This year she's given up sex."

My mouth fell open and my surprised gaze flitted back to Kami. "You gave up sex?" I sputtered. "Are you blackmailing Cox again?"

Aside from the two beautiful boys they'd produced together, Cox and Kami were notorious for two things: Fighting. And sex. All the time. If they weren't doing one, they were doing the other, or engaging in both at the same time.

Crossing one leg over the other, showcasing her expensive black heeled boots, Kami sniffed imperiously. "Fuck that asshole. Forty-three years old and he's still going at it like a jackhammer on crack every chance he gets. He was wearing me out! It's his fault I'm getting wrinkles!"

Eva rolled her eyes. "You don't have wrinkles."

"I do!" Kami protested. "You just can't see them when they're hiding behind the Botox! And these strange little hairs were appearing in the worst possible places! It is all Cox's fault!"

I was still staring at her, my mouth agape. "Wait," I said. "I'm sorry, but I'm still stuck on the fact that you and Cox aren't having sex."

Turning to me, her big eyes wide, Eva mouthed, "*Kami

isn't having sex." Then she wrinkled her nose and gave a slight shake of her head.

And I knew exactly what she was trying to convey to me. Although we came from vastly different upbringings, where Eva had spent her entire life within the confines of a motorcycle club and their social norms, I too had spent a good portion of mine here as well. And I knew exactly how things worked, more so than most.

And what she was telling me was that Kami wasn't having sex, but Cox most certainly still was.

"He's adapting," Kami added. "I've had to tase him less and less lately in order to get a good night's sleep."

Beside me, Kajika let out a long-suffering sigh, the look on her face speaking volumes about Cox and Kami's demented relationship. "One would think working for a group of bikers would be worse than being a nanny," she said, "but after living with you and your family . . . I know now there is nothing on earth worse than that."

"I don't blame you at all." Eva laughed.

"Please, Evie," Kami said. "How can *you* judge *me*? At least my husband isn't a grandfather."

"And how old is Cox's daughter now?" Eva asked, turning to wink at me. "He could be a grandfather sooner than you think."

Kami's nose wrinkled. "I'm not sure how old she is. Her mother told Cox I'm a bad influence, so she's not around much anymore."

Pressing her lips together, Eva rolled her body against mine and buried her face in my shoulder. As she shook with silent laughter, I was unable to stop the snort that escaped me. Dropping my face into Eva's mass of long brown hair, I burst into a fit of giggles.

"What?" Kami yelled. "You bitches! I am not a bad influence!"

"Yes," Kajika said dryly. "You're a pillar of female empowerment, a model all young girls should aspire to become."

"Fuck you," Kami said with a snarl. "Just because I don't wander around spouting off Indian proverbs at a bunch of biker assholes and their whores in hopes of bettering their lives, doesn't mean I'm completely useless!"

"Oh God," Eva said, breathless with silent laughter. "Just stop . . . Please, Kami, you need to get laid so badly . . . Shit, I'm gonna pee . . . Just stop . . ."

"Please pee," Kami snapped, "so we can throw out those disgusting jeans of yours! And that awful T-shirt. Who wears their husband's clothing, Evie? Who, dammit, who?"

"What is so funny?"

Glancing up, we found Tegen and Danny standing above us. Tegen's red hair hung in two long braids down her chest, and Danny was dressed in her typical pink, her blonde hair surprisingly short in an adorable pixie cut. As they peered down at us, their expressions varied between curiously amused to downright confused.

"Nothing that concerns your wrinkle-free faces," Kami said with a dramatic and dismissive wave of her hand. "You're too young to understand our suffering."

Howling with laughter, Eva fell forward, nearly falling off the couch entirely, and I quickly followed suit, collapsing on top of her. The bewildered expression on Tegen's face only served to provoke more laughter, until I could no longer control myself and I laughed and laughed until my belly positively ached.

Seated at the bar across the room, Jase watched, smiling to himself as Dorothy fell on top of Eva in a fit of laughter. How long had it been since he'd last seen her laugh? He no longer cared that Hawk was the reason she was here, because all that mattered was she was here and she wasn't avoiding him. In his mind, that was progress.

"Wanna hear somethin' gross?"

Jase didn't bother looking toward Cox. "No, I don't."

Nobody ever wanted to hear what Cox considered gross. It was usually on a level all its own, too repulsive to be considered simply "gross."

"Yeah, so, you know that new bitch that's been hangin' around lately?"

Jase cut his eyes in Cox's direction. "Young?" he asked. "Kinda fat?"

Cox nodded. "Yeah, that's her. Roly-poly little bitch. Fucked her in the ass the other day and, get this, she shit all over me. I'm talkin', this wasn't no little mess. This was Niagara fuckin' Falls pourin' outta her ass."

Jase stared at the man, cringing at the visual, wishing he had the ability to un-hear half of what Cox usually said to him. Even so, seeing Cox, a man who was covered from his neck to his toes in mostly violent and crude tattoos, who was pierced nearly everywhere humanly possible, with his eyes wide, both nodding and shaking his head, looking so damn distraught over the ridiculous story, that even in the face of his own disgust, Jase couldn't help but laugh.

"Brother, that's fuckin' disgusting."

Cox both sighed and shuddered. "Yeah, dude, I know," he said, then added rather piteously, "but Kami won't fuck me and if I don't drain this motherfucker on the regular, I'm gonna fuckin' die!"

"Goddamn it," Jase muttered, shaking his head. "Why the fuck are you always tellin' me this shit?"

Cox turned to face him fully then, his expression suddenly serious. "So you stop staring at Dorothy, wishin' for shit you lost a long-ass time ago and ain't never gonna have again."

CHAPTER 8

IT WAS EVENING BY THE TIME PREACHER AND HIS MEN had arrived, and by that time most of the club had cleared out. Only a handful of Horsemen remained, and other than Tegen and me, the women had all gone home to their children.

To my dismay, Preacher had stormed inside the club, covered in snow and looking righteously pissed off. Seeing this and fearing the worst, thinking that something had changed his mind and he was no longer on board for whatever plan Deuce had come up with to get Hawk home safely, my stomach had painfully knotted. So instead of going forth to greet him, I waited in the background with bated breath as Deuce and his boys came out to greet their guests.

"Who the fuck in their right fuckin' mind puts a fuckin' motorcycle club in the middle of goddamn Alaska?"

Preacher bellowed. "You assholes have to be outta your fuckin' minds! How much ridin' time you get around here? Two fuckin' months a year?"

Cage had laughed, Deuce had glared, and Mick had flipped him off. Several rounds of insults were traded as well as handshakes and slaps on the back, and all the while relief was shuddering from my lungs. Suddenly feeling relaxed enough to do so, I stepped forward to extend my welcome.

"Preacher," I said, smiling as I held out my hand.

His grin was that of a dirty old man with pleasure on his mind, and as he took my hand, he pulled me into a hug that ended with him taking hold of my backside and squeezing.

"You free tonight, sweetheart?" he whispered in my ear. "Always did love myself a redhead."

Laughing, I wrestled myself out of his arms. "I'm only two years older than your daughter," I scolded.

His grin growing, Preacher's head tilted to one side as he looked me up and down. "Haven't been with a woman my own age since—"

One of his men, an older man named Tiny who was anything but, slapped him on the back. "Fucker, you ain't never been with a woman your own age."

Preacher spread his arms out wide in an apologetic gesture and shrugged. "There you have it."

Eva's father was closing in on seventy, and the years of heavy smoking and drinking had begun to take a heavy toll on his once handsome features. His long hair that once had been brown was now a deep shade of gray, the deep grooves lining his face were more pronounced than ever before, but most noticeable was the change in his stature; his now imperfect posture and significant loss of muscle mass gave him an overall appearance of shrinking.

As I studied him, I couldn't help but be reminded that my own parents were around his age, which made me think of the lie I'd told Christopher. I found myself wondering how they were faring, if they were sick or in need of extra support. Almost immediately, I shook away my thoughts. This wasn't the time for trips down memory lane that would only further the already excessive load of emotions I was barely keeping in check.

Cage appeared to my right, his heavy arm landing across my shoulders. "Keep those dirty hands of yours off my mom," he said teasingly. Tegen, who'd materialized on my left, put her hands on her hips and pinned Preacher with a glare. "Seriously," she hissed. "Don't fucking touch her."

Preacher waggled his eyebrows at Cage. "It's the red hair," he said, giving Tegen a greasy smile. "Spitfires, all of 'em. Lucky little bastard."

Before Tegen had the chance to start running her mouth and getting herself into trouble, I looped my arm through hers, shot the men a brilliant smile, and dragged my daughter across the room.

As the men retreated to Deuce's office, I led her to one of the couches.

"Pigs," she muttered and dropped down beside me. She made herself comfortable, sprawling out across both the couch and me, and let out an irritated sigh.

I gave her a thorough once-over from her long braids, the thickly rimmed glasses framing her catlike eyes, down her heavily tattooed arms and long, lithe legs to the tips of her tattooed feet that were currently taking up residence on my lap.

As I studied her, with her many and largely colorful tattoos, I couldn't help but think that she was as colorful as the artwork that covered her body. Tegen was a rainbow of a woman, faults and all. A surge of pride welled up inside me. I'd made this beautiful, colorful, strong woman, and no matter how it had ended between her father and me, no matter that she wasn't a result of love, I loved her fiercely all the same.

"You look good," I mused out loud, giving her ankle a light squeeze. "Happy and healthy."

Cracking an eyelid, she twisted her lips. "Is that a nice way of telling me I look fat?"

"No," I said with a laugh. Although her once too-thin frame had rounded out rather nicely, she was the furthest thing from fat. "It's a nice way of telling you your size-four jeans suit you better than a size zero."

"Six," she muttered. "I'm a six now. See what that fucker did? Made me fat."

"Happy," I said, rubbing her calf affectionately. "Cage makes you happy. Big difference."

She snorted, looking amused, but her expression quickly shifted and suddenly she pushed herself upright and pulled her legs from my lap.

"He wants kids, you know?" she whispered. "But I'm . . . I don't think I do. He's so good with them, too, and if he wants them he should get them but . . . ugh, Mom, I don't think I can do it."

There was raw fear in my daughter's eyes, something that I knew could be attributed to me and my bad parenting, for never being there for her when she'd needed me most. She didn't know how to be a mother, because she'd never truly had one growing up.

"Tegen—" I started, but was quickly interrupted.

"No, Mom, I know what you're thinking and it's not that. I'm not scared of being a mom, or of not being able to be a good mom. I'm scared of becoming a mom and losing everything that makes me . . . well . . . me. But mostly, I'm scared of losing Cage."

Her admission caused her features to twist with shame, and her gaze dropped to where her hands were clasped together in her lap. "It's fucking selfish," she mumbled. "I know it is. But I don't want to be like these other women who have kids and suddenly their men aren't interested anymore. Sometimes I feel like that's all that keeps Cage and me together . . . the fact that he doesn't ever know what to expect from me, because, shit, most of the time I never know what to expect from me. But if we have children, I have to be dependable. I won't get to be me anymore, and what if—"

"Stop it," I snapped. "Tegen, Cage West was a whore if I ever knew one, and a man like that doesn't marry a woman just because he finds her *interesting*. He marries a woman because he's finally found the one that made him reevaluate his whorish ways and want to toss in his whoring towel.

"And," I added quickly, "I'm sure Cage wouldn't mind if you suddenly became a little less . . . interesting."

Tegen's eyes narrowed into tiny slits. "Is that a nice way of telling me I'm too interesting?"

I shrugged and smiled. "It's a nice way of telling the daughter I love and adore that she can be a little too loud and a lot too mouthy sometimes."

Tegen laughed, a sound I'd never grow tired of hearing. Leaning back into the buttery-soft leather, I laughed with her until we both fell into a companionable silence. Once again, she rested her legs across mine and I hugged them tightly to me. Time passed by slowly after that, while we waited for the men, and eventually Tegen's eyes began to close.

When she was sound asleep and softly snoring, I gently moved her legs and slid off the couch. Pressing my ear against Deuce's office doors, I found the men still engaged in conversation. Not wanting to intrude, I wandered off through the dark and silent hallways, dragging my fingertips along the smooth wall until I came to a stop outside the door I hadn't realized I was seeking.

Like most of the boys' rooms, when they weren't at the clubhouse, it was locked. But I wasn't looking to go inside. Aside from the basement, a room I'd never been allowed in, I was well acquainted with all the rooms, had spent years inside each of them, cleaning up after the occupants.

But this room wasn't just any room.

This was Hawk's room.

Pressing my palms flat against the grooved wood, I leaned forward, resting my forehead on the door and thought back to the day I entered this door, and everything changed . . .

Last night had been a mistake. A stupid drunken mistake.

While drinking heavily, reeling with self-pity after Jase had left for home, Hawk had caught me unaware with his surprising intentions.

And in my sorrow-drenched state, I'd done the unthinkable.

Now, apparently Hawk had thought he had some claim

over me, thinking he could demand that I meet him in his room.

Oh, I would be meeting him in his room, all right. Not for some sordid rendezvous, but to tell him exactly where he could shove his line of thinking.

I stormed through the club's back hall and when I reached Hawk's bedroom door, I didn't bother knocking. As far as everyone in the club was concerned, I was only here to clean. Grasping the doorknob, I pushed inside, quickly closing the door behind me.

I looked over the bare walls, the plain and minimal furniture, the lone book sitting atop his dresser, before coming to a stop on the man himself. Leaning against the window ledge, he had one arm across his chest, his hand tucked into his armpit, while the other brought a cigarette up to his mouth.

"Why?" I demanded shakily. "Why are you doing this? Is this funny for you? Is this some sort of sick game?"

After stubbing his cigarette into an ashtray, Hawk pushed himself away from the window. Folding his arms across his chest, he looked me directly in the eyes. Darkly intense and unwavering, sheer dominance radiated from his eyes, making me feel even smaller, not just in size, but worthless in comparison.

"Woman," he said, his voice a deep, rolling rumble. "I don't play games."

"Then what?" I demanded. "You just figured I'd be easy, because why? Because I'm a whore!"

The corners of his mouth began to curl. If he were anyone else, I would have thought he was smiling, but Hawk didn't smile and the expression was anything but lighthearted; it was pure menace.

"You're not a whore." He practically growled the words. "I don't fuck with club whores."

His admission gave me pause, forcing me to think back throughout the past few years, trying to place Hawk with any one of the girls that were or had been regulars at the club.

Every so often he'd make a lewd comment to one of the boys, take part in their sordid stories, and he'd definitely flirted with the girls around the club, that much I knew for certain. They'd sat in his lap, he'd done his fair share of groping, but never once could I recall a woman exiting his room. Unlike the other men, with the exception of only a few, their bedrooms were usually littered with the remnants of a long night of partying. But not Hawk's. Never Hawk's.

In fact, Hawk usually kept to himself. Aside from his club obligations, I'd only seen him sharing in the occasional drink with Ripper, and quick, quiet conversations with Blue.

With this new knowledge, I felt myself deflating, my anger receding as confusion quickly took its place.

"Why?" I whispered, shaking my head. "Why me?"

I truly didn't understand his interest. Compared to the women around the club, or even half the women in town, I was plain. Plain and boring.

Several moments of silence followed and then he began walking toward me. I stared, watching as he grew closer and closer, noting that suddenly everything about him seemed . . . different somehow. The way he looked at me, the way he held himself. All that formidable muscle no longer seemed bulky but perfectly aligned with his body, his movements sleeker and smoother.

He stopped just before me and, unsure of his motives, I held my breath, my heart pounding an unsteady rhythm in my chest. I didn't know what to expect, and certainly not what happened next.

Grabbing hold of my bicep, he shoved me in front of him and began pushing me forward. I was too shocked to fight him and simply allowed him to force me across the room where he pushed me up against the window. His arms came down on either side of me and his body pressed against mine, caging me in.

"Look at your man," he growled.

Hawk's room was located on the far side of the hall, but from his window I could see the party, still in full swing. While some partygoers still stood in small groups, most were now crowded around the picnic tables, filling their plates with the food I'd prepared only hours ago.

I found myself wondering if someone had finished making my macaroni salad . . . until I saw him. Standing beside his wife, Jase's arm was slung across her shoulders while he gestured wildly with his free hand, emphasizing whatever it was that he was discussing. Beside him, Chrissy's smiling face was upturned, utterly focused on her husband.

She was a truly beautiful woman. Her body was tall, sleek, and toned; her skin was perfectly tanned, and her long auburn hair always curled to perfection. She didn't need makeup or tight clothing; she didn't need anything to enhance how beautiful she was. She just simply was.

But her beauty wasn't why I was staring. What drew me was how comfortable they looked with each other. The two of them, perfect human specimens, talking, smiling, all without a care in the world.

Hot, humiliated tears began to fall from my eyes and slid down my cheeks.

Where did I fit in?

Any other day, I would have wrote it off as Jase playing the part of the loving husband for the sake of his children. It was something I'd told myself many, many times before. But after today, after last night, I couldn't seem to truly convince myself of anything.

What was wrong with me that I'd actually thought I could have Jase for myself?

There was no room for me here. I was the other woman. The whore. And why Jase even bothered with me when he had all that—a beautiful wife, a happy family—suddenly didn't make any sense at all.

Was I a joke to him? Did he pity me?

Had he only ever wanted a quick, easy lay, but later when he was done with me felt in some way obligated? All while I continued to put myself through this hell, letting everyone treat me like a lesser being, waiting on the sidelines for something that might never, would probably never happen.

I tried to turn away, to push back against Hawk, but his weight and his strength brooked no movement.

"Don't that shit piss you off, D?" Hawk's face was bent to mine, his breath hot and smelling of cigarettes as it breezed past my cheek. "Knowin' that he's goin' home to her, takin' her to bed."

"Don't," I whispered hoarsely. "Don't do this to me again."

"Look at the way he's touchin' her," he continued.

"Doesn't exactly look like a man who's plannin' on leavin', does it?"

I couldn't answer him, I couldn't speak, I could no longer even see. Tears were welling and falling, faster than I could blink them away, and if I spoke, I knew I'd only sob.

Everything hurt, so much more than ever before. After last night, and now this, God . . . I . . . I was so . . . so . . .

I was so damn angry.

No, I was so much more than angry. I was humiliated and hurt, and all of it was bubbling up inside me, everything I'd kept hidden for far too long was rising to the surface. I couldn't hold back, not anymore. My fears had turned to fury, and my pain had turned to rage. It was all there and Hawk was forcing me to see it, and with nothing or no one to soothe me, it had begun to boil over, leaving me shaking inside and out, craving an outlet.

"Stop!" I cried, twisting in his hold. "Stop . . . I can't . . . I can't!"

He allowed me enough space to turn and then he was back, his body pressing up against mine. I panicked then, shoving against him, beating my hand wildly against his chest. It was a useless battle. Three times the size of me and far stronger, Hawk simply grabbed hold of my wrists and pinned them high above my head.

"I'll scream!" I cried.

"Why?" he asked, sounding bored.

Through my tears, I blinked up at him. "What?" I whispered.

"Why?" he repeated. "So you can go cry some more? Go back to feelin' sorry for yourself?"

I didn't have a ready answer.

"I know you," he continued. "Wantin' everything, gettin' none of it. I get that. Hell, I feel that too. You don't know shit about me, but I know you. Fuck, I know you better than you know yourself."

He released me and all at once began backing away. Stopping in the center of his room, he gripped the hem of his black T-shirt, pulled the threadbare material up over his head, and tossed it aside. Then he kicked off his boots, sending them flying across the room where they hit the wall with a loud thud. Then in one fluid movement, Hawk had removed both his leathers and boxers.

"What are you doing?" I whispered, suddenly breathless.

"Givin' you somethin'," he said.

Giving me something. That was all he'd said.

I stared at him, both terrified and fascinated.

"Last night was a mistake," I whispered and dropped my gaze, a last attempt at trying to convince myself of just that.

"Ain't no such thing as mistakes," he said. "There's only shit that happens and shit that don't."

Raising my eyes, I found Hawk's expression unchanged. He stood there, naked as the day he was born, as stoic as ever. And, good God, was he infuriatingly cryptic, and . . . naked! He was still naked! But even as shocked as I was at his brazenness, I found myself looking him over rather thoroughly. His thick arms, his broad chest, a pair of thighs that could crack walnuts, all covered in dark, shadowed tattoos. But mostly I found myself staring at the erection, jutting out tall and proud between his legs.

He didn't care. He was standing here naked, offering

himself to what was essentially the property of one of his brothers and yet . . . he didn't care. To be this careless, to be this spontaneous, to be this *free*, I couldn't comprehend it but I was certainly envious of it.

Memories of being with Hawk last night filled my consciousness, things I'd blacked out, reminding me of the way I'd been able to let myself go. There had been no unbearable anxiety, no crippling self-doubt, but most precious of all was the lack of expectations. I'd cried and I'd laughed, not thinking, just feeling. I'd needed, and in return, Hawk had given me what I'd needed.

My nails digging into his back, him grunting in pain as I dragged them across his skin, his body meeting mine, over and over again in loud, echoing slaps, he'd given me what I'd needed.

And then holding me tightly, he'd lifted me off the countertop and I'd found myself flat on my back on the floor behind the bar. The rigid bar mat, wet with spilled alcohol, dug uncomfortably into my skin. But I had little time to dwell on it as Hawk rose to his knees above me and lifted my legs, positioning them over his shoulders.

Then he'd taken me so hard, so fast, that I'd forgotten everything else—where I was, who I was, and most importantly, who I belonged to.

Giving me what I'd needed.

He'd made the whole world disappear.

Oh God, was I considering this? Being unfaithful to yet another man?

What had happened to me? The girl I'd once been never would have entertained this.

But the girl I'd been never would have married a man

she didn't love; she never would have taken up with a married man to fill a void inside herself. I was no longer that girl, filled with dreams of love. I was a woman now, whose mistakes and circumstances had forced her down a very different path. Who had time and time again chosen the wrong direction.

Once again I was at a fork in the road. If I chose right, I could remain faithful to Jase, forever waiting and watching from the sidelines. If I chose left, I could forge a new path, destination and consequences unknown.

"Stop thinkin', D," Hawk said, and I almost laughed. Stop thinking? It was like telling me to stop breathing.

"It's real easy," he continued. "You leave and Jase finds out. You stay, and Jase never has to know."

And just like that, he'd made it easy. By taking away my choice, he'd made it easy.

I didn't remember who moved first, all I knew was I was moving and he was moving and when we collided, it was a collision of mouths and groping hands, the ferocity of which I didn't recognize. It was awkward at first, wildly different from anything I'd experienced with Peter or Jase, but at the same time it was oddly filling. Frenzied, messy kisses and touches that were anything but gentle were filling me, replacing my anxiety with an overwhelming sense of desperation. Desperation for what, I didn't know, only that I couldn't stop. That I needed more.

More and more, until I felt myself capitulating, both mind and body, letting go entirely. When I grew weaker, his strong arms held me up. When my hands hesitated, his were sure and steady, and when I fell apart, he put me back together.

I had left Hawk's bedroom on shaking, trembling legs, but feeling stronger than I had in a very long time.

After that day, I might have still been Jase's secret, but then I too had a secret. And for some reason that secret had suddenly made all the difference in my world . . .

So much wasted time I'd spent waiting on Jase, so many tears spilled in the wake of Jase's lies, and then there was Hawk, always waiting in the shadows . . .

"You need somethin' from me, baby?"

And, *good God*, those words. My chest would begin to heave with wildly exhilarated breaths, stripping my brain of basic reasoning skills, leaving me emotionally naked and vulnerable. Hawk might have forced his way in between Jase and me, but it had been my decision to keep him there as long as I had.

"*Yes*," I would whisper. Because I always did. I needed something, someone, to count on for once in my life. Because I had always been forever lacking.

"What do you need?" he would always whisper back.

"*You*," I would tell him. "*I need you.*"

With a heavy sigh, I lifted my head and pushed myself away from the door.

"I need you now," I whispered to the door. "And I need you to be okay."

Doubling back the way I came, I retook my place on the couch beside Tegen. After rearranging her legs so they once again rested atop mine, I leaned back against the couch and closed my eyes.

Once again I felt it, the odd and unwelcome sensation

that everything was about to change. That my world was once again about to spin out of control, and as usual, I would be helpless to stop it.

But instead of fearing it, surprisingly . . . I welcomed it.

CHAPTER 9

"**M**MM," I MURMURED, TURNING MY FACE INTO THE soft pillow beneath my head and inhaling deeply. I loved the smell of Jase's aftershave. Understated, yet softly spicy, I could often be found sniffing around his face and neck.

Wait . . . what?

Jase's aftershave?

I blinked against the pillow, feeling confused and disoriented.

Why in the world . . . ?

All at once my eyelids flew open as I scrambled into a sitting position, the sudden onslaught of sunlight streaming into the room through the partially open blinds jolting my mind back into conscious awareness. Looking wildly around the room, blinking rapidly, I tried to make sense of what was going on.

Wait . . . not only was I surrounded in Jase's scent, but I was in Jase's room!

How in the world . . . ? My gaze landed on Jase, seated on the floor, slumped against the wall and still sound asleep.

"Oh good God," I muttered, flinging the covers off me, noting with relief that I was still fully dressed in yesterday's jeans and sweatshirt. Being in this room again, near this man, was the very last thing I needed complicating my life at the moment.

To ensure the bed didn't squeak, I climbed out as quietly as possible and began tiptoeing my way past Jase and toward the door.

"Dorothy."

I froze, closing my eyes in dismay. Why? Why! Why couldn't I ever catch a break? My mother had been right when she'd told me all those years ago that I'd been a disappointment not only to my family but to God as well. God must really and truly hate me.

Crossing my arms over my chest, an attempt at shielding myself from the emotional curveball Jase would surely fling at me, I turned to face him.

Standing only a few feet from me, he scrubbed a hand across his shadowed jaw and attempted an awkward smile. If he were anyone else, looking as disheveled as he did, his short hair a matted mess and in need of a good shave, I would have found him endearing. But he wasn't anyone else, he was the one person on this earth I couldn't stand to be around. His face, his body, everything about him was nothing but a painful reminder of the series of tragic events we'd set into motion by simply being together.

"We found you and Tegen sleepin' on the couch," he explained, nodding toward his bed. "Cage took her to his room and I just couldn't let you sleep out there. Gets fuckin' cold in the middle of the night."

I nodded briskly. "Thank you."

He dipped his head but said nothing, just continued to stand there, regarding me in that god-awful needy way he always did.

"Okay," I said. "Well, uh, thanks—"

"Do you love him?"

My eyes rounded with surprise. "Excuse me?"

"Hawk," he said. "You were sayin' his name in your sleep."

I felt my face heat, flushing with both anger and embarrassment. "That is none of your business!" I whispered harshly.

"How is it none of my business?" he demanded. "You were mine, I thought that baby was mine! It was MY FUCKIN' BUSINESS! And I get it, I fucked up, and I deserved everything that was tossed my way because of it but, god-fuckin'-dammit, it's been seven years. You got your fuckin' memory back, and you still can't say more than two words to me!"

Startled, I took a small step back. Jase's mood swings had always been unpredictable, but since my injury and my refusal to have anything to do with him, he was downright manic at times, especially when he overindulged in alcohol, which made his temper even worse.

"It's been seven fuckin' years, Dorothy!" he repeated. "And you owe me a goddamn explanation!"

My shock bled quickly into anger. "I don't owe you a

damn thing," I said, seething.

Nostrils flaring, he took a deliberate step toward me. Despite wanting to flee the room, to run from him, I held my ground.

"But you owe *him* something?" he gritted out. "Why? Why would you come back for him? Why is he any different from me?"

"What is wrong with you?" I cried. "You're so selfish, Jason! With everything that's going on right now, you're still only thinking about you, you, YOU!"

I spun away from him and reached for the door. My fingertips had barely brushed the knob when I was crushed from behind, Jase's body pressing up against me, forcing me to flatten uncomfortably against the door. Lowering his head, he buried his face deeply into my hair.

"Do you love him?" His words were spoken softly, his breath warm and familiar against the back of my neck. As he inhaled deeply, purposely breathing me in, I shivered against the sudden onslaught of feelings that were danger-ously close to erupting.

"Go to hell," I whispered.

"I'm already there," he shot back.

"You have no idea what hell is," I said, my voice trem-bling. "You have no idea what it feels like to know that your own selfishness is the reason your son could have died! Or how it feels to be unable to recognize your own daughter's face, not knowing how to comfort her as she tries desper-ately to make you to remember her and fails every time. You have no fucking idea what hell is!"

I found myself being spun around. Jase's hands came down heavy upon my shoulders, weighing me down as he forced me back up against the door.

"I've got nothin' left," he gritted out angrily, tears filling his eyes. "My girls won't speak to me, you won't speak to me, and my brothers think I'm a worthless piece of shit."

"You're projecting!" I cried, batting at his arms, trying to free myself. "You think you're a worthless piece of shit, not them!"

"I AM A WORTHLESS PIECE OF SHIT!" he bellowed, using his grip on my shoulders to shake me. My diminutive size in comparison to his was no match for his strength, and my head smashed repeatedly into the door, causing me to cry out in pain.

Then he was gone, backing away from me, his eyes wide with shock, holding his hands up in the air.

"I'm sorry," he whispered, blinking rapidly, shaking his head. "Fuck, I'm so sorry."

Fists clenched, teeth gritted, my chest heaving, I glared up at him. I was so angry with him, but it was more than that, it was so much more. I still hadn't forgiven him; that was painfully apparent now. The longer I stared, the angrier I grew, and the angrier I grew, all I could seem to focus on was everything I'd ever done wrong—and almost everything I'd done wrong could be attributed to this man standing before me. We weren't good for each other, we never had been, but we'd both been blinded by different things, and it had taken far too long to realize it.

He still hadn't realized it.

But I had.

And once I had, it was as if a dam broke and I could feel myself splitting apart from the inside out. Everything I hadn't realized I'd been keeping hidden within me for so very long now, it all just burst forth in a rush of mangled emotions and I couldn't stop it. Nor could I stop what happened next.

I ran at him, sending first my right fist into his chest and then my left, and then I slapped him across the face, over and over again until my hands burned and his face was bright red. Tears streamed down both our faces but still I couldn't stop. Jase didn't move; he just took it and the more he took it, the more I wanted to hurt him—for hurting me, for hurting his wife, for hurting our children, for hurting himself, for hurting everyone and ruining everything.

"Look what you did!" I sobbed. "Look what you made me!"

"MOM!"

I hadn't heard them come in, hadn't even heard the door open. I was so consumed by emotion, so lost to my rage and my pain, that it wasn't until I was dragged off Jase, and Tegen was standing between us shoving Jase backward, that I realized we were no longer alone.

"What did you do?" Tegen screamed, slamming her palms into Jase's chest, sending him staggering backward. "What the fuck did you do?"

"No!" I cried out, trying to wrestle free from my captor's grip. "No, Tegen! It was me! Stop it, right now!"

Everything and everyone seemed to stop what they were doing, all eyes suddenly on me. The hands gripping my arms fell away and I turned, finding it had been Cage who'd dragged me across the room.

"Out!" I shouted, pointing to the door. "Both of you, get out!"

Looking confused and upset, Tegen shook her head.

"Mom?"

"Ouuuuuuuut!" The gravelly scream exploded from the bottom of my lungs and rang loudly throughout the small room.

"Babe," Cage said softly, stepping forward. He reached out, his large hand engulfing Tegen's small and trembling one. "Let's go."

Reluctant to leave me, she looked between Jase and me, indecision creasing her face. She'd always taken care of me when I hadn't the strength to do so. When I'd been too weak to stand up for myself, Tegen had been there, fighting my battles, defending my honor.

That would end today.

Today, I wouldn't spend another minute hating myself for the sins of my past, but instead would draw strength from them.

Today, a lot of things would end.

"Go," I repeated, my tone softer, more controlled. "Trust me when I tell you that I'm fine."

She said nothing, but didn't fight him when Cage tugged her forward. I waited until the door was firmly closed behind them before turning back to Jase.

He stood before me looking as broken on the outside as he was on the inside. Both sides of his face were red and mottled with quickly forming bruises, his bottom lip was split in two places, and two thin trails of blood dripped down his chin.

I stepped forward, staring up at him, into those deep blue eyes I'd once thought I'd never see enough of, had never wanted to look away from.

"Do you remember the day we met?" I whispered, my

voice hoarse from screaming.

More tears fell from his eyes as he nodded. "Local store," he said, his voice cracking. "On the county line."

"Tegen had the flu," I said, looking past him at the wall behind him. "My sister was watching her and I was picking up medicine—"

"You had puke on your shirt," Jase whispered.

"You were wearing your fatigues," I said. "You were the most beautiful man I'd ever seen."

I closed my eyes, picturing him as a young man dressed in military fatigues, holding a large green duffel bag as he stepped inside the small shop.

"You said, 'Name's Brady,'" I whispered. "Jason Brady."

Despite my closed eyes, I could hear Jase's approach, could feel the heat from his body as he stopped directly in front of me. And when his arms wrapped around me, against my better judgment, I sank into his embrace.

I smiled against his chest. "I remember you asking me, 'You got a nickname, little Dorothy Matthews? 'Cause that's a fuckin' mouthful, right there. Not that I mind a mouthful of pretty girl.'"

Beneath my cheek, Jase's chest heaved as he snorted. "I was an asshole."

I nodded. "The worst kind of asshole," I whispered. "The kind who thinks he's a good guy."

Through my shirt, I could feel Jase's fingertips dig gently into my back, could feel the tension in his arms as he fought to restrain himself from touching me further, more intimately. Good God, I knew this man like the back of my hand. Even after all these years apart, I knew every inch of him, every nuance, every quirk. I knew everything.

That knowledge, how wasteful we'd been, devastated me.

"I'm sorry, Dorothy," he whispered raggedly.

More tears fell from my eyes. "I'm sorry too."

Jase's hand dragged slowly up my back, up into my hair and softly gripping a fistful. I opened my eyes just as his other hand cupped the side of my face, tilting my chin. As he lowered his head, his lips descended upon mine.

I didn't turn away; I didn't flinch. I just waited until our lips were almost touching and then I reached up, standing on my tiptoes to wrap my arms around his neck, and I kissed him.

It was a gentle kiss, nothing like the passion-filled ones we'd once shared. A stark difference from the chaotic lives we'd once lived.

It was a forgiving kiss, soft and sweet.

It was a good-bye kiss.

I pulled away from him, licking my lips and tasting his blood.

"You were my first love, Jason Brady," I whispered, swallowing back the urge to sob.

His hands dropped to his sides, his expression crestfallen. "Don't," he rasped. "Don't leave me again."

God, my chest was going to collapse in on itself. Who would have thought after so many years apart that finally saying good-bye would hurt this badly? Especially when it would be so easy to say yes, to kiss him again and seal my fate. There was nothing standing in our way anymore, nothing holding either of us back.

Except there was. There was someone very much in our way. And I couldn't ignore him anymore.

I took a deep breath, and that breath entered my lungs like a thousand shards of glass exploding. "I left you a long time ago," I whispered, reaching up to place a hand over my breaking heart. "I just didn't realize it."

Jase's features twisted with raw pain. "You love him." Those three words were barely a whisper, just a rush of air, as if he couldn't say them fast enough, as if speaking them aloud physically hurt him.

My mouth opened and my lips trembled violently. I'd only said it once before, and only to Tegen in an attempt to explain something to her. No one else had ever known, not even the man himself.

"I love him," I cried out softly, realizing just how true the words were.

It was true that I'd loved Hawk for a long time, but what I hadn't realized was the extent of that love, or how deeply ingrained it was within me. Not until this very moment.

I hadn't rushed home, desperate to find out Hawk's fate for the sake of his son. Knowing this might be my last chance, I rushed home, desperate to right things with the man I loved, had loved all along.

That realization, that *truth*, was the single most freeing experience of my entire life. And by far, one of the most painful.

Jase was glad for the pain radiating from his cheeks and lip; he was so fucking glad for it. Because if his damn face weren't throbbing, he'd be forced to focus on the pain in his chest, that empty, aching, broken feeling that never seemed to leave him, but had suddenly just amplified in the wake of what had just transpired.

It shouldn't hurt this badly.

It just shouldn't. Not after all this time.

But even after all this time, he'd stupidly held out hope, hadn't he? He'd clung to the memories of their time together like a fucking child clings to its baby blanket, unable to give it up even after that blanket had been chewed on, bled on, tattered, and finally shredded to pieces.

Even after that blanket was no longer a blanket but just a memory.

That was all he and Dorothy were now. Just a fucking memory.

As the door closed behind her, Jase staggered sideways, collapsing backward onto his bed. He needed a drink, but more than that he needed to ride. Seeing as there were several feet of snow on the ground, he wouldn't be riding anywhere except into a snowbank.

Jesus Christ, he couldn't stay here in this clubhouse with Dorothy, and he couldn't go home to that empty house. So now what? What did he do? Where the fuck did he go?

For years now he'd been doing absolutely fucking nothing, just wallowing through life—eating, drinking, sleeping, but barely existing.

So now what?

WHAT THE FUCK NOW?

He sat upright, pushing himself up off the bed. His gaze landed on his leather jacket slung across his dresser top, and the keys to his truck that lay beside it.

"Fuck it," he muttered. He might not be able to ride, but that didn't mean he had to sit around this fucking place, feeling sorry for himself, for one second longer.

Grabbing his jacket and cut, he pocketed his keys and then crossed his room, flung open the door, and stalked down the hall.

"Jase?"

Ignoring Cage, he picked up the pace and kept walking.

"JASE!"

"Fuck!" he shouted as he stopped and spun around. "What?"

Jogging down the hall, Cage quickly closed the gap between them. "Where you headed?" he asked.

Cage's face, a younger but otherwise exact replica of Deuce's, was filled with concern. And didn't that just make him feel like an even bigger piece of shit.

"Out."

"We're in the middle of some big shit, dude. You sure that's a good idea?"

"You aren't president yet," he shot back.

Cage's expression didn't change. "No, but I'm your friend. Your brother."

His shoulders slumping, Jase closed his eyes. "I just need to get outta here, get some air, get some road time in."

A jingling sound had him opening his eyes and he found Cage holding out his own keys in offering.

"Take my truck, dude. It handles better than yours."

"My truck is vintage," Jase protested.

"Yeah, whatever. Vintage, a piece of shit on wheels . . . same difference."

Snatching the keys from Cage's hand, Jase resumed storming down the hall.

"Call if you need somethin'," Cage yelled after him. "And don't drink and drive!"

"Fuck off!" Jase yelled, even as he cracked a smile.

No one could ever replace Deuce, at least not in Jase's opinion, but if the man was eventually going to pass the gavel, Cage was . . .

Well, even if he was married to one of the most feral bitches in the history of bitches, Cage was a good guy and dedicated to the club. Which was more than Jase could say for himself.

CHAPTER 10

IT WAS EARLY WHEN THE CARAVAN REACHED WILLARD Bay Reservoir. The sun was just barely cresting on the horizon, and most of the boys were still sound asleep in the back of the vans.

Deuce pulled off the road and into a snow-covered parking lot. Leaving the engine running, he exited the vehicle. As he slammed closed the driver's side door, a rush of cold, frost-bitten air smacked into him, sending a chill straight through him.

Beneath his cut, he pulled his leather jacket closed and began fumbling with the zipper, until he realized that would only impede him if shit went south and he needed ready access to the twin pistols he kept holstered under his arms. Pulling the guns free, he tucked one into the back of his leathers, the other into the holster inside his cut, and proceeded to zip up his jacket.

With a large exhale of air, his breath appearing before him in a large white puff, Deuce slipped his bare hands underneath his armpits and leaned back against the van. They'd driven all night to make it to the meeting with the Russians, and they'd chosen Utah for two reasons. One, because it was halfway to Vegas, and two, because it was neutral ground. Neither party, under these circumstances, would risk a meeting like this one in compromised territory. Still, as he looked out across the quiet water to the left of him and the empty plot of land surrounding him, he couldn't help but wonder if they'd walked into a trap.

Despite the fact that they'd had countless friendly dealings with the Russians in the past, they were coldhearted motherfuckers who didn't care who kicked it, as long as the end game resulted in their favor. Finding out it was in fact Yenny who was running things, who had been running things this entire time since betraying his own blood, only furthered Deuce's disgust for them.

Deuce might live outside the law, but he and many others like him had a set of rules they followed. Because if they didn't keep some sort of system in place, a chain of command and honesty among thieves, it would be absolute anarchy.

Even criminals should have a code; if not, then it was a free-for-all. If you couldn't trust your own damn brother, then what was the fucking point?

And all this time he'd thought it was that Russian moron, Valentin, running the show when really, that fat fuck had just been the figurehead. Yenny had been the man behind the curtain, hiding much the same as Hawk had been doing all these years.

The Russians' lack of honor was one of the reasons Deuce had done his damnedest to steer the club away from dealings with them. Since working side by side with Preacher and the Silver Demons, he'd grown accustomed to buying from and distributing for the Chinese. It had been a deliberately slow transition, since he didn't want to cut ties with the Russians all at once in case he needed their backing at some point, but his dwindling dealings with them had apparently been noticed and they obviously weren't too happy about it. Now they were using Hawk to blackmail Deuce back into exclusivity, and using Deuce to blackmail Preacher into expanded distribution, all to their benefit. Greedy fuckers.

Preacher, his hands stuffed inside his pockets, his shoulders hunched forward, came to stand beside him. "What happens if your boy has already kicked it?" Then pulling his cigarettes from inside his coat, he lit one up and blew a long stream of smoke into the wind.

Deuce closed his eyes, wishing he could do the same. Since his heart attack, Eva had been a goddamn vigilante, hell-bent on denying him even the simplest of pleasures. Like a motherfucking cigarette. Or salt. Yeah, Jesus fucking Christ, he missed salt.

"They wouldn't risk it," Deuce said. "They want your business and they ain't gonna get it if they kill my boy. They're smart enough to know that. But if they did kill 'im, then they're goin' to ground." He turned his gaze back to the water. "Every last one of 'em."

"That means war. With the fuckin' *cartel*."

A burst of anger caused the muscles in Deuce's arms to

tighten over his chest. "Yeah."

"That means you're puttin' me in the position to be goin' to war."

Deuce cut his eyes toward Preacher. "It wasn't fuckin' me who pulled you into this shit. It was them."

"Wouldn't have been able to pull either of us into this shit if you hadn't been harboring a fugitive, one who just so happened to be one of their own."

He didn't respond. What could he say? Preacher was right, as usual. The dumbass motherfucker. But Deuce didn't regret taking Hawk in. Not for one second. That boy had proved to be one of his club's best assets.

"You let your boys in on the real plan yet?"

Deuce grimaced. No, he fucking hadn't. Other than Preacher, only Mick knew the endgame, and only because he didn't need his VP crying and whining at him again anytime soon. As for the rest of them, he couldn't tell them, not yet. He needed everyone to appear on board with taking on more merchandise from the Russians. One slipup, one goddamn wrong look could cost Hawk his life or worse, all their lives. The fallout from this motherfucking dangerous game they were all playing was going to be bad enough. No need to add fuel to the fire just yet.

"The Aces are gonna be on board with pickin' up the slack, yeah?" Deuce asked, purposely changing the subject. "If we don't have this shit in place with Slider before the Russians pick up on what we're doin', it's all gonna go bad for everyone."

Preacher's head bobbed up and down. "Hellions too. Roundman's pretty excited about the whole fuckin' deal."

Deuce let out a heavy sigh. "It ain't the East Coast, but

it's somethin', and somethin' is better than nothin'. Worse comes to worst and they don't take the bait, we at least got two more clubs backin' us."

Preacher nodded again. "Good men, both of them, with strong clubs. It'll be a bloody fuckin' war, but I ain't worried about losin' it. But, Deuce, you're gonna have to tell your boys."

"Not yet," Deuce growled. "They're already pissed at me for not tellin' them about Hawk. Can't figure out why, though, seein' as ZZ was one of 'em and he shot my boy. You think you got a loyal man when really all you got is a fuckin' shit stain who loses his balls over runaway pussy."

Pussy that had belonged to his daughter, Deuce thought, cringing. His daughter *and* Dorothy's daughter.

Beside him, Preacher erupted into a fit of laughter that turned quickly into a painful-sounding cough, and Deuce ground his teeth together. What he wouldn't give to be coughing up a lung right about now.

"Maybe you should quit," he said bitterly, hoping like hell the man would agree and hand the pack over.

"I'm already dyin'. Why quit now?"

Deuce blinked at Preacher's surprising revelation. Turning toward the man, he said, "What the fuck did you just say?"

Preacher's gaze went skyward. "Cancer."

Deuce stared at him. "Where?"

"Everywhere."

Jesus . . . shit. What the fuck was he supposed to say to that?

"Ain't there some shit they can do?"

Snorting, Preacher shook his head. "You gonna stand

there and tell me you'd let some whack-job doctor put you through the ringer just so you could die a year or two later, all shriveled up and fuckin' hairless?"

"Yeah, asshole," Deuce shouted. "I fuckin' would. I got little-ass kids and a fuckin' wife! Your daughter? Big eyes, sexy-as-shit lips and perfect fuckin' tits. You remember her?"

Preacher flicked his cigarette away and turned to face him, an eyebrow cocked and a smile on his face. "I was thinkin' more along the lines of pigtails and bad singin', but it's nice to know you're still appreciatin' my girl."

"Yeah," Deuce muttered, feeling embarrassed and wishing his words back. "Fuck you."

"Speakin' of my little girl, don't want you tellin' her 'bout me. I'll take care of that when the time comes."

The image of Eva, devastated and crying, caused Deuce's chest to tighten. Breathing through the feeling, he quickly relaxed. If Preacher wanted to be the one to tell her, that was Preacher's business, and he'd happily stay the fuck out of it.

"And I'm thinkin'," Preacher continued cheerfully, "that I want to consolidate the clubs. Hand my boys over to you. And fuck you too."

Deuce nearly choked and when he was done choking, he saw red, he saw motherfucking red. Preacher didn't just have a club or two, the man had a whole goddamn empire, world-fucking-wide.

"You crazy? I'm dyin' too! You can't put all that on me, I got enough of my own fuckin' problems!"

"You ain't dyin'."

"I am," Deuce protested, and slapped his hand over his chest. "Doctors fuckin' told me I have another heart attack like the last one and I'm fuckin' done."

Preacher rolled his eyes. "You ain't dyin', shithead. Men like you don't fuckin' die. They keep kicking and yelling their way through life until someone knocks 'em down when they ain't lookin' and even then, they just keep kicking and yelling from the damn grave."

Preacher grinned at him then. "Best kinda man," he said. "That boy of yours even got half of that shit inside him, he's gonna make us both proud."

Deuce continued to stare at him, feeling flabbergasted and more than a little uneasy.

"First you shoot me," he muttered. "Now you're handin' me your damn club and spoutin' love poems."

"She was sixteen, motherfucker, *you* woulda shot you."

"No, asshole, I woulda killed me."

At that, Preacher just kept grinning. Jesus, was he in the twilight zone?

A door squeaking open drew his attention to where Ripper was exiting the back of the van.

"We got company, Prez," Ripper said, nodding.

Deuce followed his gaze where, a ways down the road, he could see three large SUVs making their way toward them. "Right on time," he muttered.

Turning back to Preacher, Deuce glared at the man. "There is no fuckin' way I'm takin' your shit on."

Because what a mess that would be. He couldn't even keep his own boys across state lines in check. His Nevada chapter was now under the protection of the Russian mafia, and although he'd verbally stripped them of their patches, he couldn't touch a single one of them.

At least . . . not yet. But he'd find a way to kill each and every one of them for their betrayal.

But taking on the Silver Demons? He was just one man, past his prime, who in all honesty was getting more than sick of the bullshit politics that came with managing men who didn't like to be managed.

More than ever, he wanted to pass that gavel soon. He was tired, and he wasn't ashamed to admit he wanted to spend more time with his family than he did barking out orders. As for his successor, Cage still had a lot to learn.

Yeah. Like he'd said, what a mess.

But Preacher, *that motherfucker*, didn't seem to think so and just kept on grinning.

Christ. He really wanted a fucking cigarette.

Erik "Ripper" Jacobs stayed in the background as was expected of him, watching as the Russians filed out of their vehicles. Preacher's nephew Trey, a Silver Demon, had hung back with him, and together they scanned the area around them for anything that seemed out of place, looking out for potential hidden threats. Never mind that he only had one fucking eye; he was still every bit as good at his job as he'd ever been, if not better. Funny how shit like that worked. Life sure as fuck had tossed some boulders his way, small mountains he'd never thought he'd be able to climb over, but he'd done that and more. He'd smashed those fucking obstacles to pieces and ground them to dust beneath his boot.

"One of those suit-wearin' motherfuckers yours?" Trey asked, flicking his eyes toward the Russians.

Ripper scanned the line of men, counting five of them, and not finding Hawk among them. But that didn't mean jack shit. Hawk, they'd been told, had been shot. Which meant he was either dead and this was a setup, or he was still inside one of their vehicles.

"No," he said, swallowing back both his welling fear as well as his anger. He was so close to losing it, had been for days now. Finding out who Hawk really was . . . well, wasn't that some real fucking bullshit.

All those years, fucking decades, thinking you knew a man, only to find out you didn't know jack-fucking-shit about him. Hawk wasn't Hawk; everything had been a lie contrived by Deuce. Ripper didn't know how to deal with that, except for wanting to send his fist straight into both of their fucking faces. And seeing as he couldn't punch Deuce without the wrath of God falling down upon him, he would settle for venting his frustrations on Hawk. But to do that, he needed him home, and more importantly, alive. After that, the motherfucker was fair fucking game.

"So listen," Trey said, pulling his cigarette from his mouth and flicking it into the snow. "Preacher's been talkin' 'bout the clubs becomin' one."

Ripper's eyebrows lifted. This was news to him.

"'Course, not everyone's on board," Trey continued, "but ain't no one gonna argue with Prez once he's made up his mind. I figured if that's the way shit's gonna be goin' down and we're gonna be workin' side by side, then we best make sure shit's solid between us."

Whatever shit Trey was referring to, Ripper didn't feel it could be more important than the scene unfolding before him. Keeping his eyes on Deuce, he grunted his response.

Although he couldn't hear what the men were saying, Deuce appeared agitated, running his hands through his hair, something he often did when he was about to blow. And the Russians didn't exactly look too happy either. Mick, as usual, was the buffer. To the untrained eye, it would look like he was simply standing shoulder to shoulder with his prez as a show of solidarity, but Ripper knew better. Mick was waiting for the bomb to detonate, the bomb being Deuce when they found out Hawk's fate.

"That mess with Frankie, him fuckin' up your face, just wanted to make sure shit was good between you and me. No hard feelin's, right?"

Ripper's vision wavered, his fixed attention on Deuce began to wane, and for a moment he felt like he was back inside that warehouse, back under that blade and the madman wielding it. Blinking, he refocused on Deuce and took a deep breath.

"Preacher had no clue what that fucker was doin' on the side," Ripper muttered. "I let that shit go a long-ass time ago."

"Good to hear," Trey said. "Thought you might be harborin' some resentment toward the rest of us who'd been there."

Ripper froze. Everything stopped and became fuzzy as he tried and failed to process what Trey had said.

The rest of us who'd been there.

The rest of us who'd been there.

The rest of us who'd been . . .

His arm shot out, grabbing Trey's jacket collar, and then he quickly dragged the man behind the van and threw him up against the back door. Letting go of his collar, he wrapped his hand around Trey's throat and squeezed.

"What the fuck did you just say?" he demanded.

Trey didn't even blink. He was as calm as ever staring back at Ripper with those big gray eyes of his that looked so much like Eva's. In fact, Trey was the male equivalent of his cousin, minus the tits and Chuck Taylors. The only difference was the eerie chill Ripper felt slither through him while looking at the man.

"I thought you knew," Trey said quietly.

"I would have killed you if I knew," Ripper ground out through gritted teeth.

The admission made Trey smile, also super creepy. "You could've tried," he said, his tone as dead as his eyes. "Lots of motherfuckers have. And they all fuckin' failed."

"Yeah?" Ripper's eyes narrowed. "Why? 'Cause you had Frankie doin' your dirty work for you? You enjoy watchin' him fuck people up, you sick shit?"

Trey attempted to shake his head, but Ripper's unforgiving grip on his throat allowed him very little movement. "Ain't nobody wanted to fuck with that asshole and what he did for kicks. I may not be the nicest motherfucker out there, but I ain't ever carved anybody up like a Thanksgivin' turkey. If I got a beef, I shoot point-blank. Frankie was a breed all his own."

Ripper stared at him. Not the nicest motherfucker out there was putting it mildly. Trey had a line of bodies trailing behind him. But then again, so did Ripper.

Ripper released him and backed away as Trey reached up to massage his throat.

"We good?" Trey asked.

About to tell him to go fuck himself, Ripper was distracted by an angry shout. He turned just in time to see a body being tossed out the door of one of the SUVs. As

Hawk's lifeless body fell to the ground, the door slammed closed and the line of SUVs sped off. Without giving Trey a second glance, he took off running. Trey didn't fucking matter. Frankie didn't fucking matter.

Because when it came down to it, this wasn't a pretty life by any means. Bodies fell, and people got hurt. But you did your best to keep going; you found yourself a nice little patch of happiness, and you clung to that shit like it was your last fucking breath.

And he'd done just that. He'd found his peace within the arms of a beautiful girl. He'd found peace and a whole lot more.

Frankie was dead; that psychopath had paid for his sins in the worst possible way.

And someday, Trey would get what was coming to him.

Neither of them deserved another fucking thought. They weren't worth it.

But Hawk was.

"Grab his legs!" Deuce shouted, grabbing hold of Hawk's underarms and trying to pull the man's big body upward. "And watch out for those wounds!"

Shoving Dirty and Mick out of his way, Ripper dropped down to his knees and skidded across the snow-covered pavement, reaching for Hawk's unmoving body. Wearing only a pair of soiled boxers, he was covered in bruises, dried blood, and other substances Ripper didn't want to give too much thought to what that they were. On either side of his right leg, there were two shoddily stitched-up wounds, both an angry red and seeping with pus, the dirty skin around them turning unhealthy shades of black and blue.

As carefully as he could, he slipped his arm underneath his brother's thighs, and as Deuce lifted the top half of Hawk's body, Ripper lifted his legs.

"Is he breathin'?" Ripper asked, panting.

"Shallow," Mick said, "but he's breathin.'"

CHAPTER 11

They say what doesn't kill you, makes you stronger.
Well, he didn't know about all that. But it sure as shit changes
everything.
— James "Hawk" Young

PAIN WAS A RELATIVE THING.

There were good types of pain: the burning strain on your muscles when you piled on another set of weights and lifted those bad boys into the air; the feel of a tattoo machine, those tiny needles dipping into your skin over and over again, soaking it through with beautiful ink; or that crushing ache in your chest when you thought you'd never have a family again, but then a little redheaded baby boy was placed in your arms and he looked up at you with those big, wondering eyes and he was all yours, your family.

That was the kind of pain Hawk could get down with.

Then there was the other sort. The pain caused by some backroom doctor picking bone shards out of his leg, and then stitching him back up without medicating him first. The pain from an angry fist hitting his face, or a pair of booted feet sent repeatedly into his rib cage. Or the worst pain of all, seeing the laughing face of a man you once called brother, as he inflicted all that damage.

Hawk didn't remember much after ZZ had beat him senseless, no doubt retribution for Hawk having gotten him shot. Although the man had been cradling his left arm, he'd seemed just fine in comparison to how Hawk had felt.

What he did remember was the needles. Someone would come every few hours to inject something into his arm that dulled the pain, but also rendered him useless to do little more than lie there and stare at the dark, dank surroundings of whatever basement room he was being kept in. He fluttered in and out of consciousness, and each time he began to recover from the drugs, he was shot up with more.

Throughout it all there were times that he could distinguish voices, most of them speaking in Russian, sounding fuzzy and far away. But through it all, he'd frequently heard Deuce's name and he'd clung to that. While he shivered and shook, both hungry and thirsty, and repeatedly pissing and shitting himself, he'd clung to the thought of Deuce, of his club, and of the lone sliver of pride he still had left: the fact that it wasn't only him who'd dragged the Horsemen into this mess, but ZZ as well.

And then self-pity had begun to set in and he found himself going over and over again all the things he'd done wrong, all the damn mistakes he'd made. Once upon a time, he hadn't believed in mistakes; it either was or it just wasn't. He knew that wasn't true now, that one lone decision could change everything, and he'd made a lot of bad choices over the years. Too many to count. He'd been lonely and greedy and therefore selfish, he'd been desperate and therefore vengeful, and he'd been rejected and therefore indifferent. And worst of all, he'd been out of his mind with regret and therefore complacent.

All. Fucking. Wrong.

You didn't fix one mistake with another; he knew that now.

But the one person who needed to know that, to know how sorry he was for the many mistakes he'd made, was miles away, and he was beginning to think there was little chance of him ever having the opportunity to tell her.

And just when Hawk started to think he was going to die, starve to death, or overdose on whatever drug they weren't allowing to leave his system, he heard Deuce. Not his name, but the man himself.

He heard Ripper.

He heard Dirty.

He heard Mick.

At first he couldn't make out what was being said, but he recognized every one of their distinctive voices. And that was when he realized he wasn't in that room any longer, freezing his ass off and covered in his own shit.

Beyond the familiar voices surrounding him, he could both hear and feel the rumble of an engine, the faraway grainy sound of music, all blessedly beautiful sounds telling him he was inside a vehicle surrounded by men who weren't going to hurt him.

And for the first time in his life, he understood the meaning of *home* again. It wasn't where you grew up; it wasn't who you'd once been.

It was the people you surrounded yourself with.

"He's been beaten and drugged," he heard Deuce say. "Fuckin' needle marks in his arm."

"Leg's broken too," Mick said. "Shot straight through the tibia."

"Speak English, motherfucker, not Swahili!"

Hearing Ripper so agitated, Hawk smiled. Or at least, he tried to smile. He couldn't do much of anything at the moment aside from lie there like a fucking useless lump.

"I am speakin' English, you dumbass shit. Ain't my fault you never finished high school."

"Both of you idiots, shut up. Ripper, call the club, tell Cage we're gonna need a doctor."

"On it, Prez," Ripper muttered.

"And," Deuce added, "we're not takin' him to the club. Tell Cage his guest room is about to be occupied."

"Tegen will love that."

"Tegen knows her fuckin' place."

"That bitch knows her place 'bout as well as Ripper knows what the fuck a tibia is."

"Fuck off!"

"Shut your fuckin' mouths," Deuce growled. "That crazy bitch you're talkin' shit about cleaned my boy the fuck up."

"She's still crazy. Straight-up fuckin' nuts."

Hawk wanted to laugh but he still couldn't see, probably because his eyes were swollen shut. Now that he was warming up, the pain in his leg was starting to burn something fierce, causing his thoughts to muddle.

Then he felt something warm press against his cheek. Maybe a hand.

"You hang the fuck on, you feel me, brother?" Deuce said, his voice low. "You got an unhappy redhead who drove through the blizzard from hell just to see where the fuck you were. She's waitin' on your ass, probably gonna bitch you the fuck out for lyin' to her all these years. I'm givin' you permission to put that blame on me like all the rest of these motherfuckers are doin'."

For a moment, Hawk was confused, thinking Deuce was referring to Tegen, and Tegen being pissed at him wasn't anything new.

But then he heard Ripper mutter, "She's probably just pissed findin' out that little leprechaun of hers is actually a Russki, and property of the Red Mafia."

Suddenly Hawk realized it wasn't Tegen that Deuce was talking about, it was Dorothy.

So, she'd come back to Montana for *him*?

And she knew everything now? And she was upset?

Upset meant she gave a fuck.

"What?" Ripper said, sounding affronted. "No one thought that was funny? Dude, that was funny. Cox would have thought that was funny. Dirty? No? Fuck, bein' clean has made you lame as fuck."

"It was kinda funny," Mick said. "But not really."

"Jesus Christ," Deuce muttered. "Just shut the fuck up. All of you."

And if Hawk could have grinned, he sure as shit would have.

Hours passed. Days? Weeks? He didn't know.

Hawk was in and out of consciousness, sometimes shivering with unbearable cold, sometimes burning with stifling heat and sweating profusely, and sometimes both. He only caught snippets of conversations, purposely hushed voices accompanied by the sound of footsteps. He saw flashes of blurred faces, and every so often he'd feel a touch, sometimes excruciatingly painful, radiating up his leg, spreading higher and higher, gripping his chest like a vice until he'd pass out from the pain. Other times it was gentle, something soft and cool on his skin, fingertips fluttering up and down his arms, hands cupping his cheeks. A kiss pressed against his lips.

During his small moments of clarity, he tried to sort through the scrambled mess of his mind to pinpoint Dorothy, whether or not she was really here, that he hadn't just imagined Deuce mentioning her presence. He would jerk at the sound of a soft feminine voice, or when he thought he saw a flash of red, only to realize himself unable to move, unable to blink through the cloudy haze, or speak anything resembling coherent words.

And through it all Hawk dreamed. He dreamed of his childhood and having the world at his fingertips, thinking his father was a king, thinking that someday he would be a king as well. And then of the death of his father, and his time spent on the streets, afraid for his life. He dreamed of Deuce, the night the man had found him, of the club and the boys. And then he dreamed of meeting Dorothy for the first time, her long red hair and bright green eyes, and how they'd come together as a means of escaping the cruel reality of their lives, but how it had backfired on both of them.

He dreamed of the selfish young man he'd once been, thinking that the world had owed him something in return for all he'd lost.

And he dreamed of Christopher, who in a lot of ways had been the means to his end. The end of the man he'd once been, and the start of the man he'd become. A better man. A father.

He dreamed of the way things had been and the way things were now, and he dreamed of how he wished they could have been, how he wished they were now.

Until the fever finally broke and he woke the fuck up.

Blinking through the semidarkness, Hawk tried to focus on his surroundings, unable to discern a damn thing other than he was in a warm and comfortable bed, although he was anything but comfortable.

His throat was painfully dry, his head was throbbing, and his leg twice as bad. He tried to sit up and felt his leg scream in protest. Okay. Scratch that. Instead, he reached out with both hands, fumbling at his sides. His left hand found a tabletop and his right . . .

Damn.

He squeezed the soft flesh once, twice, and smiled. Yeah, sure as shit, that was definitely a breast. He reached farther, squeezing the other, his smile growing wider. He knew these breasts, had once been well acquainted with them. Perfect-sized mounds of malleable flesh covered in freckles, topped with nipples just a little too large. Nipples that would shrivel and peak beneath his fingers and mouth.

Despite his injuries, Hawk felt his body responding to his thoughts. He was considering trying to maneuver himself into a more accessible position to continue touching her when Dorothy let out a small sigh. He snatched his hand away just as she rolled toward him and into his body. Her leg nudged against his injured one, sending pain shooting through him. He breathed through it, not really caring about the pain, just wanting her to keep touching him. He'd been so long without her, without the touch of another human being who actually gave two shits about him, that whatever pain he was in didn't fucking matter. As long as she kept touching him.

Her arm crept over his midsection as her cheek nuzzled his chest, and he pulled her even closer, running his hand down her back, over the curve of her ass, and then back up again and into her hair. Feeling the scar that lay beneath it, he softly grazed the raised and bumpy skin over and over again, feeling a wave of sadness wash over him. He should have been there. If he had been there, if he would have stayed and fought for Dorothy, this might not have happened.

It was something he'd never forgive himself for, something that would haunt him until the day he died. That his ego couldn't handle another rejection from her, and because of that she'd been shot, and he'd nearly lost both her and their son.

But alongside his guilt, he felt something else, something he hadn't felt in a very long time. Holding her, touching her, even after all this time, he marveled at how natural it felt. How right it felt.

Feeling content, he closed his eyes. As he started to drift off again, both his body and mind still exhausted from all he'd physically endured, he felt her shift.

"Hawk," she whispered sleepily, her breath tickling his skin. "I love you."

He didn't respond, just closed his eyes and let those three stupid words sink inside him. She was still sound asleep, and he thought that maybe they'd had been the result of a dream, or caused by her worry for him. But regardless of why she'd said them, it was the first time he'd heard those words since his father had been killed.

And the pain that hearing them caused within his chest, the pain inside his heart, was very much the type of pain Hawk could get down with.

CHAPTER 12

FRESH FROM MY SHOWER, WRAPPED IN A LARGE WHITE towel and under the impression that Hawk was still riddled with fever and half delirious, I'd stepped out of the bathroom and into the bedroom.

He wasn't. He was wide awake, had managed to sit himself up some, and was sloppily guzzling water from the pitcher I'd left beside the bed.

Over the rim of the pitcher, his eyes met mine, those unfathomably dark eyes growing even more opaque as he lowered his drink to focus on me.

"Hey," he said, his voice hoarse and scratchy, then he wiped his mouth with the back of his hand.

Hawk's voice, that lone word, caused icy-hot shivers to race along my skin, leaving trails of gooseflesh in their wake.

Feeling suddenly flustered and strangely embarrassed, I clutched my towel tighter around me and tried to smile. "Hey," I said softly.

Glancing away from me and around the room, he cleared his throat. "Where are we?"

I surveyed the mostly barren room, containing only a bed, a nightstand, and the obligatory dresser. Cage and Tegen weren't much for decorating or personal touches.

"Cage and Tegen's," I answered.

He nodded. "How long have I been out?"

I lifted my shoulder. "About four days. You had a pretty nasty infection. The doctor Deuce brought here had to open your leg back up and clean it out."

Hawk's gaze dropped to his bandaged leg. Propped atop several pillows, it was currently wrapped in an Aircast boot. Remembering the discolored skin, how severely infected the poorly stitched-up wound had become, I internally cringed. I had begged Deuce to take him to a hospital, but the man was exasperatingly adamant that Hawk would remain where he was. Thankfully for Hawk, the doctor had been legitimate.

"You should have a hard cast," I continued. "But under the circumstances . . ." I trailed off, not knowing how to broach the subject of Hawk's true identity. It still felt foreign to me, everything Deuce had told me and, although I knew it was the truth, it didn't feel real to me. Hawk was, and to me always would be . . . Hawk.

This other life he'd once led, the son of a Russian mob boss who was gunned down, felt like some farfetched and contrived story, the stuff movies were made of, and not the former life of the man I shared a child with.

"Deuce didn't think taking me to a hospital was a good idea," he finished for me. "Bullet wounds tend to attract police. And if the police decide to dig . . ."

Hawk's eyes were still downcast, glazed over, and looking past his leg at nothing. "Guess you probably got some questions for me," he said quietly.

I did have questions for him, hundreds of them, yet standing here, looking at him, none seemed to come to mind. All that mattered for the moment was that he was home safe and he was healing from his injuries.

"They can wait," I whispered. "You just need to get better."

He let out a deep breath, and the lines creasing his face eased a bit. If I didn't know better, I would have thought he was relieved, but the Hawk I knew didn't much care what people thought of him.

Except this time, he seemed to care.

"I'm sorry I missed Christmas," he said, lifting his eyes, stopping on my chest where the little heart pendant hung from the chain around my neck. My hand went immediately to it, my fingers curled around it, gripping it tightly until I could feel the sharp point of the heart digging into my palm.

Suddenly the pendant seemed to mean so much more than it had. As if it hadn't just been a thoughtful gesture, hadn't just been a father shopping for a gift for the mother of his child.

This little heart around my neck seemed to embody the man himself, full of secrets, hidden meanings, and so much more than met the eye.

"I never thought I'd see you or Christopher again," he

said quietly. "I never thought I'd be able to . . ."

He trailed off but kept his eyes on me. Locked on mine.

I didn't say anything, didn't know what to say. And it seemed to me that neither did Hawk. He just continued to stare at me in that dark and assessing way of his, his shadowed eyes boring into me, holding me captive like a deer frozen in the face of blindingly bright headlights.

The world is full of untapped potential; everyone has experienced it. Glances across the room. Locked gazes. Secret smiles. Silent conversations. When it comes to lust, words are never needed. You feel something inside you stir, your body begins to warm, and you just know. You can feel something buried spring to life, and just like that a connection is born. You're strangers, then suddenly you're something more . . . kindred spirits, like-minded in your attraction for each other.

I'd had that with both Jase and Hawk.

But there was only one who could steal your soul, that untouchable, unreachable place inside you that existed only in your mind, that warmed and cooled, fluttered and shook without rhyme or reason, and make it theirs forever. Someone who could take your breath away with just one look, who makes all those past secret smiles and glances from afar pale in comparison to the way *he* looks at you.

The way Hawk used to look at me. Stealing glances from across the room as he stood in the shadows, his gaze running up and down the length of me, deliberately slow, drinking me in.

The way he was looking at me now.

I'd forgotten how exposed and vulnerable that look had once made me feel, yet at the same time, how wanted.

Needed. And excited.

How free.

Feeling emotion welling up inside me, I swallowed hard and whispered, "I never thought I'd see you again either."

A lengthy silence followed my words as Hawk's gaze bored into mine, and I dropped my gaze to my feet, suddenly unable to face him.

I didn't know what I'd been thinking. After my blowout with Jase, I'd had it all worked out in my head that once Hawk was home again, I'd tell him how I felt, how I'd always felt. And somehow that would make things right again, that the ever-widening span of years that we'd kept our distance from each other would instantly close.

That wasn't the case. If anything, now that he was here and conscious, I felt even more awkward than before. As if my realized feelings were new ones, instead of the old and buried ones they were, and I was afraid of what would happen if I let them blossom, let them grow. Would he return them, feeling the same? Or had too much time passed, and would he toss them away?

"I'm sorry, Dorothy," Hawk said, breaking the silence.

Surprised, I lifted my eyes to find his expression had fallen further, and his features were creased with pain.

"What I did," he said, "fuckin' with you, takin' what wasn't mine, that was wrong. I never said I was sorry 'cause I thought feelin' sorry for what I did meant I felt sorry that we had our boy, but I know that ain't true now. And I am sorry. Most of all, I'm sorry I left. If I never would have left, you wouldn't have been shot. I would have been there and you would have been safe."

I stared at him, speechless. Hawk had always been a

man of very few words.

"I pushed you away," I eventually said. "I don't blame you for leaving."

"We both made mistakes," he said.

A small, nervous laugh escaped me. What was he trying to say? That he didn't regret Christopher, but everything else? That he regretted me and us?

"I thought you didn't believe in mistakes," I said, hating the tremor in my voice that betrayed my feelings.

"I'm forty-five years old." He lifted one brow. "Got a kid of my own too. It's about time I took responsibility for my own actions, don't you think?"

I pressed my lips together, willing my tears not to betray me now. Staring at Hawk, I shook my head. "I don't understand. What are you trying to say?"

His eyes narrowed, his brows drew together, causing his forehead to furrow even more. "I'm sayin' that I'm sorry, that's—"

"Stop it," I cried out, unable to hold it in another second.

It was all too much. Not knowing what had become of him, then learning who he truly was. The agonizing wait to find out his fate, and the realization of my feelings for him. Then seeing him beaten, bloody, and broken, and all the while I was caring for him, envisioning the moment when I would tell him the truth. And now this, an apology from him, telling me he regretted what we'd done, it was all too much and released a torrential downpour of emotions that I was powerless to stop.

It seemed that the floodgates of emotion that Jase had forced open, had yet to fully close.

"You never showed up!" I shouted, swiping at the tears

on my cheeks. "You never showed up and I kept calling and I called Eva and then Deuce called me back but he wouldn't tell me anything, no one would tell me anything and then I had to find somewhere for Christopher to stay and then my flights were canceled and I had to drive all the way home in a snowstorm and Deuce told me about you and who you are and I just . . . I just, I didn't know what to think, none of it seemed real, and then I thought Preacher wasn't going to help but he did and then I beat up Jase and I told him I loved you and then he left and then Deuce left and they brought you back and I was here when the doctor came, and Hawk, oh my God, your leg, it was so bad, really infected, and you were so sick and you looked so bad, you were so beat up, and I thought you were going to die, even though everyone kept telling me you weren't going to die, and I couldn't understand anything you were saying and I was so scared that I was going to lose you again, that I wasn't going to have the chance to make things right and I couldn't . . . I didn't . . ."

Dorothy kept going and going and fucking going, flinging word after word at him like a pitching machine. Like one of those dolls with the strings and after one too many pulls, the string snaps off and the doll just keeps fucking talking and talking and talking . . .

She'd always fucking talked too much, especially when she was upset. Hawk could recall countless nights when he'd been forced to listen to her ramble on about Jase, forced to watch her cry, emotionally beating herself up over and over again for reasons he'd early on stopped trying to comprehend. He'd simply fucked her to shut her up and it had worked . . . for a while.

But she'd chosen Jase over him, and then she'd been shot, and the silence that had followed had been fucking deafening.

And, fuck, after all these years of the cold shoulder, barely speaking to each other, feeling like strangers in the same room, he hadn't realized just how much he'd missed her. Not just being with her, but *her*. All of her. Even this, her nonsensical rambling, her inability to express absolutely anything without being so motherfucking emotional. And even then, it was still a garbled mess. He'd missed every damn inch, all five foot nothing of her, the never-ending tears and all the baggage she'd always clung to, insisted on dragging along behind her.

Christ, they were both a disaster. Her with her heart exposed for all the world to see, and him with his locked up so tight, it had taken a random drunken fuck, some blackmail, a pregnancy, a gunshot wound to the head, years of emptiness, a kidnapping, and a few more gunshots for him to sort his fucking shit out.

What a goddamn waste.

The silver lining? She'd said she loved him. Last night and again just now, in between something about beating up Jase and Deuce leaving, she'd sure as shit had said she'd loved him, as well as admitting her fear of losing him again. It was a surprising and not so surprising revelation. There had been times that he'd suspected her feelings had run deeper than she'd let on, but she'd never admitted it and so he hadn't either.

But none of that shit mattered anymore. He was sick of living in the past, of living in a future going nowhere. And he didn't want to look back anymore.

"Dorothy."

She just kept talking.

"Dorothy!"

Still, she kept talking. And, goddamn it, if he didn't love the shit out of this woman, he would most certainly kill her.

"DOROTHY!" His hand flew to his throat as he instantly regretted yelling. Although it seemed to do the trick; she was no longer babbling but instead staring at him.

"For fuck's sake," he rasped, rubbing his throat. "Shut up."

"Shut up," she whispered, her face crumpling. "Shut up? You're seriously going to talk to me like—"

"Yes," he gritted out, cutting her off. "I'm seriously goin' to tell you to shut up and get your ass over here." He attempted moving himself, wincing when the pain in his leg intensified, and decided to hold out his arm to her instead. "Just come here," he said, gesturing with his hand. "Just shut up and come here."

A long pause followed, and then she stammered, "I should get dressed."

"No!" he yelled, growing increasingly frustrated with her and the fact that he couldn't get off the damn bed to go get her himself. "Get the fuck over here!"

It was slow going, but eventually she put one foot in front of the other. He waited with his arm outstretched as she moved toward him at a snail's pace, trying to maintain patience when he felt anything but.

She paused at the edge of the bed, her face still flushed and red from crying as she gripped the towel to her chest. Her gaze skittered up and down his body, then across the bed and even farther, toward the window as she looked anywhere but directly at him.

Realizing what was happening, that Dorothy was being her own worst enemy, he released a heavy sigh and let his arm drop to the mattress.

"Woman," he said softly. "Stop fuckin' thinkin' so damn much."

Her gaze lifted, meeting his, and they stared at each other, her green eyes filling with tears, his body itching with the need to bring her close, to feel her against him.

And also with the need to pee. Christ, he had to piss. Great fucking timing too. He'd waited twenty years for her to admit she had feelings for him, and for almost eight just for the chance to touch her again, and he wasn't going to let an untimely bodily function fuck this all up.

"I thought I was going to lose you," she whispered tearfully. "I thought I'd never get another chance."

"Thought you woulda figured this shit out by now," he said. "That as long as I'm breathin', I ain't goin' nowhere."

"I know that you were there . . . for Christopher," she said, her voice small, unsure.

"For both of you," he corrected her, dropping his gaze to the necklace. "I've always been there for both of you."

With one hand still clutching her towel, she reached up with the other and again clutched the tiny pendant that hung from her neck.

Remembering Christopher's attempts at trying to convince him that what she really wanted for Christmas was a new video game console, Hawk almost smiled. Almost. But knowing Dorothy, she would misconstrue his smile for something else entirely.

"I screwed up," she said, shaking her head. "I was scared and I made the wrong choice. I'll never forget the way you looked at me that night . . . like I'd betrayed you."

"I screwed up," he snapped, growing angry in the face of her infamous self-loathing, the one thing about her that he didn't miss. "Me, Dorothy, get that through your thick head. I took somethin' that wasn't mine to take and expected . . . aw, fuck!"

He clenched his fists and his breathing grew heavy. "I don't know what I expected," he gritted out. "But none of that shit matters anymore. You said you loved me, you know I love you, so I'm not seein' what the problem is and why you're not gettin' your ass over here so I can fuckin' touch you."

More tears, *goddamn her never-ending tears*, filled her eyes and overflowed.

"You still love me?" she whispered.

Jesus Christ, this woman, this silly fucking woman . . .

"Dorothy," he said. "Yeah, I fuckin' love you. Didn't think I needed to say it. Figured you already knew."

Once again she averted her eyes, and he knew she was doing what she did best. The wheels were spinning, she was overthinking every fucking thing, talking herself out of anything that could potentially serve to make her happy.

"It's been so long," she said with a shaky sigh. "We don't even really know each other anymore."

He wanted to laugh at her, maybe smack her a few times, or grab her by her foot and hang her upside down and shake all that fucking self-doubt straight out of her. Instead, he schooled his expression, maintaining the facade of calm that Dorothy had always needed from him when she was emotionally flailing.

"What's there to know," he said with a carefree shrug that caused every inch of the ravaged skin and injured muscle in his arms and chest to flare with pain. "My name is James Alexander Young. I was born and raised in New York. I was—"

He stopped talking the moment she started smiling.

"But that's not who you are," she said softly. "Not really."

"Come here," he said, crooking his finger and for once, surprising the shit out of him, she actually listened. Leaning down, using her hand to steady herself, she bent over the side of the bed. Still, she was too far away, forcing him lean to the side, which caused him ungodly amounts of pain. And yet he persisted, keeping his struggle silent as he strained his body in her direction. When their heads nearly touched, he reached up and slid his hand over the smooth skin of her cheek and into her hair.

"Luca Polachev died a long fuckin' time ago," he said. "I am James Young, a member of the Hell's Horsemen, one of Deuce's boys, and the proud father of Christopher Kelley. That is who I am now, and those are the only parts that matter."

Pressing her cheek into his hand, she gave him one of her sweet smiles, the same smile that had drawn her to him in the first place. It had made him want to take all that innocence, that inherent goodness that was Dorothy, and make it his own.

"You need a bath," she whispered, wrinkling her nose.

"Yeah," he whispered back. He needed a bath, a haircut, and a shave, as well as a couple of dozen rounds with a toothbrush. He could probably use a new leg while he was at it, but most of all he needed to take a fucking piss.

But before any of that would happen, before she could say another goddamn word, he leaned as far as he possibly could without screaming out in pain, and laid waste to the remaining inch between them.

"You know what I always regretted?" he whispered. "Never puttin' you on the back of my bike. Just me and you, out in the sun. No more fuckin' hidin'."

Dorothy had just enough time to suck in a small, surprised breath.

Then Hawk, despite feeling like anything he said or did could potentially break the tenuous connection between them, decided, *Fuck it*, and kissed her. Because when it came to Dorothy, he figured he didn't have anything left to lose.

For the first time in almost eight long years, he kissed his woman.

She was shaking, her lips quivering, but she didn't turn away or try to stop him. And he didn't waste any time, he wasn't going to waste any more time, not in a world where there were no guarantees.

They both fumbled a little at first, unused to each other. Then something clicked between them, and their eagerness for each other began to supersede any awkwardness. Her body instantly softened and she leaned forward, into his body and melting against him. One hand found his chest, her other reaching up into his hair, running through it before cupping the back of his neck.

And then, as if no time had passed, as if nothing had ever come between them, as if no tragedies had pushed them apart, she kissed him with fervor, touching him with sure hands, and he gripped her tightly, her mouth and body feeling again as natural to him as they once had.

Gently, I pulled a blanket up over Hawk's torso, tucking it under his chin. He stirred in his sleep, mumbled something incoherent, and then was quickly snoring again. Looking him over, I grimaced. He had a lot of healing left to do. He couldn't go more than an hour or two without needing more pain medication, and he was still unable to use the bathroom on his own.

But he was home, he was safe, and he was mine.

Mine.

And this time I was determined not to screw it up.

CHAPTER 13

JASE DIDN'T HAVE A FUCKING CLUE HOW HE'D ENDED UP here.

Actually, that wasn't exactly true. He knew exactly *how* he'd ended up here, he just wasn't too clear on the *why* of it.

Or how much time had passed since he'd left the clubhouse, or even what day it was, for that matter.

Just that he was here in Wyoming, in his hometown, parked in front of his childhood home, trying to recall the last time he'd been here. Then it dawned on him . . . He hadn't been back home since Chrissy had gone to trial, and he'd been too much of a mess to take care of the girls. After that they'd bounced between Chrissy's parents and his own for a while, until eventually he got his shit together, at least for the most part.

But by then it was too late, and he'd failed them all.

Ashamed of himself, of the gossip that the shooting had brought down upon his parents in their own town, and not wanting to make it worse for them, he hadn't been home since.

And now for some reason he was home, and completely at a loss for what to do next.

Did he go to the door? Announce himself? Yeah, that would go over really well.

Hi, Mom and Dad. How was your Christmas? Bet you're glad to see the son who disappointed the fuck out of you, and ruined your grandchildren's lives. Hope you don't mind the stench of vomit and booze all over me.

Or did he drive away? Go back to Montana and leave well enough alone?

Go back to what exactly? The club that pitied him? The woman who had officially said her good-byes?

And goddamn, did that still hurt like a bitch.

Whatever. He needed a drink, a little something to clear his head, and then he'd sort out what the fuck he was going to do. Leaning down, he reached for the bottle of liquor that had fallen off the passenger seat and onto the floor, when a knock on the driver's side window brought him flying back into an upright position.

Shit.

Walter Brady had aged about as well as everyone had expected. A cowboy through and through, his heavily muscled stature could be attributed to the prolific rodeo rider he once was, but the rotund belly he'd developed over the years was the result of blue-collar factory work after retiring from the rodeo, and his wife's excellent cooking. The thinning gray hair on his head, the many lines on his face, and his drooping features gave the impression he hadn't had an easy life, but anyone who knew him would know that while it might have been a struggle at times, it had been a fulfilling one.

In his early twenties, at the peak of his career, Walter had married Doreen Davies—a young buckle bunny, a rodeo groupie who'd been smitten with him—and not because of an unplanned pregnancy, but because he'd loved her. After a back injury that ended his rodeo career, together they'd worked hard to make a new life for themselves, and a home they could be proud of.

They'd filled that home with three sons and two daughters, the scent of home-cooked meals, and the sound of laughter. And for the most part, their children had made them proud—they had all eked out an honest living, were all married and filling nearby homes with children of their own.

All but one. Him. Smack dab in the middle of the brood, Jase had failed his parents' every expectation, and then made up a few of his own just so he could cross a couple more failures off his epic list.

Taking a deep breath, he rolled down the window. "Dad," he said, nodding at the man.

His father's frown stayed in place as he looked him over. "You make a habit of parking on people's lawns?"

Surprised, Jase glanced out the windshield, then to the passenger side window, noticing for the first time that he had in fact missed the driveway entirely. Thankfully, in his hometown, your closest neighbor was at least a couple of miles down the road, and no one but his parents had seen him making a fool of himself. Not that anyone would be surprised by it.

Feeling like a teenager caught with his pants down, he sheepishly turned back to face his father. "Yeah," he muttered. "I, uh, I'm sorry. The snow kinda hid it. I didn't . . . uh—"

"Scoot on over," Walter said, interrupting him. "Don't need you making a worse job of this."

"Maybe I should go," he mumbled.

"Go where," Walter demanded. "You're drunker than a damn skunk. You ain't going anywhere until you get some food in you and sleep it off."

"I don't want to upset Mama," he whispered, once again feeling like an errant child.

"Too damn late for that. Who ya think woke me up to come bring you on in?" Reaching through the open window, his father popped the lock, then wrenched the door open and climbed inside, forcing Jase to either move over or get sat upon.

"Jesus, Jason, something die in here?" His father, his facial expression pinched with disgust, glanced around the cab of the truck, coming to a stop on Jase's lap and the vomit covering his pants.

Jase momentarily thought of covering the stain before his father could see, but what the fuck for? The damage was already done. Not only had he parked on his parents' front lawn, but his dad had his number. The old man always had. Walter Brady was infamous for calling people out on their bullshit and rubbing it in their faces.

And since Jase knew that better than most, again . . .

why the fuck was he here?

Cursing and shaking his head, his father put the truck in gear and began to back up into the street. Once the truck was parked in the driveway, tucked neatly behind his mother's four-door sedan and beside his father's truck, he glanced over at his father, unsure of what to do next.

"Best git on inside the damn house before that food she's cooking you gets cold." His father gestured impatiently toward the house before pocketing the keys and exiting the truck. When Jase still had yet to do so, wondering again if coming here had been a mistake, his father began banging needlessly on the passenger side window.

"Don't make me tell you twice, son!"

With a heavy sigh, Jase pushed open the door. Vertigo hit him hard as he tried to step down, and he would have fallen on his ass had his father not caught him around the waist and dragged him back upright. Embarrassed, he cursed and spun out of his father's grip, sending his fist into the door of the truck. The metal dented under the impact, and too late he realized that this wasn't his truck, but Cage's.

"Fuck," he shouted, clutching his throbbing fist.

"Hey now!" Grabbing his arms, his father yanked him backward, quickly tucking him into his side before he could stumble again. Keeping one arm looped around Jase's waist, he started them for the door.

"It could be worse, son," Walter muttered as he guided him up the porch steps. "You just remember that, it could always be worse."

"It couldn't," Jase slurred, suddenly feeling a whole lot drunker than he had only moments ago. "I fucked it all up, everything, everyone. I made a holy fuckin' mess."

"Don't be blasphemous in front of your mama, now."

The door opened just as they reached it, and standing behind the screen was Jase's mother. Unlike Walter, Doreen had aged gracefully. Her long gray and white hair was still thick with curls, her delicate features remained intact despite the many wrinkles that had taken up residence over the years. And her eyes, his favorite feature on her kind face, were still as big and as blue as ever.

"The prodigal son returns," Walter announced flatly.

Her expression was a mixture of happiness and sadness, her eyes filling even as she tried to smile. "Jason," she said tearfully, pushing open the screen door and holding out her arms.

"He's covered in his own mess," Walter grumbled.

"I don't care," she snapped. "He's my son."

His father had to help him up the remaining step, and then he was in the house, the smells of home enveloping him as his mother's arms wrapped tightly around him.

Jase couldn't help it, he broke down, because apparently that was what he did now, he cried. All the damn time.

"Shhh," she said, hushing him while rubbing his back. "There ain't nothing wrong that we can't fix, you hear me? Nothing wrong that we can't fix."

He didn't believe her, but he didn't mind the comfort either.

Guiding him to the bench in the hall, she helped him sit before sinking to her knees and starting on his boots.

"No, Mama," he said, bending down only to get swatted away.

"Gimme that vest of yours," Walter said, already pulling it from his shoulders. "Coat too."

About to hang both up on the coat rack, his father turned back to him, his brow raised. "Deuce know you're here?"

Jase shook his head. In fact, no one knew because he had no idea where his cell phone was. Probably in his room at the club where'd he'd last seen it. Lot of good it did him there. He could only imagine Deuce's face when he tried to call him and found his phone in his room.

"All right then. I'll be givin' him a call while your mama does whatever it is she's doin'."

"Don't tell him everything," Jase called after him.

"I won't," he yelled back. "But Deuce is a smart man. Pretty sure he'll be able to fill in the blanks."

Jase sank back against the bench, feeling another wave of worthlessness slide through him.

"Jason?"

"Hmm?"

"Jason, look at me."

His energy quickly waning, Jase used every last bit of it to straighten his neck and look at his mother.

"You're a Brady, aren't you?"

Oh, fuck him in the ass with a goddamned fork, it was the Brady family speech.

"Yeah, Mama," he muttered. "I'm a Brady."

"And what do Bradys do?"

"Beer, barbeque, and rodeo?"

"Jason . . ." His mother's tone was that of a warning, and Jase fought the urge to roll his eyes.

"Bradys love each other," she snapped. "Bradys show respect for one another. Bradys work hard, Bradys are honest, and Bradys do their best."

"Mama," he said. "I've fucked up every single one of those at one point or another, some more than once."

"Last one," she continued, ignoring him. "What is it, Jason?"

Swallowing back the quickly forming lump in his throat, he looked off down the hallway to where he could see his father talking on the old rotary phone. He couldn't hear what he was saying, but he could only imagine what Deuce was telling him. The thought of them swapping stories made him cringe.

He turned back to his mother. "Bradys forgive each other."

Smiling, she gave him a quick pat on the knee, finished pulling his boot off, and then went to work on the other.

"The girls won't forgive me," he whispered.

His mother didn't even bother looking up. "They will," she said. "They're Bradys. And Jason?"

"Yeah?"

"Don't you dare curse in my house again."

CHAPTER 14

DETAILS," EVA WHISPERED, LEANING ACROSS THE kitchen counter. "I want them."

It had been almost two weeks since my arrival in Miles City, and the first time coming back to the clubhouse since Hawk had been brought home. This morning I'd woken up to Tegen and Cage and their usual bickering. Unable to stand one more second of it, I'd quickly showered and dressed, made sure Hawk was comfortable, and made a mad dash to the clubhouse.

At first I was glad to find Eva hanging around and, always happy to spend time with her, I'd offered to make us both lunch. Until she'd begun badgering me for information.

Now, I was just annoyed. Unlike Kami, I wasn't easily able to divulge the details of my romantic life, not even to the woman I considered my best friend.

Trying desperately not to blush, I feigned interest in the salad I was preparing in order to continue ignoring her.

"Sheesh, Dorothy, you've got to give me something. You have that big and sexy man laid up in bed, and I know you've kissed and made up. Cage said so."

"What?" I shrieked, slamming the wooden spoon in my hand down on the counter. "He's been spying on me?"

Eva jumped upright and did a strange celebratory dance that consisted of her shaking her backside and waving her arms in the air. It looked awkward and downright awful, and I made a mental note to tell her to never ever to do it again.

"I knew it!" she squealed, still dancing. "I knew it!"

"You tricked me!"

She shrugged as she grinned, and I sighed in defeat.

"Fine," I said shortly. "We've . . . kissed. That's it."

"Oh my God," she whispered dramatically. "Dorothy, what am I going to do with you? Who am I going to live vicariously through? Kami isn't having sex and you're not either, and my life consists of a cranky toddler, a twelve-year-old who thinks she's twenty-six, and a husband who takes heart medication."

"Join the club," I said and sighed again. "My life usually consists of a seven-year-old who wants to be either a biker or a professional paint gun warrior. But lately it's been full of my daughter and her husband who fight more than they don't, and honestly, I don't know why Tegen doesn't just get a job at the local paper instead of struggling with the publishing industry. I don't know how much longer I can take being in the same house with them. Hawk is supposed to be healing, but I don't know how much healing can happen in a house that volatile."

My daughter was a feisty one; there was no doubt about it. Belligerent and demonstrative would be putting it mildly. Tegen took opinionated to an entirely new level, and would fight to the death regardless if she was right or wrong. There were times I'd spent with her and Cage that I was truly perplexed by their interaction with each other. Always fighting, either yelling or refusing to speak to each other, yet at the same time they seemed to balance each other. It was an odd dynamic, but one that apparently worked.

I had to give Cage credit, though. Anyone who could put up with Tegen's regular blowups and her usually crude demeanor either loved her fiercely or was a glutton for punishment. Knowing Cage as well as I did, I had no doubt it was the former. But even knowing this didn't mean I wanted to bear witness to their unique way of showing their love for each other.

As for Hawk and me, there wasn't much privacy to do . . . well, to do anything at all.

Closing my eyes, I took a deep, calming breath that did nothing to soothe my strained nerves. I wasn't used to this . . . this . . . constant disruption anymore. I'd had a quiet, predictable life in San Francisco and now that I was back in Miles City, it was anything but quiet.

"And Hawk," Eva added. "Your life consists of Hawk now too."

"When didn't it?" I quipped.

"Dooooorothy . . ." Eva purposely dragged out my name in a childlike whine.

"Evvvvvvaaaaaa . . . ," I said, mimicking her.

"Dooooorothy . . . ," she repeated.

"Okay, fine," I snapped, dropping the spoon. It clattered to the countertop as I glared at her. "The truth is I haven't had sex since Jase and I were still together, about mid-pregnancy. And to be honest, I'm terrified!"

To my surprise, Eva didn't seem the least bit shocked by my revelation; instead she looked a little smug, as if she'd expected this answer from me. I didn't know whether to be hurt that she'd tricked me once again, or elated that she knew me well enough and cared about me to the extent where she'd taken the time to really know me. To see past the walls I'd built around myself.

"You know what you need?" she asked. Placing her elbows down on the counter, Eva rested her chin in her palms and regarded me with a serious expression.

I shook my head. Had I ever known what I needed? Internally, I scoffed. No, I most certainly had not.

"What?" I asked hesitantly, not sure I really wanted to know what Eva had in store for me.

"Wild pussy," Eva said solemnly.

I arched an eyebrow. "Excuse me?"

"Wild pussy," Eva repeated. "You need to just take control. Forget about everything else—the past, your fears—forget about everything but you and Hawk and what *you* want. But mostly about what you want to do to him," she finished with a sly grin.

"I'm not wild . . . pussy," I said, stumbling over the last word and feeling my face heat. Desperately, I tried searching for a word that adequately described exactly what I was and came up empty. "I'm . . . dusty pussy," I finished with a sigh, feeling ridiculous.

Eva's face went slack as she gave me an exaggerated look

of dismay. "You're in your forties, Dorothy, not dead! So go home, kick your daughter out of the house, go upstairs, get naked, and fuck your man!"

"He can barely walk!" I hissed.

"He doesn't need his leg for this!" she hissed back.

"He'll need his third leg," a new voice chimed in.

Eva and I both looked up to find Christina, Bucket's heavily tattooed girlfriend, staggering through the kitchen's swinging doors. Wearing only a black bra, a matching thong, and a pair of blood-red stiletto heels, she traipsed heavily across the linoleum before collapsing into the nearest chair.

Christina looked more haggard than I'd ever seen her before, with her long black hair a snarled mess, her dark makeup smudged around her eyes, giving her a raccoon appearance, and her red lipstick looking as though it had been forcefully smeared off her mouth and up her cheek.

I raised an eyebrow at Eva who, with a roll of her eyes, shook her head.

"So whose third leg are we talking about?" Christina asked.

"Hawk's," Eva answered, and flashed me a grin that I returned with a silent snarl.

"Oh," Christina said, sounding bored. "Just hitch up that saddle and ride, girl, ride."

"See," Eva said smartly. "Told you."

"It's not that easy," I protested.

"Why the fuck not?" Christina exclaimed. "I mean, it's not as if you haven't taken that ride before. Seriously, D, how long were you jerkin' that joystick behind Jase's back? Five, ten years? The whole damn time?"

My mouth fell open. I'd forgotten just how crude Christina could be. She had no filter, no reservations, and had always been more like one of the boys than any other woman associated with the club. In fact, she was a lot like my own daughter, aside from the fact that Tegen would never be caught dead parading around the clubhouse in lacy underwear and high heels.

Actually, the more I thought about it, the more I realized that most of the women associated with the club were a lot like Christina. With the exception of a few, they were hard women with battle-ax personalities, essentially strong enough to take on the kind of men who became part of Deuce's crew.

How on earth had I ended up here?

While I might have been cheating on my husband with a married man, and later, engaging in a sexual relationship behind my lover's back, as far as the club's female standards went, I was exceptionally tame. A gazelle thrown into a pit of lions who'd somehow managed to survive.

Although not necessarily unscathed, but I'd survived nonetheless. Life sure did throw you some interesting curveballs sometimes.

"What are you thinking about in that crazy brain of yours now, Dorothy?"

I looked up at Eva, shaking free of my thoughts, and shrugged. "Just . . . you know, how in the world I ended up here."

Eva smiled, one of her wide, warm smiles that made you feel like she knew things that others didn't. I both hated and loved that about her, the way she could light up a room with just a simple word or smile.

"You ended up here," she said, "because here is where you belong. It may not always be pretty, in fact sometimes life can be downright ugly, but everything happens for a reason, Dorothy. Everything."

Her words were nearly identical to Hawk's, and something I'd once said to Tegen in order to ease her nerves. Although I'd never been a big believer in fate or destiny, I couldn't help but think that maybe there was some truth to it. Even Hawk had admitted that he'd made mistakes.

Yet . . . maybe our mistakes were what led us to where we were supposed to be all along. Was it possible that without our mistakes, we wouldn't have become the people we were meant to be? And if we hadn't made the choices we made, what would have become of us all?

Would we still have somehow ended up in the same place?

Oh good God, my head was starting to hurt. This line of thinking reminded me very much of my childhood, when my parents had tried to instill religion in me and I fought tooth and nail against it. I might have been very much a romantic, but when it came to blind faith, I'd always needed hard proof, something they could never give me.

But maybe love was a lot like blind faith in the unknown. And maybe that was why it had been so hard for me to let go of what I'd known, instead of moving toward what I'd really wanted.

"Will you two lovesick twats get your mind off your men?" Christina suddenly snapped. "You're both making me sick."

"I think your excessive drinking is what's making you sick," Eva said dryly.

"Speaking of making me sick," she continued, giving Eva a pointed look. "One of you bitches needs to call that little dog off Cox before Kami comes in and sees what the fuck her man has been up to."

My brow furrowed. "What does Cox and Kami's relationship have to do with you feeling sick?"

"Yeah," Eva added. "And since when do you care about what the boys do?"

"Since this happened," she said, flipping us both off. Eva and I both leaned forward for a better look. Seated on her middle finger was a rather extravagant diamond ring.

"Congratulations!" Eva exclaimed with a jump and a clap. "When did that happen?"

"Last night," she said blandly. "Damn thing don't fit the right finger either."

Well, that explained the walk of shame. They must have had a very celebratory night together. And knowing Bucket as well as I did, celebrations for him usually consisted of a harem of women with Christina barking out the orders.

"It's easy to get it sized," I suggested.

She rolled her eyes. "It's a pain in my ass. But back to my point. I don't appreciate these little mutts sniffing out the club for our men. I told Bucket, no more girls now that we're engaged."

She seemed so happy—well, as happy as Christina could seem—that I just didn't have the heart to tell her that nobody ever sought out Bucket. His haggard appearance and his lack of cleanliness meant all his girls were usually bought and paid for. Dirty, another club member, had been the same way before his girlfriend, Ellie, had inspired a makeover, and together he, Bucket, and Freebird were three of the most unappealing men I'd ever met. Unkempt, ung-roomed, usually filthy, and always acting or saying some-thing absolutely disgusting.

"That girl out there is spouting off to Cox about tak-ing her out to dinner, and going home to meet her parents. Seriously, D, go look at this shit. She's all up on him like a fucking fat little dog in heat, and I'm about to go slap her down. I'm a legit old lady now, and if I ever catch her sniffin' round my man . . ." Trailing off, Christina pursed her lip-stick-smeared lips and waved a razor-sharp red fingernail in the air. "No. Just no. She needs to know her place and fast."

"Ugh," Eva muttered. "I'm not in the mood to be school-ing club rats with their eyes on the prize."

"But isn't that your job?" I jested. "God knows you don't have better things to be doing like being a mother or a wife or . . ."

"Right?" she said. "Because in my free time I love teach-ing loose women the ways of the club world, the dos and don'ts when it comes to our men. Rule number one: Don't flirt in front of the wife. Rule number two: Don't try to go down on him in front of the wife. Rule number three: Definitely don't cry in front of the wife when he tells you not to go down on him in front of his wife."

There was a time in my life when the bitter truth of Eva's remarks would have offended me, probably to the point of tears even. But I was anything but offended; after all, crude-ness aside, it was the truth and I'd lived that truth.

"I'll talk to her," I said with a sigh. "What's her name?"

"Lucy," Christina offered. "Just like her vag. Which is why Cox is always fuckin' her up the ass. And speaking of ass, I gotta take a shit." Using the table for support, she pushed herself up from her chair and tottered for a moment on her heels before regaining her balance.

"Way too much information, Christina," I muttered, walking quickly from the kitchen. "Way, way, way too much information."

I found Cox sitting at the bar among a few of the other boys: Chips, Worm, and Danny D. And Lucy was right where Christina had said she'd be: hanging off Cox.

As I headed toward them, I noted the similarities between Lucy and me when I'd first started coming to the club. She was young, early twenties, and shorter than average, as were her looks. If she didn't have so much makeup on, if her dark hair weren't cut so dramatically, she would undoubtedly appear plain, cute at best. And she was clinging to a married man she had absolutely no chance at having a substantial relationship with outside of meaningless sex, gazing up at him like he was everything she'd ever wanted, ever dreamed of finding in a man, and could do no wrong.

Cox. Do no wrong. Good God, what was wrong with this girl?

It was all so painfully familiar. The closer I drew to the bar, an odd feeling washed over me, a sense of déjà vu, and then all at once I was struck with a memory . . .

"Wat up, little D?" Ripper had greeted me with a grin, holding his arm out in welcome.

Although I'd still been feeling the sting of rejection from earlier, the same feeling I was always left with when Jase went home to his wife, I had slipped into Ripper's embrace and felt my anxiety begin to ebb. The club, the boys, they had that effect on me, giving me a sense of comfort and safety when the rest of my world was nothing but turmoil.

"Nothing's up," I'd said, returning his hug. How could I not? Ripper was so incredibly good looking. He was young, with long blond hair that had a touch of waviness, flawless golden skin molded tightly over an incredible bone structure, and an equally stunning body.

"Where's my hug, bitch?" Cox called out. Ripper's partner in both crime and humor gestured for me to come to him. Currently shirtless, his heavily tattooed and pierced body on display, the handsome Latino waggled his eyebrows suggestively.

"No way," I said, shaking my head. "Last time I hugged you, you grabbed my ass."

Cox's grin grew. "It ain't really fair that only Jase gets a piece. Gotta sample somehow, yeah?"

I rolled my eyes. "No."

Realizing I wasn't in the mood to be groped, Cox dropped his arm, and a scowl replaced his smile.

"Dude," he grumbled, pounding his fist on the bar. "That's twice now I've been rejected. Pass the fuckin' Jack."

"We're back to this shit again?" Blue asked. Sitting at his usual corner of the bar, he grabbed the bottle of liquor off the counter and tucked it inside his leather cut. Behind his long white beard, his wrinkled lips curled into a smile, his milky-white eyes sparkling with youthful humor.

Nobody knew Blue's true age, but not even the oldest of the brothers had ever known him without a full head of long white hair and an equally white beard. But despite his age, he could hold his own and liked to prove as much by drinking far more than anyone, young or old, ever should.

"Fuckin' greedy old man," Cox muttered. "Can't you see I'm fuckin' grievin' over here?"

Blue lifted a bushy white eyebrow. "Shut up, you idiot. You ain't grievin', you're fuckin' poutin' like a goddamn baby."

Confused, I glanced between the three men. "What happened?" I asked.

"Nothin'!" Ripper said, laughing. "Fuckface here is still pissed Kami walked out on us in the middle of the night."

Cox snapped into an upright position. "Fuck her!" he yelled. "FUCK HER!"

I rolled my eyes again. It had been several weeks since Eva Fox, the twenty-two-year-old daughter of the Silver Demons MC president, had shown up out of nowhere, her friend Kami in tow. Eva, who had a history with Deuce, had headed straight for him, and Kami had ended up spending three days in bed with Cox and Ripper. Then both women had just up and split in the middle of the night. Cox, who'd never been walked out on before in his life since he always did the leaving, wasn't handling it very well. And judging by the rage fest currently going on inside Deuce's office with loud cursing and crashes, accompanied by loud female moaning, Deuce wasn't handling it at all.

Actually, no one had liked what had happened. In the short time she'd been here, I'd enjoyed Eva's company immensely. Not once had she treated me like anything less than her equal. Most of the boys' families, their wives and children, paid very little attention to me, if any at all. In order to keep my relationship with Jase a secret, only known among the boys and the club groupies, I too was labeled a groupie, and was therefore considered persona non grata, not worthy of them. I wasn't an old lady, therefore, to them I was nothing. Nothing but a whore.

It had been so nice to be able to talk with another woman at the club, one who wasn't here for the sole purpose of spreading her legs. Eva was respected for being Preacher's daughter, and even holding that position she had still treated me with dignity. I could only imagine the differences between the Demons MC and the Horsemen. The club whores in Eva's care were probably treated better than the old ladies.

But the biggest difference her arrival had brought about had been in Deuce. During those three days, he'd been a different man. His permanent scowl had lifted, he'd been the bearer of jokes and smiles, he'd been happy. And when Deuce was happy, the club was happy.

Now that Eva was gone, Deuce was miserable, and so was everyone else.

Except Ripper. As usual, he wasn't bothered by any of it, didn't have a care in the world, and was laughing manically at Cox's sour expression.

"She's a stuck-up, spoiled fuckin' bitch," Cox continued. "It's 'cause I'm Puerto Rican. She's a fuckin Rican hater. Don't got no appreciation for dark meat."

"Get a fuckin' grip," Ripper said. "You sound like a little bitch."

"Wait," Blue said. "You mean to tell me you're not Mexican?" The old man shook his head. "And all this time I was over here thinkin' ya were."

Cox's eyes went wide but just as his mouth opened, one of Deuce's double office doors swung open, crashing loudly against the wall and cutting off whatever nonsense was going to come out of Cox's mouth.

The four of us turned, watching as Deuce came storming out into the room, his cut in his hand and his leathers unbuttoned, hanging open in the front. Miranda, Deuce's usual girl, came sauntering out next. Taking a seat at the bar, she pulled out a pack of cigarettes and a lighter from inside her low-cut top, placed one between her plump pink lips, and lit it up.

Miranda might be considered beautiful to some, all long legs and a luxurious mane of blonde hair, but I found the woman more trashy than anything else. Even so, I kept my feelings to myself. I was in no position to express my dislike for Deuce's taste in extracurricular activities. Not when most people viewed me as an extracurricular activity as well.

"You assholes plan on doin' fuckin' anything today?" Deuce yelled as he stalked past us. "Or you just gonna sit on your fuckin' asses, drinkin' my motherfuckin' booze?"

No one said a word, just watching in silence as he stomped across the room. He had nearly rounded the corner when he stopped suddenly and turned.

"Barbeque tomorrow," he growled. "You cookin', D?"

Startled, I could only nod in response. With an answering nod, Deuce disappeared.

"He's hurtin'." Blue nodded in the direction Deuce had gone. "Little girl shows up outta nowhere, and the two of 'em already got fuckin' history. She's tellin' him she loves him, givin' him a taste of what he's always wanted, and then poof, she's fuckin' gone."

"What the fuck you talkin' 'bout?" Cox asked. "You tryin' to tell me Prez is hard up for Demon pussy?"

"You're kidding me, right?" Miranda snorted, shaking

her head. Leaning forward across the countertop, her breasts pushed up clear to her chin. "He doesn't give two shits about that little girl."

Ignoring her, Blue looked to Cox. "You a fuckin' dumbass? Preacher told him if he touches Eva again, he's takin' him to ground. So what does he do? He touches her again. And again. I call that hard-fuckin'-up."

"Then, fuck her too," Cox growled.

"Hello?" Miranda called out, sounding annoyed. "Anybody home? Eva was a dick distraction is all. Nothing more."

Blue, looking exasperated, turned his attention to Miranda and gave her a toothless condescending smile. "You mean to tell me that if Eva Fox marched her sweet little ass back inside this club right this second, Deuce wouldn't drop you like a burnin' hot potato and take her straight to bed?"

Miranda's posture went rigid, her expression hostile, but she said nothing.

Blue shrugged unapologetically. "Might be an old man, might not know what fuckin' year it is, but I know real when I see it and Deuce and Eva, that was some real shit. You're the distraction, girl. Best get your head screwed on straight 'fore you fuckin' lose what little brains you got left up in there."

I slapped my hand over my mouth, attempting to stifle my laughter, but I was too late. Everyone had heard me.

"What are you laughing at?" Miranda demanded, her nostrils flaring with anger. "You're no better than I am! You want to talk about what's real, Dorothy? Jase and Chrissy's marriage, that's real!"

My stomach did a nervous flip, bringing all my insecurities boiling back up to the surface, and my smile slipped from my face, falling away alongside my hand.

I knew I wasn't like Miranda, was nothing like her. She didn't love Deuce; she only loved what she could gain from being with him. I loved Jase, loved him with all my heart. And he'd promised me he would eventually leave his wife.

But . . . if all that were really true, why did a meaningless insult from a woman like Miranda have the ability to wound me?

With a satisfied smile, Miranda slid off her bar stool. "It's about time you learned your place here," she spat. Spinning on her heel, she marched quickly across the room, disappearing down the same hallway Deuce had.

"Pay no attention to that one," Blue called out. "She ain't ever cared 'bout nothin' but climbin' the ranks in the club. You ain't her, Dorothy, you hear me, girl? You ain't like her. I know good people when I see 'em, and I ain't never seen nothin' but good from you."

"Yeah, fuck her, D." Ripper gave me another friendly squeeze. "She ain't got a clue what's she's spoutin' off about."

"Fuck 'em all," Cox grumbled. "Especially Kami. Stupid bitch."

"Goddamn, dude, you're actually feelin' that stuck-up, good-for-nothin'-but-fuckin' piece of New York ass?"

Cox glared at him. "You gonna try and tell me you didn't?"

Ripper shrugged. "Kami's a fuckin' party. Bitch like that ain't good for much else. 'Sides, she's too fuckin' skinny. Gotta have somethin' to grab, yeah? Fuckin' anything at all. And that bitch ain't got nothin.'"

"Then why the fuck was I sharin' her with your dumb ass?"

Ripper looked affronted. "Brother, I don't pass up hot bitches offerin' up free parties."

"Fuck off and die."

"You first, asshat."

As the two of them had continued their usual arguing and incessant bickering, a new smile began to form and I'd felt myself relaxing once again. If anyone could make me forget my problems, it was the boys. Especially these two clowns.

"Why don't ya both fuck off and die, and lemme finish drinkin' in peace!" Blue had yelled.

"Is that even possible?" Cox had asked. "I mean, dude, do you ever finish drinkin'?"

Later that evening, after a day of heavy drinking and feeling sorry for myself, I'd ended up drunk and alone at the bar. Just as I was getting ready to call it a night and head to Jase's room, a large figure stepped out of the shadows.

"Ain't no fun drinkin' alone."

"Hawk!" I exclaimed, putting my hand over my heart. "You scared me!"

Stone faced, Hawk continued his stride toward the bar. Sliding into the seat beside me, he gestured toward the row of bottles on the shelf.

"I'll have two of whatever you're havin'."

And then he smiled.

It was the first time I'd ever seen him smile.

"Wat up little, D?" Cox called out, bringing me back to the

present. "You need a drink, darlin'?"

I smiled and shook my head. "Just need to borrow Lucy for a moment."

Lucy's head emerged from Cox's neck, her lips swollen from fervent kisses. She gave me a confused look and asked, "Me? Why?"

I shrugged. "Just wanted to talk."

"Go talk," Cox encouraged her, then over her head mouthed, *Thank you, thank you, thank you,* rather emphatically.

As Lucy reached me, I looped my arm through hers and led her out of the room. "I want to tell you a story," I said, my voice hushed. "It's about a young woman who fell in love with a married man, and the many years of misery that followed."

Lucy stopped walking, forcing me to stop as well.

Looking up at me with puppy-dog eyes full of naïveté, she smiled sadly. "Am I that obvious?" she whispered.

"No," I lied. "Sadly, I'm just an expert on this sort of thing."

CHAPTER 15

HAWK WAS RECLINING IN BED, READING ONE OF TEGEN'S many publisher-rejected manuscripts that she'd forced on him, when Cage slipped his head inside the partially open bedroom door.

"You got a visitor, old man," he said, giving Hawk a grim smile.

Grateful, Hawk tossed aside the thick folder of printed pages. As far as he could tell it was a love story; at least, it was Tegen's attempt at a love story. In actuality it was more of a long-winded, hate-filled, rambling mess of words that she was trying to pass off as a love story. By two hours into it, Hawk's brain began to feel like a game of ping-pong was being played inside it.

He guessed in a way the story reflected the woman who wrote it, which made sense considering he often thought

Tegen could do with a heavy dose of medication to calm her the fuck down. How Cage dealt with that . . . yeah, Hawk didn't have a clue. If he were Cage, he would have shot out of town as fast as possible to get as far away from her as he could.

But he supposed you couldn't help who you fell in love with. He had fallen in love with a married woman, who had a boyfriend to boot. Although he couldn't help but feel like he'd gotten a better deal than Cage, seeing as the mother was a whole shitload less volatile than the daughter.

Not that Dorothy didn't have her moments, and sometimes her emotional outbursts made him want to stab himself in the eye, but Tegen . . .

Holy shit.

The walls in this house were thin, too thin, forcing Hawk to have to listen to fight after fight. They either ended in something breaking or what sounded like sex—did rabid animals have sex?—and left him contemplating smothering himself to death with his own pillow.

"Havin' fun yet?"

The bedroom door pushed open, revealing Deuce. He took a quick visual sweep of the room before walking inside. He was followed by Ripper, who immediately closed the door behind him. As Deuce crossed the room, the floor creaking heavily under the sound of his hard, booted steps, Ripper remained by the door, looking anywhere but at Hawk.

It was the first time he'd seen any of his brothers other than Cage since they'd picked his sorry ass up from the Russians, and Hawk had felt the sting of that rejection. Although he didn't blame them; how could he? In a way he'd betrayed them by lying to them all these years. Yet, he'd held out hope that once Deuce had explained everything to them, they'd forgive him. But judging by the look on Ripper's face, that wasn't the case.

Shoving his feelings on the matter aside, Hawk turned to face Deuce. There were far more important things to discuss than hurt feelings.

He'd been waiting for Deuce to show up, both dreading this moment and anticipating it. Half of him wanted this to be the outcome, but the other half desperately wanted things to be different. More so for Dorothy and Christopher than himself. Because he couldn't give two shits about what happened to him, only it wasn't just him anymore.

Funny how having a kid could change your entire perspective on life.

"Been listenin' to Tegen and Cage fuck each other up," Hawk said, looking again toward Ripper, who still hadn't so much as glanced his way. "I'm thinkin' I had more fun with the Russians."

"Yeah," Deuce muttered, giving his head a small shake. "I don't get those two, but somehow she keeps him in line, focused on the game, and that's about all that really fuckin' matters.

"And speaking of the game," Deuce continued. "Saw D at the club. She said you're feelin' better, figured it was time for us to talk."

"Two weeks, Prez," Hawk said, ensuring that every word he spoke sounded as devoid of emotion as he wished he'd felt. "I know what I gotta do. Just gimme two weeks with her, that's all I'm askin' for."

Deuce unfolded his arms and dropped his head into his

rising hands. Raking his fingers through his hair, he sighed heavily. "Brother," he started, but Hawk didn't let him finish.

"Prez, please," he said, struggling to sit up straighter. "I gotta see my boy. I gotta spend some time with them both . . . before . . ."

Realizing he'd let the very emotion he was hoping to keep in check seep into his words and body language, he trailed off.

When Deuce didn't respond, just continued to stand there, his gaze on the floor, Hawk let out a ragged sigh.

"I'll do whatever I gotta do," he said quietly. "Just promise me you're gonna take care of 'em. Look after 'em. I've been tryin' to give Dorothy money for years, but she never uses it, just keeps puttin' it into an account for Christopher. I don't want her livin' like that anymore, I want her here, near her daughter, near you. I want her in a damn house, her own place, for once."

Deuce's head raised, those cold blue eyes staring Hawk down. "You ain't gotta worry about that fuckin' shit, you know we always take care of our own. And you want two weeks, you got 'em. Hell, you want three weeks, you got 'em. I know you know what you gotta do, and I know you're gonna do it. That ain't why I'm here."

Deuce stopped talking and took a deep breath, one that caused his chest to visibly rise, then fall and rise again. It was a rare display of emotion from his prez, one that surprised the shit out of Hawk. Other than anger, Deuce didn't put his feelings out there for just anyone to see. None of the boys did, other than Cox, and even Cox kept his under the guise of humor most times.

"I shoulda never sent you to Vegas," Deuce said. "I

shoulda been smart enough to realize you coulda been made. Fact, I'm surprised it hasn't happened sooner and that's on me. I shoulda been more careful."

Hawk shook his head. "It wasn't the Russians who made me. Meant to tell you before, but I figured you had enough shit to deal with."

He had Deuce's full attention now.

"Who?" the man growled, the look on his face telling Hawk he already knew who, but wanted to hear him say it.

"ZZ," Hawk said. "It was ZZ who set this shit up. Shot me, beat the fuckin' crap outta me. He's workin' for Yenny. Fightin' for him."

The tension that gripped the room at the sound of ZZ's name grew even thicker as several silent seconds ticked uncomfortably by. Even Ripper, who'd been feigning indifference to Hawk this entire time, had jerked his head up, his expression a mixture of shock and rage.

"Prez," Hawk continued. "I wasn't so sure before that takin' him out was the best way to go, but . . . he ain't ZZ no more. The man is cold, Prez, through and through, and a walkin' fuckin' time bomb."

Ripper stepped forward while Deuce remained frozen. But even in his stillness the man was literally vibrating with rage, his nostrils flaring as the exposed skin on his forearms rippled, his muscles twitching with barely restrained fury.

"Did he say anything?" Ripper asked, and Hawk could hear the unspoken words. After all, ZZ had assumed Ripper had stolen Danny from him. And Ripper was now married to her.

"Don't think you gotta worry about Danny," Hawk said. "He's hung up on this shit, that much I could tell, but he ain't stupid enough to come anywhere near Miles City. Not with the club and the law gunnin' for him."

"I'll fuckin' kill him," Ripper said darkly.

Deuce's head swung around, Ripper's words breaking his trance-like state. "I will fuckin' kill him," Deuce gritted out. "You hear me? Me. I will fuckin' kill him."

Each of Deuce's words was fiercely punctuated with a verbal venom that Hawk had only ever heard twice before. The first, when Eva had been taken by her now-dead first husband, Frankie, and the last, when Danny had been kidnapped by Mama V, a notorious hit woman from one of the Cali gangs the Horsemen had some trouble with a while back.

But even more surprising than Deuce's unholy anger was Ripper. Having never before openly defied Deuce's orders, Ripper was staring his prez down, silently refusing to give up this kill.

"You wanna go runnin' after the fuckin' Russians?" Deuce ground out. "You wanna end up shark meat and leave my baby girl and granddaughter without you? 'Cause that's what's gonna happen if you take off, guns blazin', trying to take out an asshole protected by one of the biggest cartels in the fuckin' world."

"If I'm protectin' my family and the club," Ripper said, "I don't give a fuck if I gotta die doin' it."

All at once the anger that had taken root in Deuce seemed to evaporate. "Yeah, yeah, yeah," he said, sighing as he turned away from Ripper. "But I ain't gonna let you, so reel your fuckin' shit in before I reel it in for you."

Ripper's face gave Hawk the impression that shit was about to go south real quick. In order to avoid watching Ripper get a beat down from Deuce, Hawk cleared his throat, gaining the attention of both men, and addressed Deuce.

"You got your shit in place with the Russians?"

Deuce nodded briskly. "Got two clubs lined up, eager for the business. All we can do now is hope they ain't too mad when Yenny goes down, and take what we're offering."

Hawk didn't think there was going to be a problem. The Bratva might be greedy, but just like every other criminal organization out there, they didn't like going to war. War meant losing bodies, and losing bodies meant losing money and resources. War was a lose-lose for everyone involved.

"I think for once the law is gonna be on our side," Hawk said, feeling the weight of those words fall heavily upon him. His chest tightened, his breathing quickened, and he gripped the blanket beneath him hard enough that the soft fabric began to tear.

Get it together, he commanded himself. Get your shit together.

Only he didn't see how he could. If Deuce's actions were anything to go by, once the rest of the boys found out their plans and once Dorothy knew what he had to do, the next few weeks were going to be hell on his emotions.

Goddamn, he didn't want to hurt that woman, not again. She'd been hurt her entire life by nearly everyone in it.

"I'm sorry," Deuce said quietly.

Still gripping the blanket, Hawk swallowed hard and shook his head. "No," he gritted out through clenched teeth. "Nothin' to be sorry for. If it weren't for you, I never would've made it this long." Looking Deuce directly in the eye, he stared hard at the man. "Never would've met Dorothy, and never would've had my boy. Never woulda had nothin' worth havin.'"

Deuce's eyes narrowed, and his face contorted with angry lines. "I didn't do it for you," he spat, suddenly sounding as angry as he looked. "Didn't do it for Cox or for Ripper." He turned, pinning Ripper with a glare before turning back to Hawk.

"Didn't do it for Dirty either, didn't do it for any of you. Picked your sorry asses up off the street, gave you a place to stay, put food in your bellies and clothes on your backs . . . I did all that fuckin' shit for me.

"I did that shit for me," he repeated forcefully, slapping his hand onto his chest. "My old man had a club full of mean old bastards just like him, that's what that motherfucker left me with. I had to clean fuckin' house, bring in boys I knew would be loyal to me and only to me, and who better to be loyal than a piece of shit like you, eatin' out of the fuckin' garbage can, wanted by the fuckin' law. I knew if I saved you . . ."

Deuce glared at him through red-rimmed eyes flashing with emotion. Behind him, Ripper was staring at their prez, looking shocked. That made two of them. Never before had anyone seen this sort of show of emotion from Deuce. But at the same time, Hawk was grateful for the unexpected outburst, as it caused his own emotions to even out somewhat, allowing him to loosen his death grip on the poor, mutilated blanket and unclench his teeth. For some reason, he'd always been more apt to remain calm while others unraveled, and this was no different.

"I knew if I saved you," Deuce continued, "*you piece of*

shit, that you'd be willin' to lay down and die for me and this fuckin' club! This shit is my fault, you fuckin' feel me? My fault!"

"Prez," Hawk said quietly. "This ain't your burden to bear. It's mine, always has been. Fact is, no matter your reasons, you gave me a life I never woulda had, and whether you want to accept it or not, I'm thankin' you for that. Now, the club comes before anything else, always has, always will, and I'll do my part because I'm a Horseman first, and we do what we gotta do to keep the club goin'. No matter what."

His words didn't have the calming effect on Deuce that he hoped they would have; if anything, they seemed to agitate him further. No longer still, Deuce was shifting from foot to foot, his brow furrowed, his features pinched.

Hawk didn't know what to do, what to say, so he did and said nothing at all, planning to just wait out the tumultuous storm that was Deuce West. But no storm came, and surprisingly enough, Deuce seemed to be able to get himself under control before the impending explosion could happen. Shoving his hands into the pockets of his leathers, Deuce schooled his expression. Although his body remained rigid, not a trace of anger could be found in his features.

Odd, Hawk thought, that so much had changed in such a short period of time. Looked like he wasn't the only one who had done some growing up recently.

"I'll get Christopher here," Deuce said shortly. "I'll send Tegen and Cage tomorrow. Ain't like they got shit better to do than slap each other around anyway."

And with that, he left. Just turned and marched across the room, shoving Ripper out of his way, and then he was gone, leaving Hawk staring after him.

As Ripper and Hawk turned to look at each other, Hawk found the man looking him over, his expression rather sad.

"Prez told you?"

Ripper nodded. "Cornered him, made him tell me what the fuck was goin' on with you."

"You still pissed?" Hawk asked.

Ripper shrugged. "No." A couple of silent seconds followed, then, "Wanna play video games?"

"Brother," Hawk said. "If you can get the TV up here, I'm fuckin' down. I've been stuck readin' Tegen's damn books."

"Say no more," Ripper said, grimacing.

When Ripper disappeared into the hallway, Hawk sank back down into his pillows and closed his eyes. Blowing out a deep, noisy breath, he willed himself not to be a pussy. After all, he'd spent the second half of his life expecting this day to someday come, waiting for it even.

He just hadn't expected it to come after he'd finally gotten everything he'd always wanted. That, more than anything else, really fucking sucked.

CHAPTER 16

"**Y**OU FORGET HOW TO CHOP WOOD, SON?"

Jase glared at his father.

No, he hadn't fucking forgotten how to chop wood; he'd fucking forgotten how to function without some sort of liquor coursing through his veins.

After sleeping off his hangover, he'd woken up in need of a drink only to find that the remaining liquor in Cage's truck had mysteriously disappeared, as had his keys. At first he'd been pissed off, storming through his parents' house, wildly searching through the cupboards and ransacking the closets. And then he'd been desperate, even going as far as to look under beds and in his parents' dresser drawers for a bottle of anything. Any-fucking-thing. Only to come up empty. Not only that, he'd ended up with his father's meaty fist slamming into his face.

While lying on the floor, his vision going in and out, he'd thought he'd heard his father calling him a goddamn drunk and his mother arguing that he wasn't, but was only in need of a good cleanup.

After that, everything grew a little fuzzy. The next thing he knew he was in his old bed, hanging over the side, puking up whatever was left in his empty stomach into a small trash can his poor mother held beneath his head.

He spent the next few days either in bed sleeping away the physical misery his body was enduring or pacing his room, trying to walk off the constant nausea and the need to make a liquor store run. Which he would have if his father hadn't been standing guard outside his bedroom with a .22 rifle cradled in his arms. Even Jase's oldest brother, Daniel, had joined the party, and was taking turns with their father to babysit him.

It was both humiliating and sobering, pun fucking intended.

And now that he could walk without shaking and speak without retching, his father had a list of chores for him to do. But instead of calling them chores, his dear old dad was fondly referring to them as necessary punishments for being such a dumbass.

Shoveling the driveway and sidewalk had been first on his list of dumbassery punishments, followed by cleaning the windows from the inside, scraping the grime off the old claw-foot tub upstairs, straightening up the holy mess that was the attic, mending a broken log in the backyard fence, and now, God help him, he was chopping wood in the snow. Had been at it all day because, for reasons unknown to him, his parents had a deep-rooted love of wood-burning stoves.

Then, to make already shitty circumstances even worse, his other brother had shown up this morning with his wife and two little kids in tow. One girl, one boy, dressed in the obligatory blue and pink, both cherub-faced, well-behaved little fuckers who adored their parents and only served to agitate Jase when everyone else was fawning over them. In fact, he almost preferred being outside, freezing his ass off, turning his hands into blister-ridden messes to being cooped up inside the house with the happy fucking family.

Over and over again he'd continuously asked himself why he'd come here, and he'd still be asking himself at that very moment if he hadn't already figured out the answer.

As usual, his old man had been right about him. He was a drunk. He'd started drinking heavily the moment he'd found out the baby Dorothy had given birth to wasn't his, that Hawk had betrayed the bonds of brotherhood, and to top it all off, Dorothy didn't even remember him and subsequently wanted nothing to do with him.

So he'd kept drinking all through Chrissy's trial, and throughout the years that followed. He struggled to be a father, but instead ended up as a nuisance to his girls, a motherfucking embarrassment too caught up in his own bullshit to be able to pay any attention to them.

And then even later, after Dorothy's memories had returned and he kept trying to speak to her, each time getting rejected, he turned time and time again to the bottle to stave off the pain she caused him with every word she wouldn't speak, every look she wouldn't give, every touch she withheld from him.

As the years rolled by, he continued throwing drinks back until drinking had become a part of his daily routine.

He could function better with alcohol in his system than he could without it.

But truth be told, hindsight was 20/20. After the surprisingly awful bout of withdrawal he'd just endured, he'd come to the conclusion that his old man, as fucking usual, was right.

He, Jason Brady, was a goddamn drunk.

And despite his liquor-soaked brain cells, coming home had obviously been an unconscious cry for much-needed help.

So he was chopping wood, or rather he was trying to chop wood. Not an easy task when his muscles felt like jelly, and the sharp smell of cedar wasn't helping his constant nausea.

Even though he was taller and in much better shape than his father, Jase could barely lift the ax, let alone get enough momentum to split logs in one swing, leaving him feeling like a goddamn little girl. Except a little girl would probably be far more useful to his father than he currently was.

"You thought about whatcha gonna do after this?" Walter asked. Not waiting for Jase's response, his father swung the ax and the thick log split a good ways down the center. Pausing, his father used the woolen sleeve of his thick flannel jacket to wipe the sweat from his brow before he swung again.

As the wood split into two separate pieces and fell from the chopping block, his father tossed the ax aside and turned to look at Jase.

"So?" he asked. "Whatcha gonna do?"

Jase stared at him, confused by the question. What did

he mean, what was he going to do?

"Go home," he started off slowly. "Go back to—"

"The club," Walter finished for him. "And sleepin' around and drinkin', no doubt."

Jase paused for a moment, letting his father's words sink in. And when they did, he couldn't help but realize that, yeah, that was more than likely exactly what would happen. But what other choice did he have? He couldn't live with his parents. Men in their forties didn't live with their parents, not if they could help it, and he damn sure couldn't stay in this town. Not with the threat of running into Chrissy's family. If his arrival here was made public, there wasn't a doubt in Jase's mind that a lynch mob, complete with pitchforks and shotguns, would be gunning for him with Chrissy's father in the lead.

So then, what was left? He couldn't very well rejoin the reserves, not at his age and with his record. All he had was the club. It was all he knew at this point.

"The club." Jase nodded slowly. "I ain't got nothin' else."

His father frowned at him, not that the man wasn't already frowning at him to begin with. In fact, all his father had done since his arrival was frown and shake his head while grumbling under his breath.

"You know what they say about makin' the same mistake over and over again, and thinkin' it's gonna be different this time?"

"No, Dad." Jase sighed. "What do they say?"

"They say it's damn crazy is what they say!"

Jase scrubbed his gloved hand across his jaw. "Then what, Dad? What the fuck do you think I should do?"

"No!" Walter shot back. "What the fuck do *you* think

you should do? You're a grown man, son, not a little boy. And it's time you start actin' like it."

Jase knew his father was right, was dead fucking right, but still, hearing the man say it, call him out on his bullshit point-blank . . . didn't feel so good.

"Get a job?" Jase suggested with a limp shrug of his shoulder. He really didn't know what his father expected of him. How could he leave the club? Leave Deuce and the boys? It wasn't computing in his head.

"You're gettin' warmer," Walter said with a sigh. "Get a job where?"

Jase stared at the older man, utterly perplexed. "Anywhere?"

His father, despite the man's love of calling people out on their wrongdoings, had always been a fairly even-tempered guy. So when he suddenly lurched over and grabbed the collar of Jase's jacket, using it to wrench him forward, Jase was shocked speechless.

"What do you want most in the damn world?" Walter gritted out, his breath smelling of the butterscotch candies he'd always loved.

"More than anything else," he continued, tightening his grip on Jase's collar. "What do you want from this life you're so quick to give up? 'Cause you aren't gonna get another one. There are no second chances once you've closed those eyes for the last damn time. So I'm gonna ask you again, Jason, what do you damn well want?"

Jase's thoughts went wild, spinning around before fanning out in a mad scramble. What did he want? *What the fuck did he want?* What did he really, truly want more than anything?

He didn't have to think about it for very long.

"I want my girls," he said quietly. "I want my kids back."

"And how you gonna make that happen?" Walter asked.

Jase didn't know how he was going to make that happen, but he knew one thing for certain. As long as he was a Hell's Horseman, his girls would have nothing to do with him.

"I gotta leave the club," he whispered, dropping his gaze to the snow-covered lawn. "Get a job, somewhere near the girls, maybe."

When his father didn't readily respond, Jase glanced up to find the old man smiling at him. It was a satisfied smile, and one that Jase had never seen before. Correction, it was a look that Jase had never seen directed *at him* before.

"You've always been a good mechanic," Walter said, releasing him. Bending down with a grunt, his father grabbed the handle of the ax and swung it up over his shoulder.

Then, in typical Walter Brady fashion, without another word he turned around and walked away, leaving Jase standing there alone with his thoughts, staring off across his parents' acreage, feeling as empty and as cold as his surroundings.

The very thought of leaving the club left him with a fear he'd never felt before. When everyone else had left, the club had always been there. It was his foundation. His safe place. His whole world.

And maybe that was his biggest problem. The club was his crutch, the one place he could hide from the mess he'd made of his life.

He swallowed back a wave of sickness that had nothing to do with his detoxing body and everything to do with the fear of living outside the club. He'd be a regular joe. No band of brothers, be it military or motorcycle club, to tell him what to do, or catch him when he fell flat on his face. And he always did fall flat on his damn face.

But his girls . . . Without them, what was he?

As far as he could see, without them he wasn't worth a damn.

"Uncle Jason! Uncle Jason!"

Jase turned, barely having time to jump out of the way as his niece and nephew came barreling through the snow, nearly waist deep on them both. They were wearing matching pink and blue snowsuits that made them look like tiny colorful marshmallows.

"Build a snowman with us!" the girl yelled as they ran past him. Jase tried to smile at them, but failed. Neither child had ever met him before, yet they'd instantly accepted him as their uncle. It only deepened his yearning to be reunited with his own children, who wouldn't be nearly as accepting, if at all.

His younger brother, Michael, who'd been quickly following his children, paused beside Jase with a smile on his face. Of course he was smiling at him. Michael was a Brady, and Bradys loved their family despite their faults.

"How's it going, big brother?" he asked, knocking Jase softly on the shoulder with his fist.

Brother.

It struck him then they he might no longer have the reserves, and if he left the club he'd no longer have the boys, but he'd always have his family, complete with two brothers who would always have his back.

"Listen," Jase said. "I owe you an apology—"

Michael shook his head. "Nah," he said. "We all knew you'd come home again."

Jase studied the younger man, almost a mirror image of himself back when he was still in his thirties. Yet instead of the hard lines and firm jaw that Jase had inherited from their father, Michael had a more rounded face with wide blue eyes like their mother's that gave him a perpetually youthful appearance.

Remembering when they were kids and how Michael had always looked up to him, Jase felt a wave of guilt wash over him. Michael might easily forgive, but Jase couldn't forgive himself for not being there for his little brother's marriage, or for the birth of his children. Those were things Bradys did simply because they loved their family.

Jase didn't deserve to be a Brady.

"Help me out?" Michael suggested. "Those two monsters can go all day, and after Mom let them eat a plate of her sugar cookies . . ." He shook his head. "I'll be running out of energy long before they do."

Jase glanced to where the kids were unsuccessfully trying to roll a ball of snow, but instead of seeing his brother's kids, he saw his own girls in their childhood, running through the snow-covered backyard, bundled from head to toe, grins gracing their innocent faces.

He'd tried so hard to keep them innocent, separate from his other life, from what he did for a living and his numerous indiscretions.

He'd never wanted to hurt them, but he had.

And now it was time to make a change.

"Build a snowman," he said, giving his brother a sad smile. "Why the hell not?"

Jase wasn't stupid enough to think that redemption would be handed to him on a silver platter. But as he walked side by side with his brother, leaning down to grab handfuls of snow as he went, he figured he had to start somewhere.

Might as well start with a snowman.

CHAPTER 17

"WHAT DO YOU MEAN, TEGEN AND CAGE ARE bringing Christopher here?"

With my hands on my hips I glared at Hawk, who was still in bed, looking much the same as I'd left him this morning. Only now he was sitting up, the bed a mess with papers that had been strewn across it, along with bits of food and an ashtray that looked precariously close to spilling over and covering the white sheets in black ash. And someone had lugged the flat screen up the stairs, along with both of Cage's video game consoles.

It appeared that the boys had been visiting, and nobody had bothered to clean up.

This disgusting mess, coupled with the fact that Hawk hadn't consulted me about bringing Christopher to Miles City, had taken me from feeling a sort of nervous excitement for what the night might have brought, to being downright irritated with him.

"I didn't want him seeing you like this," I continued. "What's he going to think, finding his father all black and blue, hardly able to walk on his own? How are you going to explain that to him?"

Very slowly, Hawk set down the glass he was holding and turned to look at me in that maddening way he'd always looked at me when he thought I was acting like a lunatic. And maybe I was reacting badly, but if anything he should be used to me and my reactions by now. But what was really irking me, what I absolutely could not fathom, was why he hadn't grasped yet that it was that damn look that only infuriated me further.

"I missed Christmas," he said carefully, as if his words were footsteps and my temper was the thin ice he was skating on. "And I want to see my boy."

"But you didn't even consult me!" I cried. "And I'm his mother!"

"I'm his father," Hawk replied coolly. "And I was plannin' on tellin' him I wrecked. Fucked my bike up and myself."

I couldn't exactly argue with that and yet for some reason, because I had nothing to say in response and was starting to feel a little silly at my Tegen-esque outburst, I grew even more upset.

"Fine," I muttered. "Fine, whatever, I'm . . ."

I stopped talking to glance quickly around the room, looking for something that would give me an excuse to make a quick exit. My eyes landed on the closest, most plausible excuse.

"I'm going to take a bath," I said, averting my gaze from Hawk's always prying eyes, and scurried off across the room.

When the door was closed behind me and I was safely ensconced inside the little room, I leaned back against the tile wall and took a deep, calming breath. I'd been so nervous, so wound up after talking with Eva, full of expectations and excitement for the upcoming evening with Hawk, that once I'd found out Christopher was coming, it had felt as if someone had pulled the plug on my newfound happiness. It wasn't that I didn't want Christopher to come to Miles City. I not only missed him, but I wanted him to see his father. It was just that . . .

Maybe I'd wanted Hawk to myself for just a little while, before I had to share him with a child who didn't see nearly enough of him, and who monopolized the man whenever they were together. Not that it had ever bothered me before, but things were different now, things were changing, and maybe they were changing too quickly. I couldn't keep up, my emotions couldn't keep up, and I'd wanted just a couple of days where time could stop, and Hawk and I could get to know each other again. We could talk, make love, just be together for the first time out in the open, before our families, our lives, and the club all caught up to us and time started moving again.

Sighing, I pushed away from the wall and went to sit down on the edge of the bathtub. There was no use in going back out there and making more of a fool of myself, so I turned on the water and waited for the tub to fill.

I'd always loved baths, usually first thing in the morning, sort of like the calm before the storm, a way to relax before the day turned hectic and busy. Not that my days had been hectic, they hadn't been for quite a long time, but that wasn't the case anymore.

I was back home, back in Miles City, and hectic was a rather mild word for what tended to be the status quo for the good—and not-so-good—citizens of my small town.

When the tub was full I undressed quickly, leaving my clothing in a heap on the floor, and stepped tentatively into the steaming water. I sighed contentedly as I sank down, my muscles loosening as the water lapped over my body and instantly ebbed away my frustration. Letting my head fall back against the cool porcelain, I closed my eyes.

Alone now and comfortably relaxed, my thoughts returned to my conversation with Eva, and to what I'd had planned for tonight. And then they turned to the man himself, the story of us, how we'd begun, and all the stolen moments we'd shared over the years. With every latent memory I allowed to rise from the cobwebs, I found myself growing more and more aroused, excitement building inside me until I was burning, aching to be touched the way he had once touched me, hoping he still wanted me as badly as he once had.

Whimpering, I arched my back, sinking even deeper into the bathwater. Cupping my breasts, I kneaded them softly before reaching down. My fingers whispered over the soft skin of my stomach, across my hips, before sinking between my thighs.

Panting, air shuddering from my lungs, I squeezed my legs, closing them tightly around my hand, putting pressure where I needed it most.

And then, as I often did when I was alone and turned on, I envisioned Hawk. Dressed in head-to-toe riding leather, covered in road dust, his Mohawk matted and messy from his helmet. But it wasn't his appearance that was appealing to me, it was the look on his face after a run, refreshed and rejuvenated. His dark eyes would lighten, his thunderous walk would slow and relax; at those times he always looked as happy as a man who never smiled could look.

And then his eyes would find mine and in his gaze, I knew instinctively what he wanted from me. Then later, when we could be alone and I was in his arms once again, I would wrap myself around him, breathing him in, the sweat and soap on his skin, the scents of leather and smoke that always clung to him.

They were my favorite smells, ones I could conjure even now, despite the strong-smelling scents of my shampoo and body wash. All I had to do was close my eyes and inhale . . .

Suddenly my eyes flew open and my hands fell still.

What was I doing?

What in God's name was I doing?

I sat up quickly in the bathtub, my jerky movements causing water to slosh over the side and onto my clothes.

"Dammit," I whispered, slapping at the water. Forget my clothing, I was upset with myself. For doing what I did best and, once again, hiding. Here I was, about to pleasure myself while thinking of a man who was right outside the damn door! A man lying in a bed with hardly any clothing on, no less!

I didn't have to hide anymore—not my feelings, not myself, nothing. Everything was finally, blessedly all out in the big wide open. I'd said good-bye to Jase, and I'd admitted my true feelings to both myself and Hawk.

I finally had everything I wanted.

And what was I doing? I was hiding.

I shot up out of the tub and snatched the towel from the rack. Wrapping it around my body, I began internally chastising myself. I wasn't that weak-willed woman anymore, afraid of everyone, but most of all afraid of herself.

I was stronger, maybe not as sure of myself as I wished I were, but definitely stronger. I'd walked away from my demons, learned how to live on my own, living my life how I saw fit, and all without any help from anyone else.

A handful of days back in Miles City, and I was once again acting the part of a woman afraid.

Grabbing a hair tie off the bathroom sink, I pulled up my partially damp hair into a messy top bun and continued drying myself off. My thoughts were spinning, my nerve endings flaring to life as my stomach tingled with nervous excitement.

I was going to leave this bathroom a strong woman, a woman sure of herself, one who knew exactly what she wanted. For the first time in my life, I was going to take what I wanted without having to worry about the repercussions, without having to worry about hurting anyone in the process.

Until I caught a glimpse of myself in the mirror.

For a moment I simply stood there, gazing into the reflective glass, feeling a strong sense of detachment. Unlike when I'd lost my memories, I wasn't greeted with a sense of unfamiliarity, but I was still left wondering where the time had gone. Where I had gone.

The image in the mirror didn't mesh with the one in my dreams and fantasies: a younger woman, her days and nights filled with hot, sweaty lust and love. And men—their big, tall bodies hard and thick, their skin inked, their hands strong and calloused from years of hard work, covered in dirt that had coated them so long, it would never wash away.

This woman was getting older, had lost her youthful cuteness, and although I'd never classify myself as ugly, I still felt inadequate.

Letting my towel fall to the floor, I cupped my breasts, pushing them up as high as they would go. Turning sideways, I studied my self-imposed lift. Yes, my face wasn't the only thing that had changed.

"Saggy boobs," I said softly with a sigh.

This wasn't the body of a woman who should be standing beside a man like Hawk. This was the body of a woman who . . .

I thought of Richard, a local butcher back in San Francisco I'd gone on a few awkward dates with. He was a kind man but as far as his looks went, he had been balding and rather rotund. The longer I stared at myself, the more I thought of myself as Richard's physical equal, a woman you would expect to see with a man like him.

Not with a man like the tall and astoundingly muscular one lying just outside this room. Covered in tattoos, oozing strength, Hawk had never looked his age. Visually, he was such a strong presence, giving the appearance of both an outer and inner strength, both qualities making him appear somewhat ageless.

And I was . . . me.

"Screw it," I said under my breath, turning away from the mirror. If I continued to stare at myself, beating myself up over every little imperfection, I would talk myself right out of what I wanted.

I could be like Eva or Christina, I could be wild . . . *pussy*. Couldn't I?

I could, or at least, dammit, I could try.

Even as I was wrinkling my nose up at the thought of referring to my anatomy as "wild pussy," I grabbed hold of the doorknob and pulled open the door. As if he'd been watching the door the entire time I'd been inside the bathroom, Hawk's eyes were on me. Or rather, they were on my breasts.

Be brave, I silently told myself.

Fighting the urge to cover myself, I proceeded quickly, marching forward like a woman on a mission, until I'd reached the end of the bed. It took him a moment, but eventually Hawk pried his eyes away from my body and looked up into my eyes.

"I've always loved you," I said, sounding as breathless as I felt. "And I'm sorry I waited so long to tell you. I'm sorry for my outburst. I was being silly and selfish, wanting to just spend a few days alone together before I had to share you again."

Hawk stared at me, looking confused. "You're . . . naked?" he said, sounding as perplexed as he looked.

"Yes, I'm naked," I snapped. Annoyed by his response to my nudity, or rather, his lack of response, I put my hands on my hips and narrowed my eyes. "I'm naked because I want to be with you, you big, dumb man."

The slow smile that lit his face, painting creases around his eyes and highlighting his hard features with a sexy sort of softness, was breathtaking. Hawk hardly smiled; his expression was normally as stoic as he usually was. But on those precious occasions when he had smiled in the past, it had always taken my breath away. How incredible that such a small, simple gesture could transform a rather frightening-looking man with hardened features into a softer, more beautiful one.

But his smile, as it always had been, was short lived, and as it slipped away from his face, replaced by his usual indifference, my heart sank and anxiety filled me. I wasn't a sexually confident woman, no matter how much I pretended to be. I couldn't be like Eva or Christina, not really. And now I was left standing here, completely nude, wondering what I'd been thinking, walking out here like this and putting myself on display, ripe for rejection.

"I'm kinda broken," he said, nodding down at his leg.

And just like that my anxiety slipped away. It was rare for Hawk to show any sort of vulnerability, and in the face of his admission it became instantly clear to me that I wasn't the only one feeling a little unsure. Just knowing that this formidable man had fears too was what encouraged me to move forward with my original plan.

"We're all a little broken," I whispered, reaching up into my hair and brushing my fingers over my scar. "And you don't have to do anything, just lie there and I'll do it all."

I nearly clapped my hand over my mouth, disbelieving the words that had just come out of me. Those weren't my words, they were the words of a confident woman, a worldly woman who could make her own decisions, one who saw what she wanted and went for it, no outside persuasion necessary.

I wasn't that woman.

But just maybe . . . I could pretend to be.

"Woman," Hawk said, his voice growing significantly

deeper, more lyrical than before, something I'd learned long ago was attributed to his arousal. "You can't say somethin' like that, then just keep standin' there. Get your damn ass over here."

Burning with a sudden blossoming embarrassment, I slowly began rounding the bed. I was overly aware of Hawk's gaze on me, traveling up and down my body, and desperately trying not to blush because of it. As it was, my stomach was once again fluttering, and worse, I was starting to sweat.

Reaching his side of the bed, I paused, searching out a way to climb atop him without hurting him, but Hawk's hand stayed me. Reaching out, his palm grazed my side and ran down the length of me before settling on my hip.

My breath hitched and my eyes fluttered closed. His touch on my naked skin, so familiar yet so foreign, was both comforting and disconcerting. I had to remind myself that this was Hawk, and that my love for him superseded the years we'd spent in limbo.

"I missed you," he said hoarsely. "I fucking missed you, D."

My eyes flew open to find him staring up at me, at my body, with an almost reverent look on his face. It was moving in a way that left me unable to find the right words to describe it, and crushed to dust any lasting reservations I'd been feeling.

Tears burned behind my eyes. To hell with being a strong and sure woman. This was the man I loved. I didn't need to be strong or sure; I just needed to be with him.

"I missed you too," I whispered. It was a seemingly silly thing to say to a man I saw on a regular basis, but it was the truth. I'd missed him terribly, in the way of a person who has loved and lost someone who'd remained a part of their life—close, yet never close enough.

Death would have been a much easier loss than to have to live every day with the guilt of a mistake, a misstep that you couldn't fathom how to ever again make right.

But none of that mattered anymore.

And maybe there really was something to what Eva said about fate.

Maybe there was . . .

Hawk squeezed my hip lightly, abruptly ending my train of thought. Slowly, as if I were made of glass, he began to slide his hand across my stomach. His touch was so unbelievably light, a barely there fluttering sensation that caused my eyelids to grow heavy. The sensation only grew as he traveled higher, his fingertips drawing invisible lines on their upward journey between my breasts. Dancing over the top of them, he paused, hovering over one breast, his calloused palm causing the nipple to tighten beneath it, and a shiver to slither down my spine.

"Hawk . . ." I breathed his name, nothing more than a puff of air slipping from my lips. At my sides my fingers began to twitch restlessly, my body aching for more.

And he gave me more.

His hand closed around my breast, squeezing and kneading the soft flesh, leaving me breathing harder.

It was a beautifully tortuous game he was playing with me, and one I wouldn't have any other way. I might have walked into this room with the silly notion that I would take control of the situation, when in reality I needed him to go as slow as he was, to be as careful as he was being, working me up to the point where he knew I'd be comfortable and ready for more.

His hand dropped from my breast, traveling slowly down the same path back to my stomach and then lower, running his fingertips between my legs, but just barely touching the sensitive skin. I swallowed back a threatening whimper. It had been so long since I'd been touched like this and my body was a veritable volcano, threatening to erupt from the simplest of touches.

He saw this, my response to him, and his pupils began to dilate; his breaths grew louder, and more pronounced. All his reactions told me I wasn't the only one so affected, and that knowledge—knowing he was feeling every bit of what I was—was so incredibly intoxicating,

My moans came out in staccato breaths as his fingers began to play, his touch still so astoundingly gentle that I was beginning to have trouble concentrating on anything other than the feel of him and the deeply buried sensations he brought to life, to light, within my body.

My name was a low rumble past his lips and then he slid a finger up inside me. I cried out, biting down on my bottom lip as heat roared through my trembling body, filling it with the sort of heart-pounding adrenaline that made me weak in the knees, leaving my body a mass of quivering muscle and skin. I didn't know where I was, who I was, and didn't care to ever know. All I wanted, all I needed, was this.

Him.

"Come here," he said, his voice a throaty growl as he removed his hand from my body.

It took me a moment to regain my bearings, but only a moment as I was more than desperate to touch him now, desperate to have him inside me again.

Quaking knees aside, I managed to climb up over him without hurting him. It helped that I was so much smaller than him, so as I settled myself over his hips, he didn't as much as flinch.

"Is this okay?" I whispered.

"This is more than okay," he said, and through his boxers, I felt him jerk beneath me, hard and ready. The movement caused my body to clench, to fill with a rush of eager need.

Leaning forward, I placed both my hands on his chest and pressed my mouth to his lips, and just celebrated in the act of touching him again.

Hawk's body, like his mouth, was warm, and as I stroked his chest, his tattooed skin twitched beneath my palms. I took my time with him, kissing him slowly while tracing every line on his body—his thickly defined pectorals, the indented muscles over his abdomen, the dipping grooves of his hips . . . Until finally, I couldn't take another second of waiting, and lifted off him just enough to slip my hand inside his boxers.

My shaking hands fumbled a bit as I tried to align our bodies.

Unused to the act of sex, unused to having a man inside me, I could only slowly move up and down, easing him gently inside me with unsteady and unsure maneuvers until finally, I felt my body give way and allow him full entry.

"Dorothy . . ." Hawk more groaned than spoke my name.

Breathing hard, I raised my head to look at him.

"You're so crazy tight," he whispered, his eyes unusually

wide, surprise tingeing his tone.

I blushed, partly because Hawk was inside me and instead of making love we were having a conversation, but mostly because I *was* so incredibly tight. I could feel everything—every ridge, every pulse, the way my body was throbbing around his, absolutely everything. And although it was slightly uncomfortable, it was beautifully filling.

"It's . . . been a while," I whispered.

"How long?" he whispered back.

I looked down at his chest, feeling silly, and even more embarrassed that all our foreplay had led to this. Talking about how tight I was. Good God.

Then I felt Hawk's fingertips touch beneath my chin, lifting my head.

"How long?" he repeated. But he already knew the answer. The look on his face was one I'd only seen once before, the one and only time we'd ever been able to spend an entire night together. It was years ago; the club had been empty, everyone had gone to a bike rally across state lines. I'd woken up curled beside him to find him already awake and watching me sleep.

"Good morning," I'd said sleepily that morning, stretching as I'd yawned.

He'd never answered me, just given me that look, a look that spoke more than words ever could. A look that told me I was his world.

"Was it me?" he asked, and I could tell, not by his tone but by his eyes, the way they darkened when he asked, that he wanted it to have been him.

And, oh God, I wished it had been him, more than anything I wished that now. But it wasn't true and I refused to ever lie to him again.

I opened my mouth, an apology already forming on my lips, but he cut me off by pulling me forward and into a kiss.

"Never mind," he mumbled against my lips. "That shit don't matter anymore."

And then, when I couldn't take much more and had to break the kiss in order to start moving my hips, needing to relieve the building pressure inside me, I pushed myself upright and, gripping his pectorals, began to rock my body over his.

"Hawk . . ." His name fell from my lips, over and over again, each time more and more breathless, while I grew more and more senseless.

His eyes, firmly fixed on me, were black liquid fire, searing every inch of me, his body a hot and throbbing volcano below me, within me. Me, I was mere kindle, alit with his every attention. And together . . . together we burned.

Gasping, whimpering, crying out his name, clawing at his skin . . . I fucking burned.

We burned the way I'd remembered us, young and full of lust, and then it was more than that, more than it had ever been. It wasn't just sex or lust, it wasn't just love, it was something else entirely, a feeling I couldn't explain, a word without a sound.

But it was everything I'd been searching for.

He was everything I'd been searching for.

What filled the unfillable hole inside me.

And when it was over, when I was lying on my back half atop him, half on the bed, and Hawk was running his hands over my body, he paused over the scar on my abdomen, softly tracing the result of my C-section.

I couldn't help but think of Christopher in that moment. And Hawk's eyes, when we turned to face each other, softened exponentially. His son did that to him. To us. Made him a different man. A better man. And me a better woman.

However brief the moment was, the warmth it left me feeling as Hawk's hands resumed their traveling was unparalleled and left me reeling. To love someone was one thing, but to share a child with someone you love, to share the love you both had for that child . . . together . . .

It was a heartbreakingly beautiful revelation that gave me the insight I'd been missing.

And suddenly I knew. In that very moment, I just knew. It all made sense.

It had always been meant to be.

My lifeless marriage had led me to Jase, and Jase had led me to Hawk. And Hawk and I had created a child we both cherished.

None of it had been a mistake. It had just been my path, my cracked and broken road to home.

And if I hadn't loved him already, I would undoubtedly love him now.

It had taken me half a lifetime, years filled with heartache and one bad decision after another. But I'd finally found him, my prince, hiding inside a man who'd been there all along.

Dorothy had been naked.

Granted she was still naked, had been naked for a while now and they'd already fucked, but still, Hawk couldn't get that image of her walking out of the bathroom butt-ass naked out of his head. She'd never done shit like that, not in all the years they'd been together. It had always been him who'd made the first move, him who'd undressed her, him who'd initiated sex.

This. Her. Naked. Them. It was like Christmas fucking morning.

Now she was lying on top of him, her back to his front. Because he couldn't lie any other way except on his back without the accompanying pain, he'd had a hard time touching her while they'd fucked. Unable to touch her the way he'd wanted had pissed him off so badly that for the last hour, he'd forced her to lie on top of him so he could easily grope all those parts of her he'd missed out on. Because of how short she was, this worked out perfectly for him, and also allowed their heads to rest side by side.

At the moment he had one hand between her legs, a finger up inside her, softly stroking inside and out, over and over again, while his other hand alternated between stroking her breasts when he could focus long enough to switch it up.

When he bit down softly on her shoulder, she let out a small gasp, and Hawk grinned against her skin, biting down harder, thrusting his fingers faster.

He knew he should tell her what the coming weeks were going to bring, but for some reason he couldn't force himself to do it just yet. He needed this, her and him, her content and happy because of him. He didn't want to ruin the moment, or be the cause of any more tears that would inevitably flow from those beautiful green eyes of hers once he told her everything.

That and he really wanted her to come again. Wanted to feel her little body tighten up, see her hands clench into fists, her toes curl, all while making those incredibly sexy mewing noises she always made. Increasing his speed, he gripped her breast, biting first her shoulder, then her neck. Then, as her back bowed, her whimpers catching in her throat, he took her mouth, sending her over the edge. Finishing hard, she cried out loudly as her body squeezed around his fingers.

While kissing the single tear sliding down her cheek, he had a fleeting thought that he should thank his traitorous uncle. After all, it was Yenny's doing that had brought this about, brought Dorothy and him back together. This time, and for the first time with no secrets.

"I love you," she whispered, turning her face, nuzzling her nose against his cheek. He turned to meet her and their mouths met. Slow kisses ensued, wet and soft, making him hungry for more, making his body twitch with the need to intensify this insatiable pull between them.

And goddamn it, he just wanted to be able to throw her off him, climb on top of her, and hammer the hell out of her.

"You're beautiful, D," he said softly.

"I'm getting older," she whispered, her smile suddenly waning.

He almost snorted, but reminded himself how insecure she'd always been and held his solemn expression. He'd dealt with her insecurities back then, and knew exactly how to deal with them now.

"Woman," he said, slipping another finger inside her. "Quit your fuckin' nonsense."

Then he kissed her before she could say another word.

He'd fucked a lot of women since going nomad, all younger than her, and yet not one of them could hold a damn candle to the way he felt about her, the way he saw her.

So her skin wasn't as smooth as it had once been, her breasts weren't as high and her stomach not quite as tight. None of that mattered to him.

Dorothy was still herself, still beautiful, and she was still the lone woman on this earth who'd been able to give him any sense of comfort. She was the one woman who'd grounded him when he'd needed it most, who'd given him the one thing he'd thought he'd never have again: a flesh and blood family.

No matter how much she aged, when her hair turned white and her skin was a cascade of wrinkles, he'd find her beautiful, above all others, and love her still.

"I feel like we should be talking more," she mumbled against his mouth, "but we've barely spoken, it seems like."

He kissed her again, her mouth, each cheek, and then her pert little nose. "When the fuck have we ever needed words?"

Because they hadn't needed them, not back then and not now. Maybe a few would have come in handy toward the end there, and maybe getting to this point wouldn't have been such a long, hard road, but it didn't matter anymore because they were here. They'd both made it to the finish line.

And words weren't fucking needed.

Except when they were.

"D," he whispered, removing his hands from her body. "We need to talk."

Slowly, looking slightly dazed, her lips swollen from kissing and her skin reddened from his touches, she rolled off of him and onto her side.

"Hmm?" she murmured, nuzzling into his arm. As her hand slid over his stomach, her nails lightly grazing his skin, he closed his eyes, biting back a groan. He wanted to do this, do her, all night long, all week long. Hell, he wanted to make up for lost time and do this for a year straight.

But he didn't have a year. He didn't even have a month.

And if he didn't tell her now, she'd hate him for it later. That wasn't something he could live with.

Wrapping his arm around her back, he said, "There's somethin' you need to know, baby."

"Deuce already told me everything," she whispered, kissing his arm.

"No," he said. "He didn't."

All at once her body language shifted from languid and soft to rigid and alert. Shifting off of him, she moved to a sitting position and pulled a pillow in front of her, covering herself and hugging it to her chest.

"What?" she asked, sounding wary.

It hurt. It was physically hurting Hawk to try to get the words out, because once he freed them, there would be no taking them back. The damage would be done and he'd spend his last few weeks with her trying to repair that damage instead of simply being together. It would be the elephant in the fucking room, too momentous to ignore.

But even though he hated it, hated the very idea of hurting her, there had been enough secrets between them in the past. He didn't want that to be who they were anymore.

"This shit with the Russians," he said, his voice giving

away the emotional strain he was feeling. "It's . . . not over."

Her eyes narrowed. "What do you mean, it's not over?"

He took a deep breath, a blatant and unlikely show of emotion that surprised both himself and Dorothy.

"Hawk," she said, her voice small and unusually high, a testament to her growing fear. "What's going on? You're scaring me."

"There's somethin' I gotta do," he said, reaching for her. Cupping her cheek, he smoothed his thumb across her bottom lip, trying to stop it from trembling. "Somethin' you're not gonna like."

CHAPTER 18

IFE WAS MADE UP OF MOMENTS, BIG ONES AND LITTLE, the good and bad, dark and light. We never remembered the gray, the times in between, but instead only the moments that had the ability to transform us in some way, affect us so completely that the memory would be forever etched upon who we were, who we are, and who we would become.

My moments were many. Becoming pregnant at fifteen, married to a man I didn't love at eighteen, falling in love for the first time while I was still married to a man who was also married.

Losing the respect and support of my family.

And then falling in love again, this time for the last time with a man who was virtually a stranger to me, and again becoming pregnant.

The day Chrissy shot me, the first time I saw Christopher's face and innately knew he was mine, the day my memories started to return.

All a mixture of devastation and happiness that I'd never forget.

My daughter falling apart in my arms after Cage had been shot, and then the look on her face when she'd married him and finally had the one thing she'd wanted most in this world.

Each and every one of Christopher's smiles.

Hawk not showing up for Christmas and all the events that followed, leading to me finally having the courage to face Jase, to let him go, and by letting him go finally allowing myself to accept my true feelings for Hawk.

And Hawk. Having him, for the first time, really, truly having the man I undeniably loved, a man who loved me unconditionally in return, having him in my heart and in my arms, and unashamedly, unapologetically, finally being able to tell the world that he was mine and I was his.

Those were the moments I'd remember forever, the moments of my life, the story of me.

And it was all ending with Hawk leaving.

He was leaving me.

Not by choice, but because of his sense of duty—to Deuce, to all the Horsemen, even to Preacher.

Neither Deuce nor Preacher would ever allow another organization to dictate how they ran their businesses, who they bought from, who they sold to. And because of that, in return for saving Hawk's life, Hawk had to sacrifice his freedom for the good of both clubs.

In a few days there would be a meeting with the club's

lawyer to discuss their strategy, and in three weeks' time, Deuce would accompany Hawk to the FBI headquarters where Hawk would reveal who he really was, ultimately turning himself in.

And I would lose him all over again.

Moments.

Good . . . and bad.

My life.

At first I'd cried.

Then I'd asked Hawk, my voice a hoarse whisper, "How long will you be gone?" And he couldn't give me an answer, just a look that told me, in no uncertain terms, that he didn't have an answer for me but he expected the worst and so should I.

"What exactly are you wanted for?" I asked meekly, dreading the answer.

He didn't want to tell me, that much I could discern from the deep frown that formed on his usually unmovable features.

"Weapons, drugs, human trafficking." He sighed. "You name it, my father had his hand in it."

Then I'd yelled while I'd cried, I'd beat my fists against the bedding and pillows instead of the man. Because even though I wanted to blame him, I couldn't. I couldn't blame him for the sins of his father, or that his father had been careless enough to let his teenage son be a part of such a dangerous game.

Then I'd cried again. I'd cried because I could have spent the past eight years in his arms. I could have looked past my pain and allowed him in, opened that door he'd been waiting outside the entire time and just fucking let him in.

But I hadn't, because even though I'd thought myself stronger, I hadn't been. I'd still been hiding, still scared of myself and my feelings, of what my future held.

And now it was too late.

Then I'd kissed him. Cupped the sides of his face, dug my fingers through his scruffy beard and into his skin, then up into his hair and while raking my nails across his scalp, I kissed him hard. A ferocious, tear-drenched kiss, full of my anger and pain, pouring it all into his mouth, into him. Because I had to do something or I would scream and scream, and I'd feared that if I started screaming, I'd never stop.

We made love again, this time without my insecurities and without Hawk's restraint. Despite his limited range of movement, he was aggressive, demanding, and equally as passionate as I was needful. I wasn't gentle; I couldn't be. I didn't have time for gentleness, didn't have time to take things slow, to get to know each other all over again, discovering what he loved best and what I enjoyed most.

All I had was right now and I didn't want to waste it. Him. Us. Our moments.

These moments that I would remember for the rest of my life.

Him, so deep inside me that I could feel him, large and heavy with need, the blood pumping through his body, beating in time with my own heart.

And me, so full, so utterly satiated, surrounded and infused by him, both too much and not enough, and ultimately heartbreakingly satisfying to levels of gratification only known by a woman who has experienced what true love is.

Moments.

I cried again when I came. Breathless and still quivering from my release, with Hawk still inside me, I collapsed onto his chest. His arms wound around me, squeezing me tightly, his face buried into my hair while my eyes overflowed, wetting both of us, and neither of us spoke.

When my tears had run dry, when I was finally able to release him, he refused to let me go.

"You're my woman, Dorothy Kelley," he said, his deep voice soft. "Always have been, always will be. I've waited a long-ass time for this, for you, so havin' to wait a little longer ain't gonna kill me."

I raised my head to meet his eyes. Eyes that were surprisingly moist. Hawk really had changed. Finally being free of his past, his secrets, no longer in hiding, had brought out the man he always should have been, a man I loved even more because of it.

"I'll wait forever." I whispered the words, willing myself to stay strong, at least for this moment. "I will wait for fucking ever," I repeated, this time with more force, every fiber of my being afire with the truth of those words. I could feel it, breathe it, that I would undoubtedly wait forever for this man to come back to me.

Hawk's lips split into a smile so big, so bright, that even his beard couldn't hide the intensity of it.

I couldn't help but grin in return.

Hawk didn't grin. There were those rare occasions that one of the boys at the club would say something juvenile, causing him to laugh, but a grin, a cat-that-ate-the-canary sort of grin? Never.

A hand came down hard on my backside, a sharp slap that echoed throughout the room, making me jump.

"Woman," he said, barking out a laugh. "I fuckin' love it when you curse."

CHAPTER 19

EREDITH JAMISON WAS A POWERHOUSE IN HEELS IF Hawk had ever seen one.

In her white button-down shirt hidden behind a silky-looking black pants suit that hugged her barely there curves, her shiny black hair pulled back into a tight ponytail, her hard and all-knowing brown eyes, and an expression as unyielding as her tone, she was a woman who gave the impression that she could take on the world, bring it to its knees, and make it her bitch.

Which was great.

Fucking perfect.

She was the kind of lawyer Hawk needed if he wanted to avoid spending his golden years behind bars.

Out of all the club's affiliations with lawyers over the years, she was by far the best. She worked as hard as she

"I'll be in touch soon," she said without looking back.

As she opened the doors, the sounds of the party going on outside Deuce's office filled the air, a good-bye party for Hawk that the boys had decided to throw in his honor. As the doors closed behind her, cutting off the sounds of music and laughter, Hawk envisioned a prison cell door slamming shut, cutting him off from the world entirely.

And to think he'd once thought he didn't have shit in this world. In reality, he'd had so much. More than most.

"I ain't never served any real time, just a few short stints here and there, nothin' more than a few months," Deuce said as he got up out of his chair and rounded his desk. Coming to sit beside Hawk on the couch, he sighed heavily. "Thanks to Mick," he finished, rolling his eyes.

"But you'll do okay. Just keep your head down, keep your mouth shut, and if you have to, if someone's got a beef with you, fall in line with a crew that'll have your back. And you run into any real problems, you let me know. Preacher's got eyes all over the damn place. Whatever joint you end up in, I'm sure Preacher knows someone who knows someone who knows someone, and I'll take care of that shit real quick."

Hawk couldn't tell if it was him that Deuce was trying to convince that everything was going to be all right, or himself. But he didn't doubt the man for a minute. After all, it was Deuce who had his own father put down while in the joint. Had him shanked in the showers.

And wasn't Hawk happy he'd done just that. Without the fortunate death of Reaper West, who knew what the hell would have happened to him, Cox, Ripper, or Dirty? Reaper certainly wouldn't have done a couple of homeless teenagers any favors.

While killing your own father might seem to others the actions of a cruel, coldhearted man, it had been Reaper who'd been cruel and Deuce anything but. He was just a man who did what he had to do to keep surviving. He made his own rules, lived his own way, and anyone who fucked with him or what was his . . .

Somehow, someday, Deuce would serve them their punishment.

"Speaking of takin' care of shit," Hawk said. "What are you gonna do about the Vegas boys, or . . ." He hesitated, not wanting to bring up the biggest traitor of them all, but it didn't matter. Deuce knew exactly who he was talking about.

"They've all been stripped," Deuce said. "Can't do much else while they're in bed with the cartel, but you know the Russians, they never like to keep outsiders on the inside for too long. Liabilities. One way or another, they'll all be goin' to ground.

"As for ZZ," Deuce continued, his jaw hardening to the point where Hawk could see his facial muscles twitching. "I don't give two fucks who he thinks is protectin' him. I ain't gonna stop lookin' and when I find him, I'm goin' to rip his fuckin' heart out."

Deuce's nostrils flared, his cold blue eyes burning with vehemence. "He shot my boy, he betrayed me, and then this shit with you . . ."

Resting on his knees, Deuce's fists clenched.

"He still loves her," Hawk said.

Deuce's head jerked, his eyes flicking to Hawk. "Danny?" he asked.

Hawk nodded. "Gathered that much after he shot me, before he started beatin' the fuckin' shit outta me. Didn't really want to spell it all out in front of Ripper."

Deuce's expression seemed to slacken some, but the underlying anger remained. "Don't matter," he growled. "You been pinin' after D all these years, and you didn't start shootin' up your brothers."

Hawk bit back a laugh. There were times when he'd wanted nothing more than to put a bullet in Jase's spoiled, selfish, useless brain. But hurting Dorothy was something he'd never been able to stomach, and killing Jase . . . Well, no matter her feelings for the man, it would have hurt her.

"Fuck all this woman talk," Deuce suddenly spat, pushing himself off the couch. Grabbing Hawk's crutches, Deuce held out his arm for him to take. "You got a party goin' on out there, and people wantin' to see you."

Hawk grabbed hold of Deuce's offered arm and with a good bit of struggling, managed to stand up. While he balanced on his good leg, Deuce shoved the crutches under his arms. It took Hawk a moment to adjust to them, having never used them before recently, but it was either use the crutches or be stuck in a wheelchair, and crutches seemed a hell of a lot more appealing than trying to maneuver around on fucking wheels.

Deuce was about to open the doors when a loud knock sounded from the opposite side, making the wood vibrate.

Hawk took a limping step backward as Deuce pulled the doors open, revealing . . . Jase.

"You're back," Deuce said.

"I . . . uh . . ." Jase's gaze flickered to Hawk, who held his gaze with narrowed eyes. Dorothy had explained to him what had transpired between the two of them. He knew that Dorothy had slept in Jase's bed, and ended up kissing him good-bye the next morning. But even knowing that had been their last kiss, Hawk wasn't happy about it. Not that he'd had any claim on Dorothy at that point in time, but he did now and he couldn't help but feel a little territorial. Or maybe a lot territorial.

Looking between the two of them, Deuce ushered Jase inside before giving Hawk a grim smile and a slap on the back.

"Go," Deuce said, pointing to the room beyond his office.

As Hawk hobbled through the doorway, he knew there was nothing on this earth aside from a bullet to the brain or a fatal drug overdose that was going to make him forget about what was coming, but as he was greeted with grins and shouts and cheers, bottles being held up in the air, and the sad smile of a pretty little redhead, he could almost forget.

Almost.

Even before Jase watched Hawk limp across the room, heading straight for Dorothy, grabbing her in a one-armed hug and yanking her against his body to lay a kiss on her that would have made porn stars blush, he'd already known something had happened between the two of them.

Whereas Hawk and he might have a history of disliking each other, they usually spent the very little time they were forced to spend in the same room together ignoring each other. Not since the day Hawk had showed up at the hospital, informing them all that Dorothy's baby was his and then beating Jase senseless, had Hawk given him the time of day.

Until today. As soon as he'd seen Jase, his hard expression had hardened further. Even injured, the man had squared his shoulders, rising to his full height. It was the human equivalent of an animal sensing a threat, and Hawk's figurative hackles had risen.

As they'd stared at each other, Jase had felt an unspoken tension begin building between them, worse than it had ever been before. Yeah, something was very different this time, and once he saw that kiss . . .

Deuce shut the doors with a slam and Jase closed his eyes. He'd felt that kiss, felt that shit all the way down to his toes. No smack down Hawk could have ever laid on him, verbally or physically, would make him feel worse than seeing the woman who'd once put him on a damn pedestal, had faithfully waited on him to choose her for years—

Wait. Scratch that shit. She hadn't been faithful. Not even close. But he couldn't even bring himself to be pissed about it. Talk about the pot calling the kettle black.

Even so, seeing her publicly claimed by another man made him feel like shit.

"Reel it in," Deuce muttered, "and sit the fuck down. I got a fuck of a lot of shit to fill your sorry ass in on."

As Deuce headed for his desk, Jase dropped into an armchair and sighed. "'Bout that shit, Prez, I don't think you should be tellin' me anything."

Deuce took his seat, but instead of leaning forward onto his desk like he usually would, he pushed back, folded his arms across his chest, and stared blankly at Jase.

"Yeah?" Deuce asked. "And why's that? You quittin' me?"

"I got kids that won't fuckin' talk to me," Jase said, beginning to worry about whether Deuce was going to let him retire in good standing, or boot his ass out of here for being a quitter and force him to cover up his club tattoos.

"Been with you a long time, Prez," he said nervously. "Half my damn life, just about. I gotta go. I ain't got no choice. Gotta make this shit right with my girls."

"So that's where you're headed, then? Upstate? Near the college?"

Jase simply nodded.

Unfolding his arms, Deuce sat up and yanked open a drawer that Jase couldn't see into. He pulled out a pack of smokes, shook one out of the box, and lit it up.

Jase glanced to the door, expecting Eva to charge in here and begin busting the man's balls, but when nothing happened, he shrugged and looked back to Deuce.

"Don't give me any bullshit," Deuce grumbled. "I got two of my boys leavin' me, think I deserve a fuckin' smoke."

Jase wanted to ask who else was leaving, but decided against it. If Deuce allowed him to pull out on good standing, he'd technically still be a member, just a retired one. And being retired from an MC was a hell of a lot like military service—you could be called back to duty at any time if you were needed.

"Ahhh." Deuce sighed as a long stream of gray smoke poured from between his lips. "Fuckin' beautiful shit right there."

Jase stayed silent, letting the man enjoy his cigarette as he glanced around the office for what was more than likely going to be the last time. The thought of leaving, saying good-bye to everything he knew was terrifying, yet at the same time there was a tiny part of him that felt . . . excited at the idea of starting over.

Deuce abruptly stood up, jerking Jase's attention back to him. "Hand over your cut," he said, and Jase's stomach sank.

Slowly he pushed himself out of the chair, and even more slowly, he let the black leather vest slide from his shoulders. He turned, catching it before it could fall to the floor. Then, clutching it in his hands, he stared down at it a moment, at the patches on it, thinking of the million memories such a small scrap of material contained.

"Picture stays on the wall," Deuce said, regaining Jase's attention. "Colors stay on your skin. And I ever need your ass, you're back here faster than shit stains a white fuckin' carpet, you feel me?"

After stubbing his cigarette out, Deuce headed back around the desk and toward him. Holding out his hand, he said, "Give it here."

Looking at Deuce, Jase was reminded of his father. Despite aging better than his old man had, Deuce had been like a father to Jase. Saying good-bye to him felt like losing a family member.

Still, he handed over the vest, and once it was in Deuce's hand, the man turned around and pointed to where Blue's cut was hanging on the wall above his desk, encased in glass and framed.

"It's goin' there, brother," he said. "You'll be in good fuckin' company."

It was both surprising and heartwarming. To have his cut hung on Deuce's wall, and near Blue's, no less? That was an honor of epic proportions, and one given to very few brothers. Jase wasn't being dismissed or cut off, not at all. He was simply moving on in a way that was reminiscent of leaving your parents' home once you were old enough, once it was finally time.

And it was time for Jase to move on.

"Thanks, Prez," Jase said quietly.

"Deuce," he said, turning back to him and holding out his hand. "My name is Deuce, brother."

Jase clasped the man's hand and gave it a firm shake that ended with Deuce pulling him forward into a quick hug. He'd barely had enough time to feel surprised when he was suddenly being pushed away and Deuce was jerking his chin toward the door.

"There's a fuckin' party goin' on out there. Go say goodbye to the boys."

Jase knew when he was being booted, but he also knew that Deuce, judging by the man's expression, was only doing so because he needed a moment alone. Whatever was going on that had him hurting, Jase had only added to it.

"And Jase?"

Looking back at Deuce, he arched an eyebrow in question.

Deuce smiled grimly. "Some of the boys might not like what you're doin', leavin' the club and all, but don't pay 'em no mind. Ain't nothin' more important than family. Took me a long fuckin' time to figure that shit out."

Closing his eyes, Jase took a deep breath. When he opened them, he gave Deuce a long, hard look, willing himself to be strong. Strong like Deuce always was.

"Thanks, brother."

"Now go," Deuce ordered, turning away from him. "Get to livin' again."

Jase's muscles tensed and his jaw locked up tight. He wasn't going to be a pussy now; he was going to walk out those doors, his head held high, proud of what he was finally getting around to doing. His fucking emotions, goddamn them, were not going to get the better of him this time.

Wrapping his hand around the doorknob, Jase pulled open the door.

"Fucker!" Cage yelled, pointing as he stormed towards him. "What the fuck did you do to my truck? You don't fuck around with another man's truck!"

"Stop whinin'!" Ripper shouted from across the room. "Your truck ain't shit!"

"Jase!" Cox pounded on the bar. "Get your ass over here. I got stories to tell and ain't nobody listenin'!"

Grinning, Jase closed Deuce's office door behind him and slowly headed out into the club.

For the last time.

CHAPTER 20

I T WAS BEING TOUTED AS A PARTY, BUT I KNEW WHAT THE reality of this impromptu get-together at the clubhouse really was. A good-bye party. Everyone had come—the boys, their wives or girlfriends, and all of their children. Even the nomads, the men who didn't live in Miles City, had shown up.

Feeling pride in Hawk's sacrifice, his true past all but forgotten, they'd all come to pay their respects, as well as say good-bye to one of their own.

As much as I appreciated their efforts, I didn't feel much like a party, and so I stayed on the sidelines, avoiding everyone. I wanted nothing more than to be curled up in bed beside Hawk, running my hands over him, every inch of him, memorizing every plane and hollow of his body, the feel of every muscle and bone beneath his skin, every line on his face, every callus on his hands, every hair, both coarse and soft, upon his body.

I wanted to stare at his face, into his eyes, until it was all I could see, so much so that every time I would close my eyes from now until forever, it would be those fiercely handsome, dangerously dark features that would form in the blackness of my subconscious.

I wanted to keep him with me even when he couldn't be with me himself.

But I wasn't the only one who loved Hawk and wanted to spend much-needed time with him before he left us. He might have never been much of a talker, always more of a doer than the others, but that didn't mean he hadn't formed bonds with them over the years.

I surveyed the room, my gaze dancing across the many faces until I found the one I sought. Hawk was seated on a bar stool, leaning heavily to his right with a crutch nestled under his arm, bearing most of his weight. His head was freshly shaven, his Mohawk gone, and all that remained of his beard was a couple of days' worth of prickly growth.

But it wasn't his handsome features that held my gaze. It was the strength behind them. The inner man.

I loved him for that strength. For being the devoted father he was, for never once giving up on me despite my reluctance. But mostly I loved him for loving me in the face of my many, many weaknesses.

Jase and I were never meant to be. Jase and I were one and the same, both weak minded, and weak willed. We'd both felt trapped, stuck in lives we'd never wanted, and because of that had come together during a dark and seemingly hopeless time in my life.

For a short time, he'd been what I'd truly wanted.

But never what I'd needed.

Hawk was the strong, sturdy, emotionally solid man I needed, and I could only hope that one day Jase would realize this truth as well and find a woman who provided him with the same sort of support and unconditional love.

My only solace in losing Hawk was the knowledge that I would never lose that love. He might not be able to physically be with me during the time he'd be gone, but he'd never leave me. And not even the thick concrete walls and steel bars of a prison could take that from me.

"I'd be willin' to bet he'll be in for ten years, max."

The couch dipped as Deuce dropped down on the cushion beside me, startling me out of my thoughts.

"Five to seven with good behavior," Deuce continued. "It'll go by before you know it, and he'll be home again."

Sighing, I turned away from Hawk to give Deuce my full attention. God knew the man wouldn't deal well with being ignored.

Holding a drink in his hand, Deuce offered it to me. "You'll get through this, D."

Deuce said ten years as if it were nothing, as if ten years were just a blip in the span of a life that usually only consisted of sixty or seventy, and that was if you were lucky.

Ten years meant ten long years without the man I loved, and Christopher growing up without his father. Ten years was ten goddamn years, and it was most certainly not a blip.

I would be in my fifties, Christopher would be graduating from high school, and Hawk would have missed it all. Swallowing back a wave of sorrow, I chased my feelings with a large gulp of whatever Deuce had brought me and ended up nearly choking to death. What was this? Rubbing alcohol?

"He wants you here, you know?" Deuce said quietly, leaning toward me. "He wants you and the boy here so he knows you're bein' takin' care of. I gotta say, D, that I agree with him. I can help you find a house, a job, whatever you need."

As much as I hated uprooting Christopher from his school, his friends, and his city, I would be a liar if I didn't admit I didn't want to return to San Francisco. Especially with the loss of Hawk's visits, I would have no one but Christopher. Tegen's friends were nice enough, but I was never able to connect emotionally with them. I wanted to be with my daughter, to be around women my own age . . . and of course, the club.

But I didn't need Deuce to find me a house, not when I was related to the only real estate agent in town.

And it was about time I faced my family.

"I'll call my sister," I said. "See what's on the market."

"How long's it been since you and her spoke?"

I shrugged again. "A very long time."

"Your folks too?"

Sighing, I nodded. "I know they've reached out to Tegen a few times, and so have her father's parents, but she's told me she made it clear to them that she wants nothing to do with them." I shook my head. "Then of course she had to take it one step further and tell them her name was Tegen West, ensuring they knew exactly who her father-in-law was."

I gave Deuce a pointed look. "I can only imagine the looks on their God-fearing faces."

Deuce barked out a deep belly laugh that drew the attention of nearly everyone around us.

"You better put that shit on my tab," he said, still chuckling. "And, D? I ain't takin' no for an answer."

I didn't think he would. He never had, and I'd learned that back when he'd insisted on paying for Tegen to live in San Francisco. I wasn't dumb enough to refuse his offer, not when all I had were my disability checks, and what little was in my savings. It wasn't nearly enough to purchase a decent home for my son to grow up in.

"I'm on it, Prez," I teased. "But only if you can promise me that it's safe."

Deuce gave me a sidelong look. "Safe?" he asked, perplexed.

I shrugged, feeling out of place talking to Deuce about his business. "The Russians? From everything Hawk has told me, and what he plans to do . . . Won't there be some sort of retaliation? What if they find out Christopher is Hawk's son?"

Deuce grimaced. "I've got some shit lined up as a fuckin' safeguard. I can't promise they ain't gonna hit us back, but I can promise it ain't gonna be in my fuckin' town, and ain't nobody gonna think that little leprechaun is Hawk's boy."

His gaze shifted to Christopher. Seated on the floor, his legs crossed into a pretzel, my son and a few of the other children were sitting in a circle.

"Looks like you made him all on your own, darlin'."

I laughed even as I squinted to get a better look at what the children were doing. "What are they doing?" I said. "Is Ivy teaching them . . . ?" I trailed off, my eyes widening.

"My God, Deuce, she's only twelve and teaching them to play poker!"

Deuce shrugged. "Devin, that little fuckin' shit, taught her." He shrugged again. "At least it ain't strip poker."

As I gaped at him, he gave my leg a conciliatory pat. "Anyways, you let me worry about the Russians and my daughter's gambling problem. You just raise that boy and live your life, you feel me?"

I looked back at Christopher, then at Hawk, who was engaged in conversation, before looking again at Deuce. His eyes were the softest I'd ever seen them, the kindest too.

"I feel you," I whispered, grateful for his support, but also beginning to feel very overwhelmed.

"And wherever Hawk gets put away," he added, "I'll be takin' you to see him once a month. Myself."

It wasn't much, a visit once a month, but it was something. And it would have to serve in tiding me over for the next . . . ten years.

"This is nice," Dorothy said, snuggling closer to Hawk.

Lounging in one of the club's many reclining chairs, Hawk was able to keep his leg propped up as well as have Dorothy, as tiny as she was, seated on his lap, her body wound around his.

It was nice. Strange and really fucking nice. Nice because the pain meds he'd taken just a short while ago were kicking in, and strange because he and Dorothy had never done this before . . . just hung out, being lazy and stupid.

And even stranger because not only had they spent the day at the club together, they'd spent it as a couple in front of everyone, but especially in front of Jase, for the very first time.

As far as Jase was concerned, while Hawk didn't have the warm fuzzies for the guy, even he had to admit that losing a brother pretty much sucked, even if that brother was a complete fucking asshole. But Jase had always been looking for something more; any moron who knew him knew that. The only problem was that the biggest moron of them all, Jase, never had a clue. Now that he was moving on, finally taking control of his life, Hawk hoped the man could find what he'd been searching for all these years.

And if whatever that was kept him away from Dorothy, then great. Super. Hawk was a happy fucking guy.

"It was nice of Tegen to take Christopher home," she said. Running her hand slowly down the front of his chest, she pulled the material of his T-shirt up over his abdomen and began giving his bare stomach the same treatment.

"Nice that everyone got the fuck outta here," he said, closing his eyes. Yeah, this was nice.

Dorothy snorted softly, causing her body to shake lightly against his. "Cox came back," she whispered. "Three guesses what he's doing?"

Hawk didn't give a shit about what Cox was doing. Actually, he didn't give a shit about what anyone was doing other than Dorothy and the way her fingers had crept down his stomach and were now dipping below the waistline of his sweatpants.

"Feel fuckin' ridiculous in these giant fuckin' pants," he mumbled. Even more ridiculous than the sweatpants were the fact that one of the legs had been cut off in order to provide room for his fucked-up leg and cast.

"No way," Dorothy cooed, kissing his neck, reaching even farther down his pants. Beneath her small hand his dick, thankfully not affected by his pain pills, was instantly alert. "They're so easily accessible."

Yep. This was nice. Probably surpassed even nice, but Hawk was really feeling the effects of those pain pills and his brain wasn't exactly functioning on all cylinders. Nice was about the best he could come up with.

"So I was talking with Deuce earlier," she said.

Hawk's upper lip curled in disgust. Why the fuck was she talking about Deuce? Stroking his cock and talking about Deuce? Those two things definitely did not coincide happily.

"And I'm taking him up on his house offer," she continued.

"Yeah?" he asked, looking down at her. "You're gonna move back here?"

She smiled up at him, and he noticed for the first time how relaxed she looked. Too relaxed for Dorothy.

"Woman, you been drinkin'?" He got his answer when she giggled in response.

Grinning, he let his head fall back and closed his eyes. Thank fuck Deuce had made good on his word. Nothing made him happier than knowing Christopher was going to grow up here, among his family and the club. He'd never liked the fact that Dorothy had hightailed it out to California, and had figured once Tegen had moved back home, Dorothy would follow, but she hadn't. And since shit between them had been as awkward as all hell, he'd never suggested it.

Didn't matter now, though, did it?

He could rest easy inside whatever fucking prison the Feds ended up locking his ass up in, knowing that Dorothy and his son were going to be living in Horsemen territory, under Deuce's certain protection.

"I want every report card," he said. "Every disciplinary notice, every school picture. I want it all, D."

"I promise," she whispered.

"And no wrestling," he continued, letting his hand drop down her back and onto her backside. His hands were big enough, her ass small enough, that one entire ass cheek fit perfectly in the palm of his hand. Yeah, real fucking nice. Jesus, was he that high that his vocabulary suddenly only consisted of "nice"?

"Wrestling?" she asked.

"Yeah, don't let Christopher wrestle for school. Don't want my boy wearing one of those gay-ass singlets. Football's okay, baseball, basketball, fuck, even soccer. Just no goddamn wrestling."

Dorothy giggled again. "No wrestling," she said. "Got it."

"I mean it, woman," he growled, playfully squeezing her ass.

"Did you wrestle as a child?" she asked, laughing. "Are you having painful singlet flashbacks?"

Hawk fell silent. He hadn't had the luxury of an average, everyday childhood. He'd gone to a private school and rather than engaging in sports or typical extracurricular activities, he'd both attended and thrown lavish parties. Even as a young child, his life had never been ordinary. Going as far back as his memory would allow him, he could recall piano lessons, suit fittings, and an army of nannies, all of them more for his father's personal enjoyment rather than to fulfill childcare duties.

"I'm sorry," Dorothy whispered. She stared up at him, her expression full of worry, and asked, "Did I say something wrong?"

"Nah," he said. "Just thinkin' back."

"You should tell me," she said, sounding hopeful. "About your other life. I feel like there is so much about you I don't know and—"

"No," he said with more force than he'd meant to, and Dorothy flinched.

"Shit, I'm sorry, D," he said quietly, squeezing her closer. "Like I already told you, that ain't my life anymore. You and Christopher, the club, that's who I am now. Don't need to be lookin' back at bullshit."

She was about to smile, he could tell by the way her eyes had lit up, and he was about to smile in response until just as quickly her bottom lip began to tremble and those eyes of hers filled with tears.

"No, no, no," he muttered, rubbing his hand across her back in large circles. "No crying, D. More dick touching."

A sort of sputtering sob erupted from her and her body began to shake. Hawk bent his head to the side to get a better look at her face, and found she was laughing. Well, still crying, but also laughing.

And just as he was about to insist that he hadn't been joking and definitely wanted more dick touching, the gate monitor behind the bar began to buzz.

"The gate is opening," Dorothy muttered, stretching her body to look over the back of the chair.

"Means whoever it is has the code and key," he said,

then added, "and whoever the fuck it is, is going to die for interrupting us."

"Oh shit!" she exclaimed, startling Hawk.

Suddenly Dorothy was cursing up a storm, scrambling off his lap and nearly falling flat on her face on the floor beside the chair. "Shit!"

"What?" Hawk shouted, looking around for a threat. "What the fuck, woman?"

"Kami!" Dorothy screamed, pointing to the window as she made a mad dash for the front door. "Kami is here!"

"So fuckin' what?" he muttered, slumping back down.

"So what?" Dorothy shouted, throwing herself against the door. "Cox is in the back! With that girl!"

Annoyed, Hawk closed his eyes and lifted his shoulder. "His funeral."

"OPEN THIS DOOR!" came a very familiar and annoying high-pitched scream from outside the clubhouse.

"Are you kidding me?" Dorothy exclaimed, grabbing the doorknob as it began to jiggle. "What about brotherhood? You're just going to let Kami kill him?"

He cracked an eyelid at her. "Never did much like all the fuckin' cheatin' that goes on around here."

Dorothy paused and as she turned to look at him, her mouth slightly agape, she loosened her grip on the door. When it came swinging open, Dorothy was knocked backward and into the wall, where she fell to a heap on the floor.

"Where is he?" Kami screamed, her blonde hair flying wildly around her face as her head whipped back and forth. "Where is that cheating motherfucker?"

"Jesus Christ, Kami!" Hawk shouted, struggling to sit up, wishing he could reach his crutches and get the fuck out of this chair. "D! Are you okay?"

"I'm fine," she called out, and when she lifted her head so he could see her face, he relaxed back in his chair, relieved that she wasn't hurt.

"Fuck you both," Kami snapped, marching forward.

"Kami!" Pushing herself up off the floor, Dorothy struggled to stand upright. "Kami, do you have a weapon?"

"No, I do not have a fucking weapon!" Kami screamed over her shoulder. "Do you really think I'd risk going to jail for that Mexican whore?"

"Puerto Rican," Hawk muttered, rolling his eyes.

"Shut up, Gorbachev!"

"Real original!" he shouted after her, wishing now more than ever that he could reach at least one of his crutches, if only to throw it at that bitch's damn head. "Real fuckin' original!"

Rubbing the back of her head, Dorothy made her way back to him, her eyes wide as she stared down the hallway at Kami's retreating back.

"We should go," she whispered. "Before this gets ugly."

"Why?" he asked. "His stupid ass got my dick touching interrupted. It's only fair that I stick around to watch his get interrupted."

Just as the last word had left his mouth, both a crash and a scream echoed from the back hall and Hawk smiled.

"One," he muttered under his breath. "Two . . ."

Just then a fully nude, rather chubby-looking girl came running into the room, clutching her clothing to the front of her body. "Help him!" she screamed, running for the front door. "That crazy bitch is going to kill him!"

"Three," Hawk finished.

"You're so bad," Dorothy said, fighting a smile.

He held his arm out to her, gesturing for her to climb back on top of him but instead, her gaze flickered to the hallway. "They're going to kill each other . . ."

"So fuckin' what? How is that any different from any other day?"

Still staring off down the hall, Dorothy shook her head. "But did you see her face? This is different. She's hurt, Hawk, really hurt."

"Yeah, and Cox ain't doin' so well lately himself but that's their business, their fuckin' marriage, not ours."

Another shout sounded, this time sounding more like a sob.

"BITCH," Cox bellowed. "You won't fuckin' touch me, YOU WON'T FUCKIN' LET ME TOUCH YOU!"

"It doesn't matter!" Kami screamed. "You are mine! You are mine and you don't get to be with another fucking woman!"

"THEN FUCKING TOUCH ME, KAMI! AT LEAST FUCKING LOOK AT ME ONCE IN A WHILE!"

And after hearing that, even Hawk had to admit that maybe this wasn't Cox and Kami's typical MO. But there still wasn't a chance in hell he was going to interfere.

"D," he growled. "Sit the fuck down."

With a sigh, she shook her head again and then finally, fucking finally, crawled back into his lap. Replacing his hand on her ass, he used his other to shove her hand back down the front of his pants.

And as the screaming and crying down the hallway continued, Dorothy glanced up at him, her freckled nose wrinkled. "This isn't so nice anymore," she whispered.

"Just keep playin' with my dick," he whispered back, giving her backside a light slap.

"You're never going to change!" Kami screamed.

"Give me a fuckin' reason to!" Cox shot back.

Keeping a firm hold on Dorothy, Hawk closed his eyes and sighed. Couple of crazy assholes. But he was really going to miss this place. Crazy assholes and all.

CHAPTER 21

I T WAS THE NIGHT BEFORE HAWK WOULD BE LEAVING, and I'd spent the majority of it making a rather extravagant dinner for my family. Tegen and Cage were spending the entire day out of the house in order to give the three of us time together, and Hawk had spent most of the day with Christopher, doing as much as he could with his son despite his limited mobility.

As for me, I couldn't sit still. I was in a constant state of nervous anxiety, full of so much dread of what was to come that I had to stay busy in order to keep from crying, or screaming, or both.

After prepping a seven-pound ham, I'd begun preparing asparagus, homemade mashed potatoes, and gravy. Then I finished with a traditional Irish apple and bramble cake with whiskey custard, made from scratch and my memories of baking alongside my grandmother.

When there was nothing left to prepare and I was only waiting on the cake to finish cooling, I took off my apron and headed upstairs to shower before dinner.

Once clean, my hair blow-dried and as straight as I could get it, I sorted through the limited clothing I'd brought with me, finding nothing I wanted to wear. I had no desire to slip into a pair of worn jeans and a faded T-shirt, but instead wished for tonight to be special, a memory Hawk could think back on and smile about.

Giving up on my own belongings, I headed into Tegen's room to search through her closet in hopes of finding something simple yet sexy. No longer stick thin, her clothing might be long on me, but at least it would fit my width.

After sorting through her vast variety of band T-shirts, assorted colorful tank tops, long flowing skirts, and numerous holey jeans, I was just about to give up and head back to my own room when I found it.

It was a silky black halter dress with a deep V-neck and a cinched waist. It would hit about mid-thigh on Tegen, but on me would reach my knees. It looked expensive, and after finding the tags still on it, I found that it was indeed a small fortune and surmised that it was probably a gift from Kami. Knowing my daughter, I knew she'd never wear it.

But for me, it was perfect.

After applying more makeup then I'd ever worn before, including foundation, powder, a shimmering dark eye shadow, and a healthy amount of mascara, I brushed my hair out one last time, slipped in a pair of Tegen's black feather earrings, and then for a moment simply stared at myself in the full-length mirror.

Much like when I'd lost my memories, I didn't recognize the woman staring back at me. Even with my lack of a bra, which left my breasts sloping naturally, and my older and softer body, despite the lines beginning to frame my eyes and my more mature features, I looked the most vibrant, the most beautiful I could ever remember myself looking or feeling before.

Feeling nervous but surprisingly confident, I descended the stairs, happily inhaling the smells of my mouthwatering meal as I breezed past the kitchen and turned left to enter the living room.

Both Hawk and Christopher were utterly immersed in whatever video game they were playing, their eyes glued to the television screen while their fingers worked the controllers with swift and sure movements.

I stared at them for a moment, just drinking in the sight of father and son, knowing this was the last time for a long time that they would be able to just be together in this way. It made me incredibly sad to think that another of my children would grow up without their father.

Hawk and I had both tried our best to let Christopher know what was coming, without giving away the grittier aspect of things. Although the time would soon come when he would be visiting his father in jail, neither of us wanted to taint Christopher with the brutal details of his father's past. And while Christopher had become upset hearing that his father would no longer be coming for visits, he didn't truly understand, and both Hawk and I decided to leave well enough alone for the time being.

"Mom!" Christopher exclaimed, dropping his controller into his lap. His eyes widened into big green saucers as he took in my appearance. "You look so pretty!"

I smiled at my son, but my attentions were soon divert-
ed to Hawk, who had also released his controller and was
raking me over with his eyes.

He looked surprised, but even more he appeared . . .
turned on.

Despite the heat of the room, his unspoken thoughts
caused icy-hot shivers to race along my skin, leaving trails
of gooseflesh in their wake. He was more than aware of my
reaction to him, aware of his effect on me, and I watched
with the utmost delight as those unfathomably dark eyes
grew even more opaque, as the swell of his muscles grew
strained, as his body tightened with need, the sight of which
was holding my eyes and my body hostage, frozen like a
deer in the spotlight of his hungry gaze.

It was a look I hadn't seen since we'd both been in our
twenties, a heavy look, one laden with hidden meaning and
secret emotion, both of us despairing over different things
and secretly using each other to soothe the desperate burning inside us.

But this time it was different.

This wasn't a secret look.

This was all for me, for all the world to see.

All for him.

All for me. *All for me.*

I stared at him, my thoughts and body afire as he
mouthed the words, *You're beautiful.* And I could have
sworn I felt his breath, cool against my overheated body,
cascading over my skin, causing it to ripple and pebble with
gooseflesh all over again.

"Dinner's ready," I whispered hoarsely, then lifted my

hand to my throat, to the necklace that I never took off, surreptitiously hiding the large swallow of emotion that had welled up within me.

Christopher leaped off the couch and bounded past me while Hawk remained unmoving, his eyes still on me.

"I don't wanna go," he said softly, surprising me.

Those words, so full of raw emotion, caused a tidal wave of pain to come crashing over me, coursing through me at an alarming rate.

Its impact on my heart was devastating.

He looked so vulnerable, so unlike any way he'd ever looked before, that I couldn't stop myself. I rushed forward, dropping onto the couch beside him and wrapping my arms around his neck.

"Let's leave," I whispered frantically against the soft cotton of his T-shirt. "Let's just go, run away. We could move somewhere remote, where no one would ever find us. We could be a family."

His body heaved as a heavy breath fled his chest, and in that breath I heard his answer. We wouldn't be leaving, or running. We wouldn't be together.

"D," he said gently. "I've been hidin' most of my life. I don't wanna hide anymore."

"I can't lose you," I whimpered. "Not after I just got you back."

"Someday," he whispered, sliding his arm behind my back and pulling me into a one-armed hug. "I'm going to finally take you for that ride. Just you and me, D. Me wearing my cut, you with all that red hair flying in the wind. Both of us finally out in the wide fuckin' open. No more hidin.'"

And after hearing that, there was no way on earth I

was going to make it through a three-course meal without crying.

I fell apart for what felt like the millionth time, ruining all my carefully applied makeup, smearing it all over Hawk's T-shirt as I clutched him so tightly my knuckles began to throb.

"I want tonight to last forever," I whispered brokenly.

Because it had to last forever, or at least for the next ten years.

The last three weeks had been full of surprises, the biggest of which Hawk had thought was him and Dorothy finally coming together.

He'd been so fucking wrong.

The biggest surprise was just . . . Dorothy.

With as much rational thought as he could manage while being slowly ridden by the beautiful woman on top of him, he stared up at her in wonder.

The dress's halter top was pooled around her waist, leaving her breasts exposed. Her body was arched, hands clutching his knees, and her head was thrown back, making the tips of her long red hair brush the tops of his thighs. With closed eyes and parted lips, she ground back and forth over him in a maddening, painstakingly, yet magnificently slow pace.

She was not the same woman he'd fallen in love with. But he was pretty sure he loved who she'd become even more.

And he was insanely terrified that he was going to lose her again.

She'd promised him over and over again that she would wait. But he didn't expect her to wait, to be alone for years. She'd already been alone for far too long, and he wanted her happy.

Even if that meant she'd be happy without him.

Of course, he'd never in a million fucking years voice his feelings to her or anyone else on earth. Because as much as he wanted her happy, he wanted her waiting at those gates when he was finally able to rejoin the world.

It was selfish. Hawk knew that.

But he'd always been selfish when it came to this woman. He might have let her be, but he'd never given her up or really truly ever left her side.

He'd always been right there, whether she wanted him there or not.

And now that she wanted him there, for good this time, to make something solid out of their choppy history . . .

He was going to be fucking selfish.

Even locked up, he was going to be selfish.

With one hand under the skirt of her dress, clutching her hip, he reached up with the other and cupped her breast, lifting and squeezing the soft flesh. In response she moaned loudly, her breathing grew more uneven, her movements sped up, becoming less rhythmic and jerkier than before.

"Faster," he rasped.

She tried to do as he asked but she was beginning to waver, her body quaking as she reached the beginnings of an orgasm. Releasing her breast to grab her other hip, he gripped her tightly and despite the pain in his leg his movements were causing, thrust his hips upward, over and over again, as fast as he could manage until he too was finishing with her.

As he released inside her, staring up at her beautiful body, he was struck with most profound sense of home-coming. Maybe he hadn't realized it back then, when he'd first set his sights on her, how much this woman would come to mean to him, but he knew it now.

Breathing hard, blinking rapidly, Dorothy released his legs and straightened above him. Her hair, the way it fell forward covering her breasts; her eyes, the way they shone even in the dim light; her lips, plumped from her own bit-ing, glossy from licking them; her body, the way it curved like a woman's should, soft in all the right places—he took it all in, taking his time in order to capture it all, to memorize every inch of her.

Just like this.

This was how he wanted to remember her.

"Fucking hell, woman," he said hoarsely, unable to stop the words, unable to keep himself from letting it out. "*I fuckin' love you.*"

Her eyes caught his, her lips slowly curved into a smile that, sure as shit, was sexy as hell.

Yeah. This was how he wanted to remember her.

This was what would get him through.

CHAPTER 22

OR JASE, FINDING A HOUSE TO RENT HADN'T BEEN difficult. Neither had filling it with the minimal furniture he had brought with him.

And after Deuce had called in a favor at the local auto body shop in town, obtaining employment had been a piece of fucking cake.

What hadn't been easy was having to say good-bye to everyone. Even Hawk, despite his scowl, had shaken Jase's hand. During the party, he'd come to find out that it was Hawk who was leaving, was turning himself over to the law in order to take down the Russians blackmailing Deuce and Preacher. Despite how he felt about Hawk and Dorothy being together, you couldn't hate a man who would sacrifice his own life for the good of the club.

In a way, Jase felt like Hawk had everything Jase never

had. The woman they both loved belonged to Hawk, the respect of everyone in the club belonged to Hawk, and whereas Jase had left the club behind, Hawk would never. Even in the face of his imprisonment.

He was a far better man than Jase would ever be, as well as being a better father than Jase would ever be.

Hawk deserved both Dorothy and the club.

And Jase deserved . . .

Well, he didn't know what the fuck he deserved, but his father's words had been playing on repeat over and over in his head. He only had one life to live, he only had this one life to make things right, and, Jesus Christ, he was going to do his damnedest to do just that.

His first week in town had been quiet, and other than watching his girls from afar, he'd left them alone. The twins lived together in a large apartment building not far from the college they were attending, but Maribelle lived alone in a studio apartment above an antiques store. Unlike the twins she was often alone, her only social interaction with the customers at a nearby café where she worked.

Several days in a row after work, Jase had stood across the street, hidden by his heavy winter wear, just watching her through the foggy glass windows of the café. While she might smile at the people she was waiting on, Jase knew it was fake and forced. Maribelle, when she was truly happy, showed her teeth when she smiled. These smiles looked almost painful, her lips pressed tightly together, her brow furrowed and pinched. And the dimple he knew to be on the left side of her cheek never once revealed itself.

Unlike the twins, who were happily behaving as most college students do and seeming to have a booming social life, Maribelle had shut down. No longer was she the ambitious girl she'd once been, peppy and spunky, and who'd graduated from college with honors. Ignoring her degree, she'd become a waitress, and had taken to hiding from the world instead of participating in it. He could only attribute her downward spiral to the many responsibilities she'd been laden with after her mother had gone to jail. Taking care of the twins, being the mother they no longer had, as well as keeping up with Chrissy's legal matters, Maribelle had forgotten to take care of herself.

He could have gone straight to the twins. Without Maribelle around to influence them, he didn't doubt he'd at least get them to hear what he had to say, but it was Maribelle who was suffering the most, and going behind her back to her sisters wouldn't earn him any favors with her.

It was Maribelle's love and respect he needed to win back first, and then the twins would follow.

And so, on his seventh day in town, he decided to finally show his face. Once he'd parked his truck across the street from where she worked, he tried desperately to clean the grease from his hands. After succeeding in wiping most of it onto his coveralls, he took a glimpse in the rearview mirror at himself. Gone was the good-looking, cocky son of a bitch he'd once been. He was looking his age lately, older and infinitely more tired. Most days he went without shaving, and he hadn't gotten around to getting a haircut in quite a while.

Sadly, he was beginning to look the part of a man who'd lost everything.

The bells on the door jingled as he pushed it open, and everyone in the small café turned to look at him, even

Maribelle. Standing beside a small round table with two seated customers, she was wearing a small black apron, her hair pulled back in a ponytail, and she had a pen and pad of paper in her hand. In the process of scribbling something down when she'd heard the bells, she glanced up and then back down, instantly dismissing him.

As she went back to writing on her pad, Jase's heart started to pound in his chest. He was entertaining the thought of turning around, his tail tucked between his legs, when her head snapped back up. Her eyes looked him over, from head to toe and back up again, before growing wide with surprise.

Grabbing the bill of his ball cap, Jase pulled it from his head, ran a hand through his messy hair, and gave his daughter a small smile.

Looking bewildered, Maribelle glanced back down at her customers, said a few words that Jase couldn't make out, and began making her way toward him. He watched as she walked, her steps unsure and small, and remembered instead the little girl who used to come barreling down the driveway when he'd come home from a reserves weekend or a long run with the club.

Stopping in front of him, she tucked her pen into the base of her ponytail and shoved her notepad into the front of her apron.

"What are you doing here?" she asked quietly. "And why are you wearing that?" She gestured to his coveralls.

"Been workin' at Pop's a few blocks thataway," he said, jerking his thumb over his shoulder. "Doin' custom work and shit."

Maribelle's caramel-colored eyes grew even wider.

"Why?" she whispered. "I mean, what? Do you live here now?"

Clutching his hat in front of him, Jase twisted the mesh material, beginning to feel uneasy. He could almost envision the very loud, very public scene she would make if the knowledge that he'd moved to her town rubbed her the wrong way. And he didn't want to get her fired because of him. If that happened, it would just be one more thing he would have to try to make right, and the list was already too long as it was.

So he changed tactics.

"Left the club," he said, keeping his voice low and hoping she'd take the hint and do the same. "Moved here to try and make shit right."

"You left the club," she repeated dumbly, staring blankly up at him. "You left the club you've been a part of your entire life, that you've always chosen above everything else, even your own family?"

Jase's knuckles cracked as the grip on his hat tightened. Yeah, he was a crappy dad. And he deserved every single piece of shit she was going to fling his way.

"Yeah," he said hoarsely, "but I ain't been there my whole life, there was something I did before the club, somethin' I was, that was a fuck of a lot more important than a club. Took me a while to figure it out, Belle, but I was a father first and I wanna be your father again."

Uncomfortable silence filled the small space between them, during which Jase could practically feel the rejection that was sure to come, when suddenly Maribelle's gaze dropped to the floor, her lips twisting and flattening. He knew that look. That was the look his little girl made when she was trying not to cry.

"Belle," he said softly. "I didn't come here to upset you. Just wanted you to know how much I love you and your sisters. Just wanted a chance to be a family again."

"You just expect me to forgive you?" she whispered, still blinking. A drop fell from her lowered eyelashes and onto the floor near her sneakers. "Just because you quit the club and moved to my town, I'm just supposed to forget? Just like that?"

"No," he said, wishing he could pull her into a hug, wishing that things were simple again, that his girls were still little and all their hurts easily fixed with just a little bit of love.

"I'm not expectin' anything," he said. "Was just maybe hopin' for the chance to try . . ."

When she didn't respond, Jase took her silence as his cue to leave. Putting his cap back on, he pulled the bill down low and cleared his throat.

"I'll leave you alone now," he whispered. "You ever want to talk, I'm living on Forest Street. Got that little white house on the corner."

He turned to go, feeling sick and suffocated by the disappointment quickly filling him, when he felt a light touch on his bicep.

"Wait," Maribelle said.

Turning back around, he found her eyes on him, filled with unshed tears. "I have a break coming up," she said, swallowing hard.

Jase couldn't believe it, that she was actually letting him in, and despite himself, he smiled at her. A real, goddamn, genuine fucking smile.

"Great," he said, his voice cracking. "'Cause your old man would love to buy you a cup of joe."

Despite her tears, Maribelle snorted. "You sound like Grandpa."

As his daughter walked off, Jase finished stomping off the snow from his boots before heading to the back of the café to find a quiet place to sit. While he waited for Maribelle to join him, he couldn't help but think that sounding like his old man, or even being like his old man, something he'd never thought of as a compliment before, was just about the very best thing he'd ever heard.

A cup of coffee appeared in front of him as Maribelle took the seat opposite him. Placing her hands in her lap, she glanced up at him.

"So," she said softly. "What should we talk about?"

Reaching for his coffee, wrapping his hand around the warm mug and feeling the same sort of warmth beginning to spread within him, Jase shrugged.

"Everything," he said. "I want to know everything."

The road to redemption might be damn hard, but in the end—if you reached the end—his father was right. It was worth it.

Maribelle was worth it.

Funny how her birth was the reason he'd started running, but she ended up being the reason he'd stopped.

Life was really fucking funny that way.

CHAPTER 23

"To Hawk!" Cox shouted, lifting a bottle of whiskey up into the air. "A brother through and through!"

In unison, all the boys standing around the clubhouse bar picked up their shot glasses and threw back their drinks.

"To Hawk!" they shouted back.

"To my dad!" Christopher chimed in from his seat beside Hawk. He raised his glass of soda in the air and the men around him cheered again. Seeing him, so young, praising his father alongside the boys . . .

Well, if it weren't for Tegen standing beside me, for taking my hand into hers and giving me a hard squeeze, I would have lost it right then and there.

I had only one hour left. One hour left with him, and I was forced to spend it at the clubhouse sharing my last hour with everyone else. I understood that everybody wanted to say their good-byes, but after a night of making love, very little sleep, and a tear-filled morning, the club was the last place I wanted to be.

I wasn't ready to let go.

I would never be ready to let go.

"Don't drop the soap!" Tap called out, his lewd implication prompting a round of hearty laughter.

"And to Prez," Cox continued when the laughter had died down. He turned to face Deuce. "For givin' all us assholes a fuckin' home!"

Standing just outside his office doors, Deuce was leaning back against the wall, his arms folded over his chest, watching them all with a solemn expression on his face.

"And to Foxy!" Cox's gaze slid to where Eva was standing beside her husband, and his smile turned into his typical shit-eating grin. "For makin' us assholes a family!"

"And to Cox!" Kami shouted. "For giving us all something to laugh at!"

"And to Kami!" Cox shot back. "For spending all my damn money!"

"Good God," I muttered, dropping Tegen's hand and turning away from everyone. As happy as I was that Cox and Kami seemed to be back to their normal selves, I couldn't take it, not one more second of it. Everyone acting like this was just another day, making stupid jokes, completely oblivious that Hawk was about to go to jail for crimes he didn't commit. All because Deuce wouldn't be swayed by the same cartel who put Hawk in this position in the first place.

"Mom!" Tegen called out as I stormed away from her. Picking up speed I ignored her, hurrying toward the hallway that would lead me to the back of the club and away from the uncaring, unfeeling ridiculousness happening all around me.

Thankfully I found Hawk's bedroom door unlocked, and as I slammed it behind me I burst into tears.

The last month had been a whirlwind of emotions, overwhelming to say the least, and now it was all coming to a head—all the realizations, the regret, the tears, the unstoppable flood of feelings, and it was just too much. I couldn't take it, couldn't process all that had happened in such a short time. Even more, I couldn't fathom how it had all gone by so quickly and was ending before it had really had a chance to even begin.

With tears streaming down my cheeks, I took a seat on the edge of Hawk's neatly made bed, and through blurry eyes looked around the small room. The room where this had started all those years ago. Where two people had come together for reasons unknown to them at the time, but in the end . . .

I sighed. How could I be angry? Losing myself to anger at a time like this would only be selfish and serve no purpose.

Feeling calmer and more in control, I was wiping my cheeks when the door creaked open. Hawk limped slowly into the room on his crutches, and awkwardly used his elbow to shut the door behind him.

"They don't mean any harm," he said. "They're only tryin' to keep shit light for my sake."

Pushing my hair away from my face, I sighed loudly. "I know. I just . . . I just . . . I can't . . ."

Letting out another sigh, a frustrated one because I

couldn't put my feelings into words that I hadn't already used a hundred times before, I pushed myself up off the bed and crossed the room. Slipping my arms around his waist, I leaned my head against his abdomen.

"It just hurts," I managed to finish in a small voice. "Why does everything have to always hurt so bad?"

"Because life hurts." He dropped his face onto the top of my head, burying his nose into my hair and inhaling deeply. "Hidin' is fuckin' easy. It's really livin' that's hard, that sometimes hurts like a son of a bitch.

"But, D," he continued, slowly rubbing his nose back and forth across the top of my head. "We keep ridin' that shit because it's worth it, baby. When all is said and fuckin' done, when we ain't got no more time left, we're gonna be grateful for those rides.

"I'm grateful," he finished softly. "For you, for Christopher, and for the club."

I didn't say anything; there was nothing left to say. These moments, they ended here and now, and tomorrow a new chapter in my life would begin. So I just held on to him, to this moment, breathing him in, committing his scent to memory, and reveling in the feel of his big, warm body surrounding mine.

I'd always both admired and envied Hawk's strength. He was a man through and through.

But now it was my turn to be strong.

For him. For us. For our family.

And come hell or high water, I was determined to do just that.

Throughout the course of his life, Hawk had lived through some really bad days. Some real ugly shit that most times was just easier to forget than to go through the pain of working through it.

This wasn't one of those times.

This was far, far worse.

Seated on the couch beside his son, Hawk slid his arm around the boy's small shoulders. Holding him close, he gave Christopher one last squeeze.

"Gotta get goin'," he said roughly. "But I'll be seein' you soon."

As his son looked up at him, messy red hair framing a face full of confusion and hurt, Hawk had a hard time keeping his emotions in check. It was the first time in a long time that he'd so much as felt the urge to cry, the last time being the night after he'd watched a bullet tear through his father's skull. Since then, he'd felt a shit ton of emotions, some good, most bad, but none that had the ability to gut him like one look from his kid could.

"Gimme a hug," he whispered, giving Christopher a tug. As the boy turned his body into Hawk's and wrapped his skinny arms around his neck, Hawk squeezed his eyes tightly shut and put every ounce of himself into that hug.

"You take care of your mom," he whispered, burying his face into his son's hair. "Promise me you'll take care of your mom."

Against his shoulder he felt Christopher's head nod, and that was good enough for him.

Opening his eyes, he found Tegen already waiting to take Christopher. His chest aching, he nodded at her and released his son.

"Come here, little brother," Tegen said softly.

Christopher clung to him, refusing to budge, and when Hawk tried to forcefully pry him from his body, the boy let out a small sob. In that moment, at the sound of his son crying, Hawk could no longer keep it together. Cupping the back of his son's head, holding his small body tightly to him, he let his own tears fall, uncaring who saw them, and just held his boy as close as he could. Because, god-fuck-ing-dammit, the next time he'd have this chance, to be free to hold his boy, his boy was going to be a man.

He was going to miss it all.

And if that wasn't bad enough, what came next was equally as miserable.

Once Christopher was in Tegen's arms and Cage was helping Hawk to his feet, the rest of the boys began to get up from their seats. One by one they lined up by the door, their expressions ranging from solemn to just plain sad.

Holding Christopher tightly to her, Tegen grabbed Hawk's hand, threaded her fingers through his, and gave his hand a hard squeeze. It was a surprising gesture, coming from Tegen, but one that Hawk welcomed.

"Come back to them," she whispered. "Come back to them or I'll come kill you."

Using the crutch under his right arm to hold his weight, he reached for Tegen. He wrapped his hand around the back of her head and pulled her forward to kiss her soundly on her cheek. Then, after doing the same to Christopher, he started for the boys.

It was slow going with those damn crutches of his, only making the journey across the room even worse, forcing him to look longer at all those forlorn faces awaiting him.

Mick was first, and that damn softie of an old man pulled him into a gripping hug. "Might be dead by the time you get out, so I'm givin' your ass a fuckin' hug."

Beside him, Freebird snorted. "He ain't gonna be dead," the old hippie said. "But I will, so come 'ere and lay some sugar on me, darlin'."

As Freebird hugged him, giving him a purposely sloppy kiss on the cheek, a titter of laughter trickled down the line of men.

Next was Dirty, and knowing that the man hated any sort of physical contact with anyone, Hawk simply held out his fist, waiting for a tap. But Dirty surprised everyone by taking Hawk's fist between both his hands and squeezing.

"I'll see you later, brother," the man said. Touched, Hawk could only nod in response.

He continued down the line, saying good-bye to Bucket, Worm, Danny D. and Danny L., Tap, Anger, and Chips, and then to the nomads Marsh, Dimebag, and Tramp. Handshakes, back slaps, and more hugs than he'd ever been given before in his life were all exchanged.

When he reached Cox, despite his black eye and swollen lip, courtesy of Kami, the asshole was grinning.

"Remember," Cox said. "Don't be droppin' the fuckin' soap, brother."

Snorting, Hawk crooked a finger. "Come here, asswipe," he said and when Cox leaned in, Hawk grabbed the back of his head and pulled him into a hug.

"You and Kami," Hawk whispered. "Don't let whatever bullshit she's always spoutin' come between you two. You keep her happy, keep you happy, and I can fuckin' promise you, I won't be droppin' any soap."

Shoving a surprised Cox away from him, Hawk gave him a light slap across the face, flashed him a very Cox-like grin, and then turned away to face Ripper, the last man in line.

Hawk loved all his brothers, but like in all groups of friends or clubs, some people were closer than others. And although Hawk had made a point to never really get close to anyone so he could keep his past where it belonged—in the past—he'd been a loner.

So when it came to having actual friends, he didn't have a damn one, but what he did have was Ripper. They'd clicked in some way, leaving Hawk always feeling comfortable in his presence. In his own way he'd looked out for Ripper and Ripper for him, kept each other's secrets, and always had each other's back. That was mutual respect, brothers to the end, and to Hawk that was far better than having a "friend."

"My boy—" Hawk started and Ripper immediately shook his head.

"You don't gotta ask," he said. "Dude, you know I got you."

Then Hawk handed Ripper his crutches, and after awkwardly shrugging out of his cut, took back his crutches and handed over his vest.

"You're gonna be wearin' this again," Ripper said. "You fuckin' will, brother."

"Damn straight," was Hawk's answer. And as Ripper pulled him into a hug, Hawk might have hugged the man a little tighter than he'd hugged the others.

And lastly were Deuce and Eva. Standing side by side near the door, Eva gestured for him to come to her. As she wrapped her arms around his middle, Hawk rested his chin on top of her head, keeping his eyes on Deuce.

"Keep an eye on that old man of yours," he said softly. "I want him bossin' my ass around the second I get outta there."

"I promise," she whispered, sniffing as she pulled away.

With Deuce by his side, Hawk turned around to look at the club and the boys one last time. He took it all in, the building he called home, the faces of the men he called brothers, before his gaze stopped on Christopher, and the tears running down the boy's cheeks. When he couldn't take another fucking second of it, seeing all that love and sadness—especially from his son—and all of it for him, he turned around and walked the fuck out.

"I'll be in the truck," Deuce muttered, storming past him. "Take as long as you need."

Hawk took a moment to look around the parking lot, searching out Dorothy. The past few weeks had brought along a wave of unseasonably warm weather that melted most of the snow in the lot, but it was still damn cold. So when he found her leaning against her vehicle without a warm coat on, staring off at nothing for fuck only knew how long, he grew instantly pissed off.

"Woman," he growled, hopping as fast as he could in her direction.

Startled, she turned toward him, and even from this distance he could see the tears rolling down her cheeks. Judging by the red blotches covering her usually ivory skin, and her bloodshot and puffy eyes, she'd obviously been crying for a while now.

"I'm sorry," she said, hiccupping. "I'm sorry, but I just can't do this. I thought I could, that I could be strong, but who was I kidding? I've never been strong! And I can't be strong now!"

He reached her just as she was about to continue, dropped his crutches, and used his body to push her back against the car door. Standing on one leg, balancing himself with one hand on the vehicle's roof, he bore down on her with a frown.

"You are strong," he said forcefully. "You are one of the strongest females I've ever fuckin' met. And before you start spoutin' off more of your usual bullshit at me, I'm gonna repeat myself. Dorothy Kelley, you *are* strong. Look at all the shit you've lived through. All that pain, D, that would have killed most people. You aren't most people, you're fuckin' special, knew that shit from the moment I saw you. Young and stupid, not havin' a clue about life, but once life started smacking you around, what the fuck did you do? Did you lay down and die?"

Staring up at him, still crying, Dorothy shook her head. "No," she whispered tearfully.

"And you ain't gonna lay down and die now, are you?"

Her body seemed to deflate, her pinched features relaxed, and with a large exhalation of air, she shook her head again. "No," she whispered. "No, I'm not."

"Good," he said softly. Sliding his free arm around her back, he pulled her up against him.

"Good," he said soothingly. "Now say good-bye to your man."

Her trembling lips exploded in a tear-filled, snot-filled breath, and just like that she was sobbing uncontrollably again.

Shaking his head, Hawk tried to situate his body in a

more comfortable position against the car in a way that allowed him to both hold her and kiss her at the same time. Once he'd gotten that out of the way, snot and tears be dammed, he bent his head and body and covered her mouth with his.

He'd planned on kissing her slowly, thinking that was what she wanted, a good-bye that was soft and sweet, but Dorothy had different plans. With a muffled cry, she grabbed his jacket collar and practically scaled his body. As he fought for his footing, she was already clinging to him, kissing him hard and fast, messy and wet, full of tongue and full of desperation.

Clutching at whatever he could and only standing on one foot, he used all his strength to swing her around, slamming her into the car window. Her leg wound around his hip, his hand gripped her hair, and he kissed her back, every bit as hard as she was giving it to him.

And he didn't want to stop; he didn't want to fucking let her go.

He didn't ever want to let her go.

Until he had to let her go.

"Save that ride for me, D," he said softly, letting her drop to the ground.

"No," she cried, grasping for him. "No, Hawk, don't you leave!"

Clenching his jaw, Hawk reached for his crutches while she continued to grab at his clothing.

"Cage!" he bellowed, trying to hold her still, hoping like hell someone inside the clubhouse would hear him. "Cage!"

And then Cage was there, pulling her off him, and Dorothy was sobbing in Cage's arms, struggling to free herself while she screamed his name over and over again. Feeling like the biggest piece of shit to ever grace the earth, Hawk gave her one last long look before gritting his teeth and turning away.

It wasn't until they'd passed over the county line that Hawk really lost his shit. He sent his right fist flying into the dashboard of Deuce's truck, then his left. And then he just let it all out and beat the holy fuck out of the thick plastic until his hands were bleeding and the dashboard was cracked and mangled.

Through it all, Deuce never said a word.

And then silently, Hawk let his own tears fall.

CHAPTER 24

Seven years later

BENEATH THE CLOUDY GRAY COLORADO SKY, THE formidable walls of the federal prison loomed ahead of me, looking every bit as intimidating as the men it contained inside. Even after nearly eight years of visits, sometimes twice a month, seeing these walls more times than I cared to count, they still sent a shiver up my spine, filling me with a strong sense of loneliness and desperation.

Still, I'd never entertained the notion of not visiting, and I'd even been married inside those walls.

Two years into Hawk's sentence and after a ridiculous amount of paperwork and fees, Hawk and I were finally allowed to legally marry in a small and uncomfortable ceremony with the two of us, Christopher, the prison chaplain, and several dozen prison guards in attendance.

A prison marriage was never something I'd had my heart set on, but I was far from being the fantasy-driven child I'd once been. Simply having Hawk put a ring on my finger, with Christopher there to witness it, had made it one of the happiest moments of my life.

Although conjugal visits weren't allowed in federal prison—or any prison in the entire state of Colorado—it didn't matter. It was the simple act of marriage that had meant the world to me.

But this time I wouldn't be passing through those gates. There would be no paperwork to fill out, no invasive searches through my belongings and clothing.

This time I wouldn't be seeing Hawk from across a table, unable to do little more than touch his hand.

This time, Hawk would be the one walking through those gates, walking back to his life, and back to me as a free man.

It had taken seven and a half years to get to this point, but the moment was finally here and it couldn't happen fast enough. Seven years was a long time, and Hawk had missed so much.

There had been several deaths, the most devastating of which had been the loss of Eva's father, Preacher. Because he'd hidden the fact that his health was failing from his daughter, when she'd finally found out, Preacher was already in the hospital with very little time left. It had taken her a long time to recover from losing him, and then in the midst of her grief, we'd lost a fellow Hell's Horseman, Freebird. But whereas Preacher's unexpected cancer had taken him quickly and left his family reeling, Freebird's death had been a long and drawn-out battle that had whittled the once fun-loving man to nearly nothing before his passing. His wife, Apple Dumplin', devastated with grief, had followed him to the afterlife only a few short months later.

But amid the devastation there had also been joy. Several marriages had taken place, giving us reasons to celebrate even through our grief. Bucket and Christina had married, as well as Dirty and Ellie. And just a year ago, to my utter delight, my daughter had given birth to a blonde-haired, green-eyed, and dimpled little devil of a girl that she and Cage had named Samantha.

It was also around that time that the club had called a vote. Deuce's wish to step down, with Cage as his ready replacement, was unanimously voted into action.

And through it all the club had grown bigger, uniting with the Silver Demons to form an organization so large, so strong, that not even the Russian mafia had made an effort to exact revenge on Deuce for the dangerous game he'd played.

It wasn't very long after Hawk had turned himself in that his uncle and several of his uncle's men had been arrested in a federal sting operation that the Horsemen and Silver Demons had both orchestrated and participated in. Deuce told me that only a few months after Yenny's incarceration, he'd been killed in prison by his own associates.

A part of me was glad a man so twisted was no longer gracing this earth, yet I also felt saddened that the last piece of Hawk's past had been wiped from this earth.

But I'd made it a point to never again look back, so instead of dwelling on what couldn't be changed, I looked to the passenger seat, to the young man sitting beside me.

Hawk's future.

At fifteen, Christopher was quickly becoming a man, every day looking more and more like his father. He was already a foot taller than me, surprisingly muscular for a boy his age, broad and strong and always carrying himself in that stoic and sure way Hawk did.

But in so many ways, he was still a boy.

And judging by the expectant look on his face, he was a boy who still very much needed his father.

"He's late," Christopher muttered, referring to Ripper and not Hawk.

Reaching across the space between us, I covered his hand with mine and squeezed. "He'll be here," I said. "He promised your father, and Ripper never breaks his promises, does he?"

When Hawk couldn't be there to do the things a father and son did together, Ripper and Cage had been. At first it had just been the little things, wrestling around with him, playing video games together, and coming to school functions along with Tegen and me.

And then as he grew older, they took him to the school basketball court to shoot hoops, to the batting cages, go-karting, and much to my dismay, they taught him how to ride a dirt bike.

When Christopher was thirteen and his interest in the opposite sex stayed at the forefront of his mind, I'd finally convinced myself to have "the talk" with him. To my surprise, he informed me that nearly all the men at the club had already given him the talk. At first I was horrified, wondering what kind of degenerate stories they'd regaled him with, until Christopher, his face bright red with embarrassment, gave me a quick overview of the things he'd been told, as well as informing me of his ever-growing stash of condoms since the men were always shoving them in his pockets.

I'd left well enough alone at that point.

More recently Cage had been teaching Christopher how to drive, preparing him to get his driver's license. There were talks of learning how to ride a motorcycle, but I'd been adamant in my refusal. Their intentions were good and more than appreciated, but it was and always would be Hawk who would have the honor of teaching his son how to ride.

Looking at me, Christopher shook his head. "No, Ripper doesn't break his promises," he said, but his quiet tone and solemn expression told me he was still worried.

"It's going to be fine," I said softly, using a tone of voice I hadn't used with him since he'd stopped coming to me for every little thing. "Ripper will be here."

As if on cue, the rumbling growl of a motorcycle could be heard off in the distance. When the noise grew closer and louder, it became clear there wasn't just one motorcycle but an entire army of them. Christopher and I watched as, one by one, the Hell's Horsemen pulled up behind us on the street, Deuce riding point.

Christopher turned to me, his eyes wide with surprise. "Did you do this?"

I couldn't help but grin. "I wish I could take credit for this, but it was all Deuce's doing."

Christopher shot me one last look before we jumped out of the car to greet the new arrivals.

As Deuce was removing his helmet, Eva was already sliding off the back of his bike and hurrying toward me. We hugged briefly before parting and she slipped her hand into mine, a smile on her face.

"Everyone came," she said, nodding over her shoulder at the Harleys lining up on the street. She was right, they were all here: Deuce, Mick and Adriana, Cox and Kami, Ripper and Danny, Cage and Tegen, Dirty and Ellie, Bucket and Christina, Danny D. and Danny L., Worm, Anger, Tap . . .

Even Cox's son Devin had come, the spitting image of Cox in his youth, and on the back of his bike was his girlfriend, Deuce and Eva's daughter, Ivy. She too was a young woman now, and a beautiful combination of both her mother and sister.

They were all here, and seeing them here in a show of support for their fellow brother and friend warmed my heart in ways I would never be able to express with mere words.

"Do I look okay?" I whispered, gripping Eva's hand tighter. "I dyed my hair last night, but I swear the gray hairs are coming in faster and faster."

I'd done my best to look as good as I could without going overboard. My hair was freshly dyed its natural color, my makeup was minimal, and my clothes were new yet still casual.

"Stop," Eva said with a laugh. "You look beautiful. And don't talk to *me* about gray hair."

Although beginning to feel more anxious than excited, I realized my mistake and laughed as well. Eva, not caring enough to dye it, had far more gray hair than I did, and because her natural color was so dark it showed far more than mine. But even at her age she could still be found in ratty old band T-shirts, jeans that had gone out of style in the 1970s, and Chuck Taylors on her feet. Despite nearing her fifties, she was still just as unique and beautiful as when I'd met her all those years ago when she was only twenty-two.

And I couldn't have asked for a more supportive and loving friend.

While Deuce might have insisted on purchasing a house for Christopher and me, it had been Eva who'd helped me more than anyone. At her insistence, I'd finally gotten around to getting my GED and afterward, a job at the local florist. Now I was working on obtaining my associate degree, albeit online and with a great deal of my daughter's assistance.

I might be in my fifties, but in my opinion there was no time limit when it came to bettering yourself. As I often told myself when feeling discouraged, it was better late than never.

Sadly, that same line of thinking wasn't one my family shared with me. While my sister and I had reunited on well enough terms, my parents and I were still estranged. Even though a part of me would always feel the sting of losing them, I had a new family, one who accepted me despite my faults.

"There he is!"

I wasn't sure who saw him first or who announced his arrival, and I didn't care. All I cared about was the sight of the man himself. Still far off in the distance, a figure could be seen coming down the walk. Although I couldn't yet make out his features, I knew it was Hawk from the distinct limp in his stride. Despite the continued medical attention he'd received in prison, his leg never did heal correctly.

As he grew closer, slowly approaching the main gates, the crowd on the street fell silent. Searching for Christopher among them, I beckoned him to me. Releasing Eva's hand, I looped my arm through my son's and waited.

When Hawk was close enough for me to see the gray in his short beard and sideburns, close enough for me to see he was wearing the clothing I'd left for him, close enough to know that he was looking directly—and only—at me, my stomach filled with warmth, exploding quickly throughout the rest of my body.

Still, I wasn't under the silly notion that readjusting to life together would be an easy transition. Hawk had lived behind bars for nearly eight years, and whether he would admit it or not, living in prison was much like experiencing an ongoing trauma, and with each visit I'd seen the toll it took on him. His only glimpses of the outside world were through the people who took the time to come and visit, to ensure he remained a significant part of their life on the outside, and I'd done my best to see that had happened.

But at the same time, I knew there would be conflict. Voices would be raised, tears would be shed, more likely between his son and him than between him and me. But I was determined to make it work, and ready to take on any additional obstacles that life decided to throw our way. Hawk had waited for me while I'd shut myself away for years, and more than deserved me giving him that same courtesy.

After all, what kind of a life was a life without someone to enjoy it with, someone to grow old with, without someone to love.

It wasn't a life I ever cared to know again.

Suddenly the lights atop the gates lit up, a bell and

a buzzer both sounded, and my breath hitched as Hawk walked through the slowly opening gate. When he was free and clear and the gates began to close behind him, he surveyed the parade on the street with a grin on his face.

"I'm FREE!" he shouted, thrusting his arms up in the air.

With a roaring shout, the boys shot forward across the street, circling and engulfing Hawk. It took several long minutes for the reunion to calm, but when it did, when the men began to disperse and Hawk emerged from the group wearing his cut, I stepped forward into the street, still holding Christopher's arm.

"Irish!" Ripper yelled. "Go give your old man a fuckin' hug!"

Hawk's gaze shot to Ripper. "You gave my boy a nickname?"

"He did!" I called out, smiling. "They all did!"

Ripper shrugged. "Figured Irish was better than Russian, yeah?"

Releasing his arm, I gave Christopher a little shove. "Go say hi," I said softly.

He looked down at me, then back to Hawk who was just standing there, waiting for Christopher to make the first move.

Despite having seen each other throughout Hawk's prison sentence, I knew this moment had been a source of anxiety for both of them. They'd both grown so accustomed to their respective places—Hawk parenting as best he could from prison two states away, and Christopher growing up having accepted that this was the extent of his relationship with his father, and used to being the man of the house—that neither of them knew exactly how to act when the moment came that they were thrust back into each other's lives.

Just as I was beginning to worry that neither of them were going to make the first move, Hawk edged forward. And once Christopher saw that Hawk was walking toward him, he took a step as well. And although it was at a snail's pace, Hawk with his limp and Christopher full of apprehension, when they finally reached each other, Hawk pulled him into a hug that Christopher instantly returned.

With tears in my eyes, I watched as the two men in my life held each other. I felt so incredibly full, so near to bursting, that I wasn't sure I could hold out another second without running to them. But as it turned out, I didn't need to wait much longer.

I could only watch, trembling slightly, as Hawk closed the distance between us. And then he reached for me, pulling me into his arms and against his body. Crying softly, I fell limp against him and let go of all my worries, of my anxiety. Instead of thinking about what was to come, I simply reveled in the gift I'd just been given.

In Hawk.

He was here, not behind those walls, not surrounded by prison guards, but really and truly here. I was touching him and he was touching me, and it had been so long, so agonizingly long since I'd last had him to myself that the people around us, the prison behind us, the entire world seemed to disappear.

"You smell good," he said softly, dropping his face into my hair and inhaling deeply.

Gripping his back, I closed my eyes.

It was just me. Just him.

Us.

Moments.

And I was never going to let go again.

Until Ripper made me.

"Brought you a ride, brother," Ripper said, grinning as he shoved in between us. "Irish and I been plannin' this shit for a while now. Kid even helped build it."

Both Hawk and I turned to the group and as they parted, they revealed the beautiful custom-made bike that Ripper had ridden up on. Although I knew very little about motorcycles and the mechanics of them, I was aware of the many hours the boys had put into this project, and the end result was beautiful.

But Hawk was no longer looking at the motorcycle, he was looking at me. "You save me that ride, D?"

More tears welled in my eyes. "I saved you everything," I whispered. "Everything."

Reaching for me, his thumb brushed several errant tears away from my cheek. "You did good, baby," he said. "You did real fuckin' good without me."

I shook my head. "I was never without you."

And just like that, as I was staring up into those dark eyes, the gray in his beard was gone, the lines around his eyes disappeared, and in his eyes I saw my own reflection, young and pretty, smiling up at him. Ready to take that ride.

The way it always should have been.

The way it always was and always would be, inside my heart.

"You motherfuckers wanna stand outside a prison all fuckin' day?" Cox shouted. "That's on you, but I'm ridin' my ass outta here. Freakin' me the fuck out, thinkin' they're gonna come chain my ass up or somethin'!"

Shaking my head at Cox, I turned to Hawk and smiled. "Do you even remember how to ride?"

His answering laughter was the most beautiful thing I'd ever heard.

"Woman," he said, an eyebrow cocked as he looked down at me. "It's like fuckin'. You don't ever forget how."

EPILOGUE

Zachary "ZZ" Jeffries slipped the padlock onto the door of the last shipping container and slammed it shut with a loud click. After adding a metal shipping seal, he turned to leave, facing the remaining men on the docks. He gave them a nod to signify that everything was ready and they could start loading, then he walked off.

As he headed in the opposite direction, he could hear the muffled whimpers and cries from inside the container grow substantially louder. It was a heady, adrenaline-inducing feeling that powered through him, making his heart race. Unable to stop himself, his fingers curled, balled into tightly clenched fists.

He knew what those women were experiencing, locked up in that dirty, dark container, their futures unknown to them. He knew all too well that raw emotion as your heart pounded and you could barely breathe because your own fear was fucking suffocating you. He'd been running from . . . well, from everyone for a long time now, so yeah, fear was his fucking middle name.

It was also what had kept him alive this long.

He'd turned the fear into rage. Fought his way to the top of the lowest of the low, and took his place on a throne made of garbage and rot.

He didn't give a fuck if his empire was built on the blood and bones of innocent men and women, didn't care that more people would have to die so he could continue his reign, continue surviving. This was his life now, this was what they had made him, the monster they'd forced him to become.

"Boss man."

ZZ continued his stride across the docks, cutting his eyes to his right as Tommy, one of his men, fell into step beside him.

"What?" he snarled, coming to an abrupt stop.

Tommy swallowed hard and ZZ fought the urge to laugh. They were all afraid of him; even a mean old son of a bitch like Tommy was scared shitless that at any second his temper would be turned on him and once it was, no one was safe. Not a single fucking person.

"Big guy wants numbers," Tommy said quietly.

ZZ snorted. "He'll get 'em when I'm ready to fuckin' give 'em."

The Russian mafia might think they owned his ass, but the reality of it was that ZZ had ensured the loyalty of the men who worked under him. If the Russians ever decided to turn on him, make a play against him, ZZ had plans in place to start a war that would crumble the golden ground those fuckers thought they walked upon.

As Tommy reluctantly nodded, ZZ started walking again, cursing quietly over the summer heat, still suffocating even in the dead of night. But wearing short sleeves wasn't an option for him. His former loyalties, his club colors, were still tattooed all over his body, something he purposely kept as a reminder of why he'd ended up in the fucking ditch he had.

Still cursing, he reached into his pocket, pulling a rubber band from his jeans, and after tying back his long brown hair into a knot, he wiped the sweat from his forehead, cracked his neck a few times, and continued on.

Making a sharp right in the direction of the parking lot, ZZ headed straight for his truck. He was eager to get home—get drunk, get high, jack himself off—even if home was a piece of shit. It was off the grid, out of the way, and that was all he cared about.

He'd just breached the parking lot when the rumble of a motorcycle gave him pause. Self-preservation, ever present in his every move, slammed into overdrive and he side-stepped, slipping behind a nearby vehicle. Crouching down, he pulled his piece from the back of his jeans and waited.

Who the fuck was here this late? He planned his shipments down to the last second, ensuring that everyone here was on his team, their silence bought and paid for. To the best of his knowledge, no other import or export was on the schedule for tonight, and this unexpected arrival was putting a damper on his good mood.

As he waited, not just one but two, three, and then finally five bikes came to a slow stop in the center of the parking lot. Raising himself just enough to see better, ZZ looked over the trunk of the vehicle he was crouched behind, and his breath caught in his throat.

Five leather cuts were illuminated by the moonlight, highlighting the Grim Reaper on the back, the Hell's Horsemen rocker above it, and the Miles City patch beneath it.

No fucking way. They couldn't know he was here, and after all this time, why would they bother to look for him? He'd been so sure that once Deuce had come to an unhappy truce with the Russians, his former president would stop sending runners after him. And he had. For years now, ZZ hadn't heard as much as a whisper of the Horsemen sniffing around his business.

But as the bikes lined up beside one another, ZZ watching as one by one the men riding them cut their engines, toed their kickstands down, and dismounted, he couldn't help but wonder if that had been the plan all along. Letting enough time pass, letting him believe he was safe, and then pouncing when he'd least expect it.

Too bad for them, he always expected the unexpected.

"You're stupid as fuck, Dev," one of the men called out, a deep voice ZZ didn't recognize. "Prez finds out you brought along your bitch, he's gonna be puttin' you in the damn ground."

"Shut up, asshole," a female voice called out, and ZZ's eyes zeroed in on the dark figure that moved to stand beside the quickly forming circle of men. Dressed in head-to-toe leather, showcasing a body built for sin, she reached up with small, feminine hands to remove her full-face helmet.

And ZZ's heart stopped. It couldn't be . . . but it was.

The blonde hair, the killer body, the grin punctuated with dimples glinting under the parking lot lights. Danny looked just like he'd remembered her, as if she hadn't aged a day since he'd last seen her.

"She stays in the parking lot," another voice called out, this one ZZ recognized as his former brother, Bucket. As he turned to look the man over, he noticed the years hadn't been kind to him. He looked worse than ever, grimy as fuck, and older than ZZ knew he was.

"What's the big fuckin' deal?" another man said, much younger than Bucket. Coming up to stand beside Danny, he swung his arm up and around her shoulders, and pulled her tightly to him.

ZZ blinked, feeling a strong sense of déjà vu. It had been a while since he'd seen any of his former crew, but if he didn't know any better, he'd have said that man was Cox. Only it wasn't. Cox had been covered in tattoos, and this guy didn't have any visible ink.

"It's a fuckin' cash drop-off," the young man continued. "Wham, bam, we're back on the road."

Bucket shook his head. "She stays in the parking lot." This time his voice brooked no argument, and the younger man's arm fell away from Danny.

"Yeah, man," he muttered. "She stays in the parking lot. Fine."

"Fuckers," Danny bit out. "You're all a bunch of no fuckin' fun."

ZZ's head was spinning. Wasn't Danny married to Ripper, didn't she have a kid with him? And here she was with another brother?

And then all at once, his confusion, his surprise, bled

quickly to anger.

The Hell's fucking Horsemen were here, in his fucking territory, and doing some sort of business, no less.

But even worse was . . . Danielle West was here. The reason his life had gone from damn near perfect to shit staining a motherfucking gutter WAS HERE. And she was just as beautiful as ever, living a carefree fucking life doing whatever the fuck she pleased.

His anger spiking, he felt a cold tremor slither down his spine and his hands began to shake. And suddenly, he wanted more than he'd ever wanted anything to wrap his hands around her perfect fucking neck and squeeze the life out of her.

As the group turned away, headed in the direction of the docks, ZZ could no longer be bothered with their reasons for being here. He was solely focused on Danny, who was headed back to the line of bikes.

Huffing loudly, she slammed her helmet down on the seat of the Harley she'd ridden in on the back of. Then turning away from him, she dug into her back pocket, revealing a brightly lit phone.

ZZ shuffled backward so he wouldn't be seen as the men passed by him. Breathing shallowly, his heart racing, he counted under his breath as he waited, something he often did when he was preparing himself for the unknown.

Once he could no longer hear the booted footsteps echoing through the night, he shot up from his hiding place, and with careful, silent steps maneuvered through the vehicles in the lot. As he approached Danny, who was still facing away from him, entirely unaware of his presence, he raised his arm, lifting his gun.

But he wasn't going to shoot her. No, he was going to make her pay for what she'd done to him.

"Danny," he growled, feeling the muscles in his face begin to violently twitch. Rage long suppressed had been released, coursing angrily through his veins at a super speed he had absolutely no control over.

Startled, her phone clattering to the ground, Danny spun around. All that long blonde hair went flying, whipping around her as she turned to face him. As it settled away from her face, ZZ looked her up and down. Tight black leather jacket and pants, her lips painted a bright red, and eyes lined in black. This was *not* Danny. Forget that she was far too young, even younger than he'd previously thought. Now that he was standing directly in front of her, he could see the subtle differences between this woman and Danny. Her body wasn't as slim, was more curvy than athletic; her bright blue eyes were bigger, almost too big for her face; and her lips were thicker, the bottom one curving in that sexy way that was very much reminiscent of . . .

Eva.

The young woman's surprised gaze dropped to the gun in his hand and then back to his face. Just as she opened her mouth, a scream forming in her throat, he lunged forward . . .

ABOUT THE AUTHOR

Madeline Sheehan is the *USA Today* bestselling author of the Holy Trinity series and Undeniable series. She has also co-authored with Claire C. Riley the Thicker Than Blood series, and *Shut Up and Kiss Me*.

Welcome to her world of fantastical romance, full of unconventional love and unscripted emotions.

www.MadelineSheehan.com

OTHER WORKS BY
MADELINE SHEEHAN

UNDENIABLE SERIES
Undeniable
Unbeautifully
Unattainable
Unbeloved

HOLY TRINITY SERIES
The Soul Mate
My Soul to Take
The Lost Souls: A Novella

Co-Written with Claire C. Riley

THICKER THAN BLOOD SERIES
Thicker Than Blood
Beneath Blood and Bone

Shut Up and Kiss Me

Made in the USA
Coppell, TX
06 July 2022

79646020R00168